FELIX FAURE STREET

Global Black Writers in Translation

Global Black Writers in Translation

Vanessa K. Valdés, Annette Joseph-Gabriel, and Nathan H. Dize, series editors

Global Black Writers in Translation publishes texts that explore the full spectrum of Black life and expression by authors of African descent, translated from their source languages into English. The series introduces anglophone readers to the range and complexity of Black literary and cultural production, history, and political thought, expanding existing literary canons and stretching them beyond their current national, geographic, and linguistic limits to foreground global diasporic Black writers, while also increasing the number of Black translators. Although expansive in geographic and temporal scope, what unifies the varied texts is their centering of Black experiences.

TITLES IN THIS SERIES:

Camille's Lakou, by Marie Léticée, translated by Kevin Meehan and Marie Léticée

Workshop of Silence / Atelier du silence, by Jean D'Amérique, translated by Conor Bracken

My Heart Beats Fast, by Nadia Chonville, translated by Corine Labridy

We Are Still in the Fort, by Muyaka bin Haji al-Ghassaniy, translated by Richard Prins

The Noose, by Frankétienne, translated by Asselin Charles

Faith in Disguise, by Mayra Santos-Febres, translated by John A. Mundell

Felix Faure Street

A NOVEL

KEN BUGUL

TRANSLATED FROM THE FRENCH
BY JULIE ANN HUNTINGTON

VANDERBILT UNIVERSITY PRESS NASHVILLE, TENNESSEE

Originally published as *Rue Félix-Faure* in French by Hoëbeke, 2005.

Published 2026 by Vanderbilt University Press.

Library of Congress Cataloging-in-Publication Data

Names: Ken Bugul author | Huntington, Julie Ann translator
Title: Felix Faure Street : a novel / Ken Bugul ; translated by Julie Huntington.
Other titles: Rue Félix-Faure. English | Global Black writers in translation v. 7. (bcp47)
Description: Nashville : Vanderbilt University Press, 2026. | Series: Global Black writers in translation ; v. 7
Identifiers: LCCN 2026008490 (print) | LCCN 2026008491 (ebook) | ISBN 9780826500489 paperback | ISBN 9780826500496 hardcover | ISBN 9780826500502 epub | ISBN 9780826500519 pdf
Subjects: LCSH: Dakar (Senegal) | LCGFT: Novels | Fiction
Classification: LCC PQ3989.2.B78 R8413 2026 (print) | LCC PQ3989.2.B78 (ebook) | DDC 843.91--dc23/eng/20260219
LC record available at https://lccn.loc.gov/2026008490
LC ebook record available at https://lccn.loc.gov/2026008491

To Cesaria Evora,
Djibril Diop Mambetty,
and
the diva Aminata Fall

CONTENTS

Preface

Ken Bugul

I CAME TO literature out of necessity. My three works—*Le Baobab fou* (*The Abandoned Baobab*), *Cendres et braises* (Ashes and embers), and *Riwan ou le chemin de sable* (Riwan or the sandy path)—which constitute an autobiographical trilogy of novels, were written as a therapeutic process, with a sense of urgency, by necessity. I was in such a state of existential precariousness that I no longer had the choice. It was a matter of surviving madness and death. This madness and this death, which would yield the title of my first work of sociopolitical fiction, *La Folie et la mort* (Madness and death). And it is with this work that my passion for writing was born. I then alternated fictionalized autobiographies or auto-fictions with sociopolitical books. I was thrilled and excited by writing that not only mended me, but transported me into imaginary worlds that guided all of my senses. I could no longer do without writing, but what motivated me the most was the creative process and the creativity in writing. An editor of a series of crime novels invited African authors to contribute to a series with a prestigious French publishing house. The project was tempting, but nothing came of it. And a long time after that, a painful affair with a muqaddam who dragged me into a destructive relationship from which I needed to heal brought me back to the project. I was seeking an approach, a way to write a book about this traumatic story. And this is how I wrote *Felix Faure Street* as a crime novel, while, in reality, it came from personal experiences which I was unable to recount in an autobiographical genre. It was too painful for me to use the "I." It would be unbearable. I could not accept, come to terms with what had happened to me. I had to get revenge on the muqaddam. I could not imagine—with everything that I had been through, the calm that I had found in my previously turbulent life, the level of stability that I had achieved at that time—that I could be fooled, manipulated, under the cover of God. It was so unbelievable that, in order to tell this story, I needed to get creative to express everything that I was feeling, so I used the form of a crime screenplay, taking the opportunity to pay tribute to the filmmaker Djibril Diop Mambéty, who led me to come to know Felix Faure Street, a famous and out-of-the-ordinary street in Dakar, the Senegalese capital. I chose this street for the novel's setting. This street, with its seedy nightlife, allowed me to immerse myself in its setting and its characters, and to exact my revenge. And using this approach allowed me to recount this painful experience, in which I had been exploited and humiliated, by staging extraordinary female characters who, through their determination, supported me every step of the way in writing the book. I hid behind the strength of the characters of Drianké, Muñ, the four veiled women, who were all victims of manipulation and exploitation under the cover of God, by the same muqaddam. These are the characters who inspired me and supported me, in order to put an end to the leper, whose body was found chopped up into pieces, one morning, on Felix Faure Street—the street of philosophers, caramel-toned Cape Verdean women, the street of bars, and hair salons resonating with morna music. I created a cinematic atmosphere of shadows, lights, sounds, and silences, in order to dive back into everything that I had been through but did not dare to admit to anyone, not even myself. And this allowed me to satisfy my desire for vengeance and to recover, to heal in large part from this painful experience. *Felix Faure Street* is one of my books in which the magic of writing and creativity have worked best for me. Writing *Felix Faure Street* helped me to understand that I did not need to go through anyone to get to heaven. And ever since, I have been forging my own paths.

Translator's Introduction

Julie Huntington

IT IS MY HONOR to translate *Rue Félix-Faure* by Ken Bugul into English. Ken Bugul is the pen name of one of the greatest writers of her generation, Mariètou Mbaye. In Wolof, *Ken* translates to *someone* and *Bugul* translates to *not wanted* or *unwanted*.[1] Between 1982 and 2022, Ken Bugul published eleven works of fiction and autofiction. And yet, only one of these books has been translated into English, until now. That book is her first book, *Le Baobab fou*, which was translated into English by Marjolijn de Jager as *The Abandoned Baobab* in 1991, and also into Spanish, German, and Dutch. In public talks and in interviews, Mbaye sometimes refers to the book that made her both famous and infamous as *Le Baobab sacré* (The sacred baobab), since, although she has been widely praised for this semi-autobiographical work, it has also made her a subject of exoticization and marginalization, both at home and abroad.[2] She also explains that the success of this early work is part of the reason why she decided to keep writing under her pen name, upon the recommendation of her publisher. Although at first, she was not at ease with this choice, as she explains in her 2023 lecture

"Déconstruire la fatalité: Une vie, une oeuvre" (Deconstructing fatalism: a life, a work), writing under this pen name eventually allowed her to recover from a toxic and abusive relationship, while freeing her to write as she wants, to choose the projects that she wants, and to write about the issues that matter to her. Moreover, as she articulates, the name Ken Bugul is widely understood among Wolof speakers as a moniker specifically assigned to infant girls for protection and hope, in the face of human misfortune and supernatural threats:

> L'origine de Ken Bugul, quand une femme a eu des enfants qui décèdent tout bébé comme ça . . . l'enfant née, si c'est une fille, on l'appelle Ken Bugul pour exorciser . . . des mauvais oeils, des mauvais esprits, et cetera. . . . Même la mort n'en voudra pas ces choses qu'on en sous-entend quand on donne ça à un enfant. Désormais, je vais me l'approprier pour prendre toute la charge, toute la force symbolique qu'il y a dans ce prénom de Ken Bugul.[3]
>
> The origin of Ken Bugul, when a woman has had children who have suddenly died as babies . . . when a [new] child is born, if it's a girl, she is called Ken Bugul in order to exorcise . . . evil eyes, evil spirits, et cetera. . . . Even death will want nothing to do with these things that are implied, when you give this to a child. Moving forward, I'm going to own it, to take full responsibility, to claim all of the symbolic power in this name, Ken Bugul.

Over the course of her literary career, she has done just that. Unflinching and eloquent, Ken Bugul advocates for women and girls in many of her works. In so doing, she never shies away from engaging her readers in uncomfortable conversations, regardless of their positions and perspectives across geopolitical, generational, socioeconomic, ethnic, religious, and cultural divides.

•o•

In June 2024, after the Dakar Translation Symposium-Accra Edition, I reached out to Mbaye to ask for her blessing to do a translation of one of her books, one that she herself had selected. She replied with a list of five works, many of which are among my favorites. Given the choice, I could not pass up the opportunity to bring the beauty and the horror of Ken Bugul's *Felix Faure Street* to readers in English. *Felix Faure Street* is a book like no other. It opens with a gruesome scene, with two incompetent police officers standing in front of a bloody and dismembered body, found strewn across the sidewalk in a working-class neighborhood in Dakar. At the onset of the investigation, the eyes of the murdered man begin to tell the story of the events leading up to his death, but no one is listening to him. Life on Felix Faure Street goes on, just as it does every day. As the mystery unfolds, community members get involved in the investigation. Guided by supernatural elements, they will come face-to-face with a brutal truth—that the horrifically mutilated man was a religious leader who used his power to sexually abuse vulnerable women and girls.

What is striking about Ken Bugul's tale of vengeance and survival is that it shifts the reader's gaze away from the ravaged but resilient bodies of the women and girls who have suffered abuse and exploitation. Their trauma is not put on display for public consumption. Rather, it is the grotesquely mangled body of the serial perpetrator that is exposed and scandalized. The sadistic and sexualized display of the abuser's body, rather than those of the victims, is a powerful narrative strategy, one that satisfies an incomprehensible but very human bloodlust for gory and salacious details in the wake of tragedy, while shielding victims from the re-traumatization of putting their own lived nightmares on full display. Beyond calling out sexual abuse at the hands of religious leaders and putting victim-survivors in control of their own trauma narratives and healing journeys, Ken Bugul masterfully interweaves horrific imagery and biting satire with lyrical prose and captivating storytelling to confront a host of pressing social issues relevant to readers around the globe. Such issues include gentrification and displacement in global cities, police violence and corruption, abuse of religious and political authority, consequences of neoliberal capitalism and globalization, discriminatory migration and immigration policies, sexism, racism, and xenophobia.

MUSICALITY AND RESONANCE

The task of translating Ken Bugul's *Rue Félix-Faure* is akin to translating a prose poem. There is a prismatic resonance, a kaleidoscopic musicality, and a lyrical flow to her work, which is infused with the sonorities of multiple languages, vivid soundscapes, and a variety of musical and literary genres. Much like a storyteller or a singer, Ken Bugul relies on repetition and variation, interweaving various motifs and refrains throughout her novel, shifting them slightly at times, repeating them outright at others. Some of the most commonly repeated phrases are used to identify unnamed characters like *the large chopped-up leper*, *the two fat policemen*, and *the short-haired, light-skinned young woman*, as well as named characters like *the great young man*, *the filmmaker Djib*, and *Drianké, the curvy, small-statured woman*. Giving shape to her characters in this way creates a narrative style that engages with both cinematic and oral storytelling conventions. In translating these repeated modifiers, it was important to maintain the narrative flow and to respect the prosody and the musicality of Ken Bugul's original text. Moreover, because the novel is so heavily steeped in morna and blues music traditions, it was essential to get the rhythm and the lyricism of certain repeated and recast phrases just right, especially the Felix Faure Street motto: *l'espérance doublée de patience*. In this instance, rather than opting for a more literal word-for-word translation like *hope coupled with patience*, which has an awkward stutter-step kind of rhythm, I favored the stronger downbeats of *hope and patience combined*, which can be chanted or sung, at resonant moments, much like a blues refrain.

Beyond the blues and morna that resound throughout Ken Bugul's text, this English-language translation of *Felix Faure Street* has an added musical element, one that I hope will honor the legacy of Djibril Diop Mambéty, the visionary Senegalese director to whom Ken Bugul dedicates this novel in part. In line with this dedication, *Felix Faure Street* engages with characters and themes explored in many of Mambéty's films, especially his second feature film *Les Hyènes* (*Hyenas*), a tale of a woman seeking revenge against a man who betrayed and abandoned her. Moreover, Mambéty's last two films, as part of the unfinished *Les Histoires de petites gens* trilogy, highlight the resilience and the joy of working-class people in Dakar. Ken Bugul alludes to this series throughout *Felix Faure Street*, through her mentions of *petites gens*. Although the title of Mambéty's series has a variety of English translations, none of them satisfied me completely in view of the contexts, characters, and themes at play in *Felix Faure Street*. I deemed *little people* confusing, since, in English, the term often designates children or people with genetic conditions like achondroplasia. Another appropriate equivalent, *ordinary people*, also proved problematic given the importance of opposites and doubles in *Felix Faure Street*, but also because the author uses the phrase "les gens ordinaires" (ordinary people) in other passages to emphasize banal lives or lackluster characters. For these reasons, I opted for *everyday people.* In so doing, I gave a nod to the musical legacy of Sly Stone, known for his soul-infused rock songs with resonant social messages. His declarative crescendo "I am everyday people!" felt like an added point of resonance to which English-language readers could connect, even if unfamiliar with Mambéty's ground-breaking oeuvre and lasting legacy.

LINGUISTIC CONSIDERATIONS

Felix Faure Street is such a uniquely resonant work. Although written in French, it is infused with the sonorities of Wolof, which is spoken throughout Senegal, the Gambia, in neighboring West African countries, and among Diasporic communities around the globe. Although, on the surface, *Felix Faure Street* contains fewer Wolof words than some of Ken Bugul's other plurilingual works like *Aller et Retour* (2013) and *Le Trio Bleu* (2022), many of the Wolof words and expressions that appear in *Felix Faure Street* have been translated and transposed by the author herself into French.[4] In a 2019 interview, Ken Bugul spoke to the sonorous quality of her writing ("You'll immediately feel the regional difference, because with writing, you even hear the sound of it"), and characterized her use of a Wolof-infused French as: "brutal, cut-up. . . . [W]e try, in writing, to use French by twisting and turning it, by cutting it up in tiny pieces, and by sticking it elsewhere to express our ideas."[5] In following with Ken Bugul's own creative processes, it was important for me to preserve these Wolof resonances, which are threaded throughout the text, as much as possible. The most obvious examples are dialogues when characters are greeting each other or taking leave of one another. For example, when Amoul is taking leave of Drianké, he includes the word *paix* (*jàmm* in Wolof, *peace* in English) in his wishes, a word which is commonly included in greetings and sendoffs in Wolof.

> Original French: À demain. Passons une nuit de paix!
>
> Wolof translation: Ba suba. Nu fanaan ak jàmm!
>
> English translation: See you tomorrow. Let's spend the night in peace!

Although these moments may seem small, translating these quotidian exchanges to capture the beauty of the Wolof linguistic and cultural elements resonating therein is indispensable, as they help to ground the work in Dakar—a diverse, plurilingual city where Wolof, not French, operates as the de facto lingua franca.

In other moments, it was imperative to maintain some of the unique linguistic elements that speak to the complicated and interconnected histories of France and Senegal, especially in view of the painful legacy of French colonialism and its enduring impacts in the present day. Some of these signifiers, which emerged as neologisms during the French colonial era, are untranslatable due to the specific geopolitical and historic conditions that shaped their definitions and usage. Examples include words like *nègre*, which was used a racist and pejorative term throughout the colonial period, and which still rears its ugly head in hate speech today. At the same time, the term was reappropriated by Black Francophone writers living in France and its colonies as part of the Négritude movement in the early twentieth century. Leaders of the literary movement—including Senegal's Léopold Sédar Senghor, Martinique's Aimé Césaire, and French Guyane's Léon Damas—reclaimed the term and wrote in celebration of Blackness, elevating African and Diasporic histories and cultures while resisting colonial domination and hegemonic assimilation. Similarly, the signifier *beur*, a verlan construction in which the syllables of the word *arabe* are rearranged, has coexisting and conflicting pejorative and empowering connotations in the francophone world, which is why I leave it untranslated.[6]

Another term whose usage was born out of the colonial period is *hivernage*, the rainy season in tropical areas, often characterized by heavy rains. In Senegal, this period of the year (*nawet* in Wolof) can start in June and last through October. Temperatures and weather conditions vary by region. *Hivernage* is often hot in the northern part of Senegal, with temperatures tending to peak in September and October, whereas temperatures are somewhat cooler in the south. Although the weather conditions may vary from one region to another, in French, *hivernage* is applied as a blanket term for tropical areas. Curiously, it has origins in both seafaring (seasonally moving ships to shelter) and in agriculture (seasonally moving farm animals to shelter). During the colonial period, specifically during World Wars I and II, the term *hivernage* also denoted the practice of moving African *tirailleur* soldiers to camps in warmer climates from November to March.[7] In some cases, African *tirailleur* soldiers faced poor treatment, abuse, and even death, as was the case with the Thioroye massacre in Dakar on December 1, 1944. Beyond wanting to convey the specificity of feeling the heat of an *hivernage* sun in the Sahel, I did not want to strip any of these additional layers of meaning away from *hivernage* by translating it into English as *rainy season*.

Interesting challenges were how and whether or not to translate French terms that have specific localized uses in Senegal. For example, in the scene where the drunken police officer is stripping off his clothes and dancing the mayonnaise at Drianké's courtyard bar, I decided to keep the word *mayonnaise* for the dance, as I did with other dances and music genres like biguine and morna.[8]

In another instance, I chose to find an English-language equivalent for a term that is commonly used in Senegal, but not in France: *les transhumants*. This signifier *transhumants* is derived from *la transhumance politique*. Literally *political transhumance*, the expression denotes the practice of changing political parties, often for personal gain. In this light, I opted for *party switchers* as an equivalent for *transhumants*, the people who participate in this practice.

CHANGING LANDSCAPES AND LEGACIES

When this English-language edition of *Felix Faure Street* is released, over twenty years after its original publication in French, Felix Faure Street will exist only in the memories of those who have set foot there. In September 2025, the Dakar-Plateau City Council determined that Felix Faure Street would be renamed Serigne Babacar Mansour Sy Street. This street-renaming project is part of an initiative launched by Senegalese president Bassirou Diomaye Faye to replace the names of French cultural figures and colonial administrators with those of Senegalese heroes. Although these changes cannot take away the pain, injustices, and wrongdoings of the past, they represent an important step in a national healing journey, sixty-five years after Senegalese independence.

In a 2013 documentary, Mbaye recounts the pain of childhood in the colonial system, where she read stories like "Mariétou, Sabitou et le chien" (Mariétou, Sabitou and the dog) in her French reading primer. The tale casts two girls at odds with one another, fighting over meat that they bought at the market. While they are arguing, an unnamed dog eats the meat, leaving the girls empty-handed. The story is accompanied by two illustrations of the girls, whose faces and bodies are colored in with thick, black India Ink.[9] As

Mbaye explains, reading this tale and seeing these images as a child influenced her vision of her herself in harmful, self-loathing ways:

> Moi, je n'avais pas envie d'être avec les personnages réduits dans ses livres entre-guillemets africains. Moi, je voulais ressembler à la petite fille propre, mignonne, gentille qui était dans les livres français. Donc, quand on me dise que mes ancêtres étaient les Gaulois, je voulais ça pour ressembler plutôt à cette fille valorisée que ressembler à Toto, Pathé, ou Mariétou, Sabitou et le chien où les personnages étaient représentés dans l'encre de chine où c'était tout noir . . . en plus, dans des rôles réducteurs.[10]

> I did not want to be among the simplified characters in so-called African books. I wanted to look like the clean, cute, kind little girl who was in the French books. So when people told me that my ancestors were the Gauls, I wanted that, so I could look like that worthy girl instead of looking like Toto, Pathé, or Mariétou, Sabitou and the dog, in which the characters were portrayed in India Ink, with everything completely black . . . and in reductive roles at that.

Over the course of her career, Mbaye has fiercely and unflinchingly challenged and changed those reductive and limiting stereotypes. Her female characters, like Driankė and Muñ in *Felix Faure Street*, are complicated, resilient, resourceful, and worthy.[11] Like Mbaye, they refuse to let past traumas define them. On the street of *hope and patience combined*, Driankė, Muñ, and the anonymous veiled figures serve as agents of change who disrupt painful patterns and systems, and in so doing, create positive pathways for themselves and others.

Although Felix Faure Street has already been renamed, I hope that, one day, we will see a street in Dakar named for Mariètou

Mbaye, to honor her enduring legacy as a writer and advocate. I hope that, one day, I will be able to stroll down Mariètou Mbaye Street in Dakar, feeling proud, joyful, thankful, and inspired. I hope that, one day, little girls in Dakar will see this positive public representation of a Senegalese literary legend and envision bright, expansive futures for themselves, replete with boundless possibilities.

Notes

1. More directly translated into English, Ken Bugul is "no one wants." Like with the French word *personne*, *ken* can be translated as *someone* or *no one* depending on the words it is linked with. *Bug* or *Bëgg* is translated as *want* and the suffix *-ul* is a marker of negation.
2. "Le Code culturel, Un Frein pour l'activité des artistes," *Bes bi Le Jour*, no. 160 (13 June 2022), 12.
3. Ken Bugul, "Déconstruire la fatalité: Une vie, une oeuvre," Conference at Université Cheikh Anta Diop de Dakar, May 17, 2023, posted to YouTube by Université Cheikh Anta Diop de Dakar, May 23, 2023, https://www.youtube.com/watch?v=gBJZH4hGyGM.
4. *Aller et Retour* translates to Coming and Going and *Le Trio Bleu* to The Blue Trio in English.
5. Christian Ahihou, moderator. "Interview with Ken Bugul: Women's Writing in French-Speaking Africa." *Lingua Romana* 14, no. 1 (2019), https://linguaromana.byu.edu/2019/08/13/1519/.
6. *Verlan* (a play on the French word for backward, *envers*) is a common practice through which words are said backward, or their syllables are rearranged to create new slang terms.
7. *Tirailleur* soldiers were colonial subjects from Africa recruited to fight in the French army. *Tirer* = to shoot; *ailleurs* = elsewhere.
8. Dancing the mayonnaise involves standing with one's legs spread wide and rhythmically gyrating one's pelvis while moving the knees inward and outward and moving one hand in a circular motion in front of one's groin area.
9. *Les Premières lectures de Mamadou et Bineta: Livre de lecture et de français à l'usage des écoles africaines* (EDICEF, 1951), 77.
10. Silvia Voser, director, *Ken Bugul - Personne n'en veut* (Les Productions de la lanterne, 2013).
11. On the subject of names, in Wolof, Muñ denotes patience and endurance. Drianké is a female archetype of elegance, beauty, and wisdom.

FELIX FAURE STREET

1

IT WAS MORNING, Felix Faure Street. The hair salon, Chez Tonio, was still closed, but a relentless violin music was oozing, like a fluid, through its shuttered windows. On the sidewalk across from the Chez Tonio hair salon, stood two fat policemen, their legs spread wide, in front of a heap strewn across the ground. That morning, some people were already in the vicinity of the two fat policemen. Among those in the vicinity of the two fat policemen, were Felix Faure Street residents. Among those in the vicinity of the two fat policemen, were people going to work. Among those in the vicinity of the two fat policemen, were people coming home from work. Among those in the vicinity of the two fat policemen, were people who had slept on Felix Faure Street. Among those in the vicinity of the two fat policemen, were people who had woken up on Felix Faure Street. Among those in the vicinity of the two fat policemen, were people who spent every morning on Felix Faure Street. Among those in the vicinity of the two fat policemen, there was a philosopher.

This philosopher was the Felix Faure Street Philosopher. Among those in the vicinity of the two fat policemen, there was an apprentice philosopher. This apprentice philosopher was a Felix Faure Street apprentice philosopher. Among those in the vicinity of the two fat policemen, there was another apprentice philosopher, and another and another. On Felix Faure Street, there was one Philosopher, and all of the others were apprentice philosophers, wittingly or unwittingly. Everyone on Felix Faure Street had their own version and vision of the visible world and the invisible world, but the debate was ongoing. And respect for other people's versions and visions, respect for other people's ideas, respect for other people's silence was a way of being and behaving on this street. On Felix Faure Street, the acceptance of others was the motto. For philosophers—apprentices or not, witting or not—debate was important and respect was important and respect for others was primordial. Debate, respect for others, acceptance of others were just as important to everyone who was not a philosopher or an apprentice philosopher, the Felix Faure Street Philosopher would say.

It was a calm morning, so sweetly calm, like usual, on Felix Faure Street. Felix Faure Street alone had the secret to that morning sweetness. Nowhere else in this city, nearly surrounded by coastline, no matter how beautiful, had mornings like this! Felix Faure Street mornings were known for their sweetness. It was so nice to be out on that street in the morning! Felix Faure Street mornings made you want to wake up extra early and get out there. Felix Faure Street mornings made you want to spend the night on Felix Faure Street. People out on Felix Faure Street in the morning had serene faces, majestic style. Felix Faure Street residents all got up early. Even those who had hardly slept! Even those who had not slept a wink! Even those who were sleeping would get up, then go back to bed, sometimes without falling back to sleep, after making the rounds on Felix Faure Street!

Felix Faure Street mornings were the kind of mornings that reconciled beings with themselves, with each other, with life. The Felix Faure Street Philosopher would say that Felix Faure Street mornings reconciled beings with their wild imaginings, their uncertainties, their anxieties, their doubts, their selfishness, and in spite of everything, their hope. The Felix Faure Street Philosopher would say that hope was essential for sustaining one's will to live. Hope was the only notion he could come to know in this life that seemed bigger than himself. But even with that knowable hope, some beings struggled with doubt and mired themselves in impatience. Those beings had not grasped what hope could mean, or else they did not know the secret that hope contained, especially when it was combined with patience. This type of being did not exist on Felix Faure Street, or, this type of being was just passing through, and never for very long. This type of being, or this species of being (in keeping with the theory of evolution), did not feel at ease with Felix Faure Street residents and supporters, who, for their part, had stopped doubting a long time ago.

Hope and patience combined were essential for overcoming suicidal tendencies, predilections for stress, inclinations to anxiety, susceptibility to despair, and for transforming them into an existential energy. This energy was essential for human survival in life. In fact, the Felix Faure Street Philosopher would say, all of us, even those who refused to admit it, would rather drop dead than lead certain lives. We were not even living those kinds of lives. They were not lives; they were wastes of life, dregs of life, misbegotten, bottom-of-the-barrel, trick-turning lives. The kind of lives that masturbated in the face of life itself, the kind of lives that pressed us for endless arguments, explanations, justifications, concerns. Those kinds of lives were sticking to us like pieces of shit. We had not chosen, desired, wanted, or wished for them, we would say. We had not sought them out, we insisted. And so we found ourselves in an interminable series of uncertainties, anxieties, unanswered questions, ambivalence between life and survival, between survival and death. There were those days when we did not want to do anything—to live, to survive, or to die—but wanted to commit a crime instead. This urge and this temptation were simmering inside of each and every one of us. And whenever the cover of instinct was lifted, ever so slightly, we would quickly suppress that urge, we would drive it down into the deepest parts of ourselves, without ever doing away with it completely. This temptation and this urge were integral parts of ourselves, of our blood, of our breath, of our genes, the Felix Faure Street Philosopher would say. There were also days when beings, in a conscious or unconscious reversal, wanted to love and to do good. Among those out doing good, there were some who wanted to live their lives clinging to that one good deed, like to the hope for a better afterlife, one far beyond the life they were leading. "The good deed will posthumously remain, when we are no longer here," they would think. This posthumous dispensation could compensate for a life ruined by doubt or impatience. This, too, was a type of crime, the Felix Faure Street Philosopher would say. Doing good solely to justify a life, doing good solely to get to the afterlife, was criminal. If it was not criminal, it was cowardly. It was like doing good to pay down the debt of one's own anxieties in the face of nothingness, the emptiness of life and the afterlife, the Felix Faure Street Philosopher would say. And the infernal cycle continued. And in this tragic situation, hopelessness would set in for some beings with unanswered questions and unmet expectations. The hopelessness did not stem from the simple fact that we had not asked to be, but rather—why were we!? And then, there was one-upmanship, to come up with explanations, justifications for our existence, which had been so needlessly and unnecessarily foisted upon us. Perhaps we needed to include an instruction manual, a warning label with the packing materials of our destiny, which, according to some Scriptures, had been cooked up in 120 days. Which, in the Felix Faure Street Philosopher's opinion, was insufficient. One hundred and twenty days to create a man's destiny! A man? The species descended from all other species? The species descended from fish, insects, crocodiles, monkeys, dinosaurs, even cockroaches? All of those species that kept fascinating and amazing mankind! In the meantime, those species (what was left of them), instead of being amazed by man, were afraid of him. For instead of remaining men, most men had become monsters. Thrust into this life without any instructions, without any warning labels, and ever so quickly, some beings spent their time calling their destiny into question. And these irascible beings would make up other destinies for themselves—with missions! Some became scientists in genetic engineering. Others envisioned themselves as great men with grand destinies. Some would start to dance and sing at the top of their lungs. Others would write postulates, theorems, to sow discord among the hastily devised schools of each other's intelligence. In any case, everyone was looking for a role to play, since they were here. It was important to stay busy and for everyone to feel invested in a mission.

So there were missionaries.

So there were mission directors.

So there were people on a mission.

And for others, uninvolved like the Felix Faure Street residents, there was a feeling and not a mission. This feeling was hope and patience combined! Hope and patience combined were part of every Felix Faure Street morning. But hope and patience combined were not always and only tied to unfathomable, inexplicable situations; to the melancholy of life; to hopelessness, doubt, and impatience, the Felix Faure Street Philosopher would say. There was no doubt on Felix Faure Street, for example. Above all, hope and patience combined were part of what we called the good things in life. The good things in life that seemed fleeting, and hope and patience combined would make them last a little bit longer, then a little bit more, time and again. But what were the good things in life? For the Felix Faure Street Philosopher, they were Felix Faure Street mornings, among other things. They were like a child's smile. They were like pure pleasure. Felix Faure Street mornings were the epitome of hope and patience combined, but on that morning, hope and patience combined had not gotten up with the Felix Faure Street residents. The two fat policemen were standing there, with their legs spread wide, in front of a spectacle teetering between absolute beauty and absolute horror. In absolute terms, the beauty and the horror canceled each other out.

There was no longer beauty or horror.

There was a spectacle.

A magnificent spectacle.

The two fat policemen were standing, their legs still spread wide, in front of a chopped-up body. Around the chopped-up body were four lighted lanterns, placed at the four cardinal points, with their incandescent wicks glowing increasingly brightly. The pieces of the chopped-up body were big pieces. The chopped-up body seemed to be heavy with age and the chopped-up body was that of a man. The man was a leper and would be over fifty if all of his pieces were put back together. The fifty-plus years had taken a toll. The man looked older, judging by his face. Was this because of his belly too? His belly was fat and the middle of his torso looked like a mound. The man's entire chopped-up body was ravaged by leprosy. The man's body could have been strong if it weren't for that fat belly, which was throwing that big, crudely chopped-up body off balance.

What had been used to chop up that big body?

An axe?

A big knife?

That big knife, which we, as children, would imagine the monster—the big monster, the fat monster—using to chop us up and eat us?

What was it about the big monster that excited us the most?

Was it because he was going to eat us?

Or maybe because we knew that the big monster did not exist, that we had made him up, and we were excited by our own invention? Or maybe it was because the big monster did exist and did scare us, but ultimately, we knew that, one way or another, as always, he was not going to eat us?

Ultimately, had the monsters ever really existed?

Yes, yes!

The monsters had to exist!

The monsters have to exist!

We needed our monsters!

We need our monsters!

Not the kind of monsters running rampant these days—those low-level, bottom-shelf monsters; those monsters in organized crime and exploitation; those worthless, vulgar monsters; those asshole monsters! Those monsters who wanted to reinvent the world, into a world without dreams. A world where children were massacred, raped, manipulated, abandoned. A world of domination, occupation. An imperialist world, where the strongest threatened stabilities, where the wealthiest (and wealth was relative) scoffed at the poor (and poverty was relative). We needed the monsters from our childhood, the monsters from our dreams, the monsters for the dream, the monsters to keep dreaming. Whenever we thought about all of those monsters from our dreams—especially that big, fat monster coming toward us—excitement would mix with fear and it was hard to tell them apart. There was something endearingly delightful about those monsters, especially when they were big and fat and coming toward us as if to eat us. We would snuggle up in deep couches, in the strong arms of our fathers, in the comforting embraces of our mothers and grandmothers, on the laps of our big brothers and big sisters. Alas! The monsters we dreamed up, the monsters of our marvelous imaginations, were becoming increasingly rare. All that remained were increasingly monstrous monsters. Modern-day monsters who dispossessed dignities, unscrupulously stole and killed. Monsters who used God to blind, mislead, exploit, kill the innocent. Monsters who used force to dominate, crush, demonstrate, prove!

Who could have staged this spectacle on Felix Faure Street? Who had chopped up the large leper's body and stuffed his tiny genitals so deep into his mouth?

A monster?

Dracula?

No! Dracula was a gentleman!

Dracula did not chop up his victims. Dracula sucked them dry! Mmm-hmm!

The large leper's chopped-up body was lying in a pool of blood that was starting to coagulate in spots. The blood was a red blood, a red whose origin and story we will need to know, understand, and retell. That red blood, on that calm morning, was visible despite the semi-darkness bathing the street. The color of that blood, a petulant red, seemed to signify, to express, to say something. The color of that blood was unusual. That red was violent, audacious, aggressive, stifling, unwieldy, unsettling. The sidewalk seemed to collapse under the color of that blood, slipping out through his guts down along the uneven cobblestones. Usually, on that Felix Faure Street sidewalk, life resonated louder than death. Felix Faure Street was a lively street. Felix Faure Street was one of the liveliest streets in this capital city, in this country that offered its face up to the ocean. Felix Faure Street was a cosmopolitan street where you did not talk about death. It was the street of hope and patience combined. Felix Faure Street residents lived on hope and patience combined and wanted to live for that hope and patience combined. Felix Faure Street residents did not want to know where they came from, but instead dreamed of where they wanted to go. This was not afforded to everyone, a Felix Faure Street apprentice philosopher would sometimes say. And that dream was there every day, maintained, cleaned, polished, smoothed, shined, coddled, pampered, perfumed, praised. Felix Faure Street residents were completely invested in hope and patience combined. Felix Faure Street residents did not worry about their past. Felix Faure Street residents no longer had a past. On Felix Faure Street, the motto was tomorrow, one day, soon, in a while, right away, now. It was also, maybe, never. Felix Faure Street residents did not look back. They were moving forward. The beacons of their existence were hope and patience combined, were moments in this hope and patience combined. Whereas for others, the past was essential for making a present and a future for themselves. On Felix Faure Street, you did not talk about the past. Felix Faure Street was enough for anyone to make an identity, a race, a people, a history, an existence, a destiny for themselves. Passing through it was enough to feel yourself being, existing, buzzing, living, feeling. For anyone suffering or struggling to live, but nonetheless wanting and determined to live, Felix Faure Street was the street to live on, the Felix Faure Street Philosopher would often advise. Felix Faure Street offered life with hope and patience combined. Felix Faure Street was the dream. No one could escape it; no one wanted to escape it! So then, why was this the street where such a spectacle had been staged? Why had this crime been committed on Felix Faure Street?

Maybe the crime had been committed somewhere else and the chopped-up body parts had been brought here!

Who ever said that this was a criminal matter?

For the time being, it was a matter of spectacle!

Felix Faure Street was just the right street for the spectacle!

Felix Faure Street was a stage. But not for this type of spectacle, one might think!

Who ever said that this spectacle was not also life?

Who ever said that this spectacle was not also the dream?

Who ever said that this spectacle was not also hope and patience combined?

Why choose what should and should not constitute life?

Why not consider that life and death are one and the same?

The Felix Faure Street Philosopher would say—to anyone willing to listen and even to anyone unwilling to listen—that life was ultimately one big scam. And for the Felix Faure Street Philosopher, the question was: What was life? The Felix Faure Street Philosopher wondered if it was this amalgamation of big, small, good, evil, poor, rich, ignorant, intelligent, beautiful, ugly, privileged, downtrodden that comprised the substance of life. What were we trying to prove by comparing the good with the bad, the beautiful with the ugly, the Blacks with the Whites, the women with the men, the big with the small, the haves with the have-nots? To blame some and absolve others? Especially since in most cases, the guilty were exonerated and the innocent indicted. To achieve what ends? What was the moral of these opposites? This theory of opposites, like day and night, hot and cold, life and death, did it adequately account for life, did it adequately account for life's horrors, life's absurdity, life's illusions? A life in which most were searching in vain to find themselves, while others were just trying to hold on, without exactly knowing on to what! Felix Faure Street residents, they were lucky. They had hope and patience combined and the dream, whereas others did not know hope, let alone hope and patience combined. They did not know the dream either. They were those ghosts of existence, doing their utmost in vain with nothing to show for it. Those ghosts of existence were looking for reasons to live, but sometimes those reasons to live would drive them to suicide. For those reasons to live did not fill the anguish of the emptiness of their existence. Others camouflaged those reasons and camouflaged themselves and they ultimately led camouflaged lives. Perhaps this was the group that was giving rise to the new, modern-day monsters: new prophets with new temples, false gurus with new ways, false muqaddams with new places of worship.* They would take themselves for new gods at first, and become monstrous monsters. Maybe that large chopped-up leper, who no one seemed to recognize on that Felix Faure Street morning, was one of those new gods, turned monster.

Just who was that large chopped-up leper, with his tiny genitals stuffed deep into his mouth?

No one could give an answer for the time being.

And the Felix Faure Street Philosopher would wonder if, ultimately, we were nothing more than pawns that the universe needed to keep itself spinning along its absurd trajectory. That absurd trajectory required constant, perpetually renewed energy! And one day, all it would take was one slight interference for that trajectory to lead to disorder. And the intoxication instilled by that disorder would give us the feeling of being useful and important, when we were nothing more than small engines. Small engines needed to power an infernal machine, which we knew nothing about, and which was crushing us all indiscriminately. And still swept up in our intoxication, as soon as we set foot on the ravaged planet, what once was Eden, we would cry victory, when it was all just a fleeting illusion, in a disordered universe.

It was from this chaos that God came to be.

And He has been here ever since!

That spectacle of the large leper's chopped-up body, with his tiny genitals stuffed deep into his mouth, with his bulging belly, under an opaque sky at that time of morning, blended in perfectly with the setting on Felix Faure Street. No other street in this city could do justice to such a spectacle.

That spectacle belonged to Felix Faure Street.

* Literally, *muqaddam* translates to "the appointed one." The title is attributed to representatives of civil authority at the neighborhood level, but also those of a spiritual leader, authorized to provide teaching and to initiate disciples.

"It is fantastically sublime!" an apprentice philosopher exclaimed, staggering with both hands in his pockets, drunk on life, drunk on hope and patience combined, drunk on dreams. Another apprentice philosopher did a little dance while whistling a tune between aversion and admiration. He approached the chopped-up body and one of the two fat policemen violently pushed him away with the back of his hand. The apprentice philosopher backed away, with his two hands raised toward the fat policeman as a sign of peace.

"This spectacle is true art."

"Well, there is no such thing as true art and false art, there is just art."

"It is art, I tell you!" the apprentice philosopher would say, pointing at the large leper's chopped-up body.

The spectacle, you had to admit, was magnificent, sublime. The strangest parts of this spectacle were the tiny genitals, violently torn off given the way the flesh was dangling, that had been stuffed deep into the large leper's mouth. The four lanterns placed at the four cardinal points gave the spectacle an unreal feel! The glowing wicks of the four lanterns were growing bolder as if to confront, to defy a sun that had not yet risen. They seemed to highlight the leper's tiny genitals, stuffed deep into his wide-open mouth, like a bouquet of wildflowers. Such a spectacle could put the finishing touch on Bosch's *The Garden of Earthly Delights*, at the Prado museum, as a fourth panel. The large chopped-up leper's eyes, consumed by illness, barely had any eyelashes left and they were wide open. The large chopped-up leper's eyes were wide open and seemed to be moving. The large chopped-up leper's eyes were moving. The large chopped-up leper's eyes were spinning every which way, like in a tailspin. The large chopped-up leper's eyes seemed to want to say something. The large chopped-up leper's eyes seemed to want to confess something. The large chopped-up leper's eyes seemed to want to admit something. The large chopped-up leper's eyes had been sentenced to death, but were alive. The large chopped-up leper's eyes seemed to want to attract the attention of people in the vicinity. The large chopped-up leper's eyes were flagging down the two fat policemen. The large chopped-up leper's eyes were not dead. The large leper's eyes were alive and they were speaking. The large leper's eyes were saying terrible things. The large leper's eyes were telling a story, a story that had to be told to the great young man, the filmmaker Djib, to make into a film. The story that the large leper's eyes had to tell to the great young man, the filmmaker Djib, seemed to have no ending. The large chopped-up leper's eyes were there, in the midst of telling the end of the story and no one was listening, for no one was paying attention to the large leper's eyes.

Who could understand the language of eyes of the large chopped-up leper, with his tiny genitals stuffed deep into his mouth?

The two fat policemen were still there, standing with their legs spread wide. They were looking at the large chopped-up leper's body and they did not realize what was happening in his eyes. The two fat policemen were still standing there, but they were miles away. They did not even have the instincts of movie policemen. They had not examined anything. They had not tried to see if there was some clue, somewhere, near the body of the large chopped-up leper. The two fat policemen had not done anything. The two fat policemen were there as if in spite of themselves. The two fat policemen seemed annoyed. The two fat policemen were bored. The four lanterns, all around, illuminated the large leper's eyes, which were telling the story and the end of the story that had to be told to the great young man, the filmmaker Djib, to make into a film.

Who had staged this spectacle?

Was it one person or many people? No one could speak of crime.

No one should speak of crime.

This was not a crime.

This was a spectacle.

Perhaps this was why the two fat policemen did not realize what was happening in the large chopped-up leper's eyes. Like everyone else, they were taking in a spectacle illuminated by four lanterns placed at the four cardinal points. This spectacle could only have been staged by a very talented person or group.

SETTING: Felix Faure Street!

LOCATION: The Felix Faure Street sidewalk!

TIME: A Felix Faure Street morning!

OPPOSITE: The shuttered hair salon, Chez Tonio!

MUSIC: A piercing violin sound!

LIGHTING: Four lanterns placed at the four cardinal points!

And the large leper's eyes were in the midst of saying who had staged the spectacle. The large leper's eyes also seemed to be enjoying the spectacle. The large leper's eyes were admiring at times. The large leper's eyes still contained images of the mise-en-scène deep down in their sockets. But no one was paying attention to the large leper's eyes. People were looking at the large leper's chopped-up body. People were looking at the tiny genitals stuffed deep into the large leper's mouth, which was now laughing. The large leper's mouth was laughing, but the genitals stuffed deep inside of it were preventing him from letting the laughter—which could have made its way across the ocean, over to the Cape Verde Islands—escape any further. Every piece of the large leper's chopped-up body had erupted in spasms, so great was the laughter's depth, duration, and melancholy. With his tiny genitals stuffed deep into his mouth, the large chopped-up leper's laughter made its way up and down the Felix Faure Street sidewalk. The laughter escaping the large leper's mouth was like a piercing violin sound, like the blues. The large leper's eyes had been moved by the laughter making its way up and down the street and the large leper's eyes were laughing even harder. The crime must not have occurred long ago, or this misdeed rather, since this was not a criminal matter, or so they said. The large leper's eyes were watching the people in the vicinity. The large leper's eyes were laughing all the more while people-watching. A nervous laughter, a laughter that was telling the story that had to be told to the great young man, the filmmaker Djib, to make into a film! A so-called never-ending story, whose end was now being recounted by the large chopped-up leper's eyes, on a Felix Faure Street sidewalk.

Felix Faure Street was a bustling street, when the street belonged to it residents, to its supporters, to the Philosopher, and the apprentice philosophers. It was bustling day and night. It was bustling all night long until dawn, until morning, until afternoon, until evening. Some Felix Faure Street night owls would wait up for those who observed the first morning duty of prayer. They always passed through Felix Faure Street, and everyone else would merge into that blessed crowd, unwavering in their faith in that moment. So, among the crowd of morning people pacing up and down that street, there were the discreet sounds of prayer beads, of rosaries, interspersed with the clatter of girls stumbling home in their heels, buoyed by men or women drunkenly staggering after each other, everyone as blessed as everyone else. Felix Faure Street was the street of the blessed! And that morning, Felix Faure Street was offering up another spectacle, another prayer! That morning's prayer was the large leper's chopped-up body, with his tiny genitals stuffed deep into his mouth and his eyes wanting to say something, saying something even.

"Violent death!" said one apprentice philosopher.

"Atrocious death!" said another apprentice philosopher.

"Horrible death!" said one apprentice philosopher.

"Sublime death!" said another apprentice philosopher.

The two fat policemen were too big and too fat, in front of the large leper's chopped-up body, with its big belly visibly ballooning in size. The two fat policemen were too big and too fat for their profession. This trend of too big and too fat policemen should alarm police commissioners everywhere, but apparently, this was the trend, because the commissioners—everywhere and as a general rule—were even bigger and fatter. But what were these policemen (from near and far) feeding on? Perhaps on billy-clubbing, unwelcome frisking, ass-kicking, swearing, arbitrary profiling—facial, racial—of brown- or olive-sounding names. Beur, Arab, Osama, Nègre, Saddam, Gypsy, North Ivorian, South Ivorian, undocumented, and even documented. And as of late, new usual suspects, stereotypical Europeans, Asians, and what have you! And the time-honored Romani, Rom, Romansch, Jew, Towelhead! The Felix Faure Street Philosopher would say that this was highly indigestible as food. They needed someone to make them a strict diet plan, an apprentice philosopher would say. To start, they had to carry out their work as officials properly, conscious of what they represent in society, instead of playing tough guys and flexing their muscles. Then, they had to be less big and less fat, while ceasing to utter racist and despicable words. Ultimately, to not be policemen like themselves.

The two fat policemen, still standing with their legs spread wide, were both rubbing their bellies full of spicy gizzard kebabs, chargrilled lamb, and liters of Gazelle Coumba beer and Kiravi Valpierre wine. At that hour of morning, they were better suited for sleeping than for working. They were feeling good, and that state of well-being had just been ruined by that large leper's chopped-up body on the Felix Faure Street sidewalk. On the other hand, that large leper's chopped-up body with his tiny genitals stuffed deep into his mouth was not looking too good, the two fat policemen kept thinking. The two fat policemen did not envy the fate of the large leper with his bulging belly taunting the ever-opaque sky. The two fat policemen were wrong! The large chopped-up leper's eyes were saying something else. The large leper's eyes were saying that they had seen God at long last!

The two fat policemen did not live on Felix Faure Street, but they knew Felix Faure Street, the street of hope and patience combined. They strolled though there often, for any given reason, otherwise they would make one up. Felix Faure Street was alluring, with its lights, its neon, its music, its smells, and its copper-toned residents! Felix Faure Street was a musical street, a street where you could dance at any time. While going to buy a bag of sugar from the neighborhood shopkeeper. While going to try on a dress at the Cape Verdean seamstress's place. While going to get your hair done at Chez Tonio. While simply finding yourself on Felix Faure Street.

It was still morning and the sun did not dare to rise, much less sprinkle the street with its radiance. The sun always moved gently along Felix Faure Street. The sun did not dare to attack head-on, out of the blue, on Felix Faure Street. The sun always slipped in, almost shyly, through the centenarian trees. On Felix Faure Street, the trees were not out in the street, but instead on the inside. They had a point. It would just take one roadway construction project to raze them all to the ground! With no alternative.

For the trees?

Who would think of them?

Only the friends of the trees!

How many of them were still around?

One, three, five, seven, nine, eleven, thirteen, fifteen, seventeen, nineteen?

So, on that morning, the sun had not yet skimmed over the tiled roofs of the little houses on Felix Faure Street. The sun was modestly covering its face. The sun was flirting with Felix Faure Street. The sun knew that Felix Faure Street had its own rhythm, which it had to respect. The sun was also in cahoots with Felix Faure Street. The sun usually made its way quickly across the Felix Faure Street sky during the daytime, enveloping it in a halo of light once it reached the other side. That halo of light gave the ocher hues of the little houses a cinematic kind of feel. The Felix Faure Street sunshine could certainly be used as lighting for the film by the great young man, the filmmaker Djib, an apprentice philosopher thought. That film, the end of which was being recounted by the large chopped-up leper's eyes, on the Felix Faure Street sidewalk! Felix Faure Street was located at the dividing line between two worlds, that of night and that of day. Felix Faure Street adjoined the day to the night. And it was at this dividing line between the two worlds, that the large leper's body had been discovered, chopped up into big pieces.

The two fat policemen were afraid of suffering the same fate as the large leper.

But why would they be afraid?

And what would they be afraid of?

Did they have something to feel ashamed of?

And what if the two fat policemen had committed the crime?

The policemen, along with every uniformed officer, were generally above all suspicion, regardless of whether or not they were big and fat. On the other hand, any time an outsider would pass through, or a person of color, with cliché profiled features, the suspicion lingering over everyone would descend upon him like a swarm.

Whatever you do, do not take your beard and your *modou-modou* name with you, anywhere else!*

* *Modou-modou* is a Senegalese term designating men gone to work abroad.

And couldn't the policemen commit crimes and heinous crimes at that? Or had they undergone psycho-something tests, before being recruited? Weren't police and criminal profiles one and the same? How could they handle crimes without having somewhat of a criminal profile themselves? an apprentice philosopher might have said. Have you seen how, on occasion, and increasingly often, certain policemen treated the people they were arresting, regardless of whether or not they were guilty? They would beat them up, strike them with their batons, kick them in prime locations. They would insult them, humiliate them. Upon looking at their faces in that very moment, you could see a violent desire to take down. They would painfully hold themselves back, huffing and puffing as if relieving themselves, or possibly even coming in their pants. Some policemen could be potential criminals or perverts. Frustrated criminals, confessed criminals, were still dangerous. There was the potential for recidivism. At any rate, policemen or people in uniform were always, or often, or generally, above all suspicion. And yet, only recently, people in uniform, representatives of their great nation, charged with a so-called humanitarian mission turned horrific, had stolen artworks from the invaded country, despite any and all opposition. That was why those who wanted to commit crimes, in this day and age, donned uniforms. In uniform, you did not go unnoticed; you were even entitled to polite greetings and could easily pass through any roadblocks.

The two fat policemen above all suspicion were also poorly dressed. No, it was more like poorly decked out. Was it because of their fat bellies that two fat policemen's blue shirts could not be buttoned up properly? Did those two fat policemen not know that everyone who showed up on Felix Faure Street had to be well dressed? And that this held true for everybody and anybody! Uniformed or plain clothes! At any given time of day, Felix Faure Street residents were elegant. In the daytime, girls in shorts, little halter tops and leather sandals were like a bouquet of life, and made you want to go all out. The old folks would go outside as the sun made its way across the sky, ready to rendezvous with their street on chairs in front of their homes. The men would wear short-sleeved shirts, with bow ties. The women would wear straw hats with flowered brims. Their dresses, gathered at the waist, gently fluttered in the whispering of a light breeze, possibly providing a furtive glimpse of a knee glistening beneath a starched lace underskirt. Felix Faure Street was an elegant street. Felix Faure Street was a classy street. It was the street for classy people. A classiness unjustly undervalued by all of the people who lacked it, because they did not live on Felix Faure Street.

The two fat policemen smelled of alcohol and women. On Felix Faure Street, at that hour, this was de rigueur, or rather, required. To be a recognized member of Felix Faure Street, this too was a must. Especially at that hour when the other side of the street was about to reveal itself. And yet, Felix Faure Street residents were not the central nightlife fixtures after a certain hour. Those were other people from other places. People who lived in other places that did not live up to their dreams. When, lacking options, those people could no longer stand suffocating in those other places, they would head over to Felix Faure Street and there, they would feel alive. Upon returning to their other places, they would be filled with existential dread, and they would impatiently wait for night to fall, to rush back into the dream street, God's street, the street of hope and patience combined.

The two fat policemen were still there, standing with their legs spread wide, as if wanting to empty their bladders or their bowels onto the chopped-up body of the large leper, whose eyes were bursting with laughter at the spectacle they were offering. The two fat policemen's thick-soled shoes were warped from their weight, and their condition suggested that their insoles stunk. One of the two fat policemen, the one who seemed fatter, was small in stature. He was breathing loudly, and in front of the large leper's chopped-up body, he would cough from time to time, turning his head away. That fat policeman did not inspire confidence. He could be suspected of having committed the crime.

"What do you think?" an apprentice philosopher might have said.

"Hey, Mister two fat policemen, which one of you committed the crime? Or, did you both commit the crime?"

"Listen, this can be easily explained."

"How can someone chop up such a big body all alone? How could that someone have torn off that leper's tiny genitals so violently and how could they have stuffed them so deep into his mouth, without any help? Well, you both could have committed this crime together! What do you have to say about that, mister policemen?

"Do you think you are above all suspicion?

"Because you are policemen, fat policemen?"

The two fat policemen would not have reacted to the apprentice philosopher's accusations. The Felix Faure Street Philosopher, who would have figured out the apprentice philosopher's accusations, would have taken the floor:

"Who told you that this is a criminal matter?"

"In this case, we must call on God!" an apprentice philosopher would have suggested.

"What does God have to do with this spectacle?" another apprentice philosopher would have asked.

"We have to put the case before Him," another apprentice philosopher would have insisted. "There is a large chopped-up leper, with his tiny genitals stuffed deep into his mouth, and this is not a criminal matter! That is why we must involve God, for God is immanence in disorder. This crime, this spectacle rather, is a disorderly act. Therefore, God is concerned, since it stems from disorder."

On Felix Faure Street, God was part of everything. Every Felix Faure Street resident trusted in God. On Felix Faure Street, God was omnipresent. The street of hope and patience combined could not do without God. It was impossible. God embodied everything that Felix Faure Street residents wished for, longed for, wanted, experienced, in every moment. Felix Faure Street residents were close to God. Everything they had was God and everything else was hope and patience combined. Everything else was the dream. In the dream, Felix Faure Street residents were building another world for themselves, in another realm, but not on another street. In hope and patience combined, Felix Faure Street residents were reveling in everything about this dream, which was there with them every day, every moment of their lives.

Felix Faure Street was the dream street.

Felix Faure Street was God's street.

And yet, on Felix Faure Street, there were no temples. On Felix Faure Street, residents did not pray to God in temples. Prayer was the music of violins, guitars; the comings and goings of the Philosopher and the apprentice philosophers; mornings. Prayer was the caramel-toned backs of Cape Verdean girls. Prayer was the old folks, dressed-up, coiffed, powdered, perfumed. Felix Faure Street residents did not bow down in a temple. For them, God did not live in a temple, no matter how beautiful. God did not need a temple. A temple could not contain God. A temple could not house God. God was too tremendous to be in a temple. And God did not hide away. Felix Faure Street residents lived with God in every moment. Felix Faure Street residents did not understand how people in our day and age—after so many messengers, a son sent down, Books revealed—could go through temples, sometimes pedophile priests, sometimes lecherous muqaddams, sometimes frustrated imams, rabbis who were men just the same, false gurus, new prophets, to gain access to God. The ever-blind and ever-deaf people kept seeking Him out in other places when He was beside us, with us, all along. Felix Faure Street residents did not understand why, when people wanted to speak with God, they would wash up, get dressed, put on perfume, smile, laugh (exceptionally for some), leave their homes. Felix Faure Street residents did not understand why people would dress in white, mauve, saffron, yellow, green, black, to speak to God. Why not speak with God normally, at any time, in any place? Felix Faure Street residents did not understand the moans and the tears of the people in temples to speak to God. Why always plead with Him? Why always beg from Him? Why always ask Him for salvation, for something to eat, for something to drink? Why always kneel down, with foreheads to the ground, with heads in hands? God, who was the fruit of chaos, how could He impose these attitudes contrary to His very essence? If only people were more like birds! Birds got up early in the morning, groomed themselves, and started singing. Afterward, came love, then more songs, and (as each day had its own share of troubles), they would eat what they had hunted and pecked and start all over again. Love, songs, and loops the air! But people despised birds. They thought they were better than birds. They thought they were closer to God than birds. People, ultimately, were confused by the mixed messages. The intermediaries, the lecherous intermediaries—like the false muqaddams and the false gurus asking men, women, and children to put their foreheads to the ground, to kneel down in admiration—had confused them even more. These attitudes were degrading to human beings, humiliating to prayer, and blasphemous to God.

An apprentice philosopher would always say, "God is good, God is merciful! But do not ask, you must provide for yourselves. Everyone came into this world with their own vessel. It is up to everyone to fill theirs as they see fit. It is not up to God to fill our vessels. Because God is each and every one of us!"

Felix Faure Street residents did not understand why people kept asking God for more things, despite all of the evidence and all of the proof. Felix Faure Street residents did not ask God for anything. Felix Faure Street residents did not speak with God. Felix Faure Street residents had nothing to say to God. Felix Faure Street residents lived with God, and with God, with hope and patience combined. Felix Faure Street residents hoped, dreamed, got up early every morning, lived every day, lived every night, lived every moment.

Why, they wondered, did people spend their time holding their hands out to God, instead of living with Him?

"Ask, ask, you shall receive!" the intermediaries kept telling them. The intermediaries would tell them monstrous stories and the poor souls would hold their calloused hands up to the sky where God did not live. The downtrodden, blinded by the intermediaries, would do anything. They would crawl, kneel for whole nights through, beg for days on end, constantly implore. And still nothing! Instead of getting up and standing tall! Instead of working to earn a living by the sweat of their brows! Instead of living, while gazing upon flowers and women! Instead of loving and feeling pleasure! Instead of loving animals—cats, dogs, horses, and whatever else one might choose to love! God was freedom of love! God had said everything since driving man from the garden of Eden (where He Himself no longer tread). In His revealed Books, through His prophets, His friend, His son, the prince of prophets, His loved ones! In words, signs, symbols, parables, images, sounds, lights! God gave the Word to man, because He wanted him as His representative on earth, the Felix Faure Street Philosopher would say. Actually, God had wanted to give man the advantage, as he had been created in His own image, but man had been disappointing Him from the beginning, by wanting to be different. And the false muqaddams, the false gurus, and the new prophets were saying just the opposite.

They spoke of a god we had to beg, instead of setting us straight and being responsible for our existence and for God's existence. God was not far from us. He was with us, in us, and that was what we had to discover.

With the Ten Commandments.

With loving one's neighbors as oneself.

By completing works undertaken.

By being among the thirty-six righteous.

But the message had been intercepted, misconstrued, and distorted. Men and women were falling into darkness, blinded, led by increasingly misguided intermediaries, especially modern-day false muqaddams seeking power and might. Those false muqaddams—who had gotten it all wrong—were dragging others into their flocks, in their ignorance, and exploiting them.

2

THE FELIX FAURE Street Philosopher had happened upon the scene of the spectacle during his morning walk, a walk that Felix Faure Street residents often did. He would go up one side of Felix Faure Street and come back down the other. The Felix Faure Street Philosopher performed this routine every morning of every day that he woke up on Felix Faure Street. And he only ever woke up on Felix Faure Street! It was at the end of his routine that he noticed a crowd amassing on the other side of the street. He picked up the pace, since crowds were unusual on Felix Faure Street, especially at that time of morning. In the morning, some Felix Faure Street residents would stroll, others would walk, but they did not congregate. In the morning, Felix Faure Street residents were in a physical and mental dynamic. In the morning, on Felix Faure Street, greetings were discreet, made with a simple nod of the head. In the morning, Felix Faure Street residents did not open their mouths. The Felix Faure Street Philosopher almost did not make it to the scene of the crowd in time. Just before, on his path, he had glimpsed four veiled figures, covered from head to toe, appearing before him like an illusion. Although the veils were transparent, he was unable to make out their facial features clearly. These four veiled figures were walking slowly and seemed to be dividing themselves among both sides of the street. He passed by a few of them while crossing the street. The four veiled figures intrigued the Felix Faure Street Philosopher. He had never seen anything like it on the street, and yet, Felix Faure Street was the perfect place to happen upon everything extraordinary and incredible. Felix Faure Street, the Philosopher would say, was the center of the universe, the center of God. The Felix Faure Street Philosopher wanted to know more about those four veiled figures. He decided to go after them, but eventually gave up on it and resumed his fitness walk and meditation. While walking, the Felix Faure Street Philosopher could not get the four veiled figures that he had glimpsed out of his mind. Had he seen four veiled figures? Or, was it eight? Or sixteen? He had the impression that the veiled figures were splitting into two, were multiplying. Once the Felix Faure Street Philosopher reached the vicinity of the two fat policemen, he moved a little closer to the circle formed by the crowd. And there, he saw the large leper's chopped-up body, with his bulging belly, and his tiny genitals stuffed deep into his mouth. Placed at the four cardinal points around the chopped-up body, were four glowing lanterns. The flames from the wicks were weak, but growing stronger. He had never seen such a spectacle. The Felix Faure Street Philosopher would have never imagined it, and yet, he had quite the imagination. At least he had accepted that he was a philosopher and not a filmmaker. He was not putting on any spectacles. But this very spectacle was philosophy, he thought. He turned away from the spectacle, putting his right hand in his pants pocket and his left hand to his mouth.

The Philosopher was thinking. The apprentice philosophers were watching him think.

The Philosopher retraced his steps, crossed Felix Faure Street and went back up it again. He looked to the left and to the right, as if searching for something. The Philosopher had an idea in mind, an apprentice philosopher would say. He carefully retraced his steps, keeping his head down. The Philosopher had several ideas in mind, another apprentice philosopher would say.

"Who is this leper?" the Philosopher wondered.

The two fat policemen were still standing there, with their legs spread wide and their hands continuing to rub their plump bellies out of habit. They would yawn in unison from time to time. While the two fat policemen seemed to be getting bored, and the Philosopher—still keeping his head down—was thinking off in the distance, the large leper's eyes were answering every question. And the violin music kept oozing out of the still-shuttered hair salon, Chez Tonio.

The large leper's eyes were telling the story that had to be told to the great young man, the filmmaker Djib, to make into a film. And the flames from the wicks of the four glowing lanterns placed at the four cardinal points kept rising higher and higher, as if being drawn up by an invisible hand.

Who was this large chopped-up leper with his tiny genitals stuffed deep into his mouth? Who had chopped him up into pieces?

Before or after his death?

Was this large leper really dead?

It was still morning.

It was still quite dark.

A light and cool breeze was blowing.

A pungent and sweet smell called the sea to mind.

The sea was not far from Felix Faure Street, but it was not visible from there. It would make forays onto Felix Faure Street, and blend with the noises, smells, colors—the laughter of Cape Verdean girls, the sound of violin, the sound of guitar, hints of rosé wine, Gazelle Coumba beer, and Kiravi Valpierre wine. Felix Faure Street was the sea's favorite place to send its spray to indulge in new scents, new smells and new colors.

It was early morning before dawn, before daybreak, before sunrise. It was the time of the mysterious hours, of coolness, clearness, beneficial serenity. And those hours would fade into the pleasure of the Felix Faure Street moment. This was a moment of immense pleasure needed to face uncertain days. People would delight in pleasure as if for the last time, as if they would never again have the chance.

Live like you will never die! God advised.

Live like you will die the very next moment! God advised anew.

Live in the moment! A great Zen master taught.

At this time of day, many people would make love.

People would make love as if to defy death.

Muezzin, a man who lived behind one of the Felix Faure Street facades, was the one who had discovered the large leper's body. That morning, like every morning, Muezzin—responsible for the morning call to prayer—was heading at a lively, brisk pace to the mosque located on a street running parallel to Felix Faure Street. The atmosphere of that morning conveyed the lightness of the moment. Muezzin was practically flying. He was happy to live in the Felix Faure Street milieu. On that morning, Muezzin had also just ejaculated. He had just ejaculated, a violent ejaculation, a lengthily suppressed ejaculation. He had violently ejaculated that morning because the night before, the spectacle of the Cape Verdean girls' caramel bodies out on Felix Faure Street had driven him to the height of arousal. Until that morning, he had been thinking about suppressing that arousal, sustaining it, making it last, in order to prolong his enjoyment a little, a little more, just a little bit more. But that morning, he could not take it anymore and he exploded. While going to make the call to prayer, Muezzin knew that very few people would be going out to pray that morning, just like every other morning and increasingly so. The few people who did go to prayer were not Felix Faure Street residents. They had to have been passing through the street or living in the surrounding area. Felix Faure Street residents did not go anywhere looking for God. They lived with God and God was with them everywhere. The few people who still went to morning prayer did not dare to face God on Felix Faure Street. They surely hoped to, but did not dare. They were going out in search of gods hidden in temples with icons. As for Felix Faure Street residents, they lived with God in their homes, in the street, everywhere. In temples, Felix Faure Street residents did not find God. They found people who wanted to role play, like the official muqaddams, the muqaddams who felt called to serve, the new prophets, the new sons, the new chosen ones, the self-serving. As for Felix Faure Street residents, they had given up on temples a very long time ago. Muezzin thought that the call to prayer would rouse them from a drowsiness in which God's image might have faded slightly. Perhaps they would wake up in God, for the call to prayer would validate His existence to them. They would be reassured that God still exists. Muezzin was getting it all wrong. Felix Faure Street residents did not sleep with God's image. Felix Faure Street residents slept with God. In their sleep, in their dreams, in their daydreams, God was present and omnipresent. Felix Faure Street residents were with God in every moment. Felix Faure Street residents were in God. And God never left Felix Faure Street. Felix Faure Street residents lived in immanence, in God's presence. To settle the matter once and for all, Felix Faure Street residents had dissolved into God and had drowned in Him. So they had become one with Him. One, indivisible—which was the essence of His existence—to maintain balance in disorder! So Felix Faure Street residents were not on one side with God on the other side. It had to be that way for all creatures, all born of disorder, the Felix Faure Street Philosopher would say. It was not possible to dissociate from God. He had created us in His own image. He had created Himself in our image. Our quest for God was to perfect that image and make it divine. In this way, we will become One with God and we will be God. This was the quest for God. It was an individual, personal, intimate, dynamic quest. But the false muqaddams and other new prophets were saying something else. They were saying that to get to God, you had to be guided. That language had no bearing on Felix Faure Street. God guides who He wants. And God only guides those He knows. And God only knows those who are with Him all the time. God only knows those who live in His immanence, in His presence, those who seek to act with Him, for balance. Felix Faure Street residents had understood this for a very long time, by living each moment in God's presence. Felix Faure Street was God, especially in the morning. On Felix Faure Street, everyone would get up early with God who had spent the night with them. They would wake up that way every morning, divine. Felix Faure Street residents wanted to ensure that their street would always be there, now and forever. And their street was still there, so God was still there! Felix Faure Street residents too!

The sounds of bells and calls to prayer from temples devoted to other gods rang out every morning in the surrounding neighborhoods. There were no temples on Felix Faure Street, but all of the desperate calls to other people's gods could be heard all the way over there. While God was there on Felix Faure Street, with the Felix Faure Street residents! And God did not hear anything, did not see anything, did not say anything, did not feel anything, did not taste anything. God did not have senses. God was essence! Whereas man had five senses, plus a sixth sense— which was sex— the visionary Bentounès had said. He might even have a seventh sense: the belly!

So while he was en route to play his role like the others—all of those actors for so many gods—Muezzin tripped over a heap and fell onto it. The levity of the moment is what made him fall down. Muezzin was feeling so carefree on that morning. Carefree to be part of Felix Faure Street (even if that was not completely true). Carefree to be alive, that very morning, on Felix Faure Street. Carefree, perhaps, from spending half the night out on Felix Faure Street, ogling sights which he tried to deny himself, but which turned him on even more. Ah! All of those girls prancing around the streets at night! Their dresses were light and breezy. They were laughing, living life to the fullest, in the arms of men who were defying the destinies that had been mapped out for them by society, religions. What turned Muezzin on the most was the freedom with which those women would speak while roaring with laughter. And their mouths seemed to drag him down into a deep abyss. An abyss in which he delighted in wallowing. On Felix Faure Street nights, those women and girls did not dress like his two wives and three daughters, did not talk like them. Muezzin's two wives and three daughters lived in a rear lot off of Felix Faure Street. They were turbaned, covered, swaddled, like ghosts. For some time now, Muezzin's eldest daughter had been covering herself completely in veils, from head to toe, and had stopped speaking. Muezzin's two wives and three daughters did not live on Felix Faure Street, were not part of Felix Faure Street. Whereas Felix Faure Street girls just wore little things that barely concealed what tempted Muezzin the most. Muezzin would often say to anyone willing to listen—on Felix Faure Street or anywhere else—that he did not want to have any problems with God.

What problems?

God did not have any problems with anyone, an apprentice philosopher would have replied.

Muezzin did not have any sense of responsibility, another apprentice philosopher would have surely said. Muezzin refused to admit that he loved the good things in life. Muezzin was uncomfortable with himself and could not handle his inclinations, another apprentice philosopher would have added.

Oh, he could handle them, another apprentice philosopher would have said!

And whenever he did take matters into his own hands, Muezzin would always say that God was the one who had made him that way. God was an easy scapegoat, another apprentice philosopher would say. People lacking any notion or sense of responsibility always blamed everything on God. People uncomfortable in their own skin—who did not question or reflect on themselves, who could not handle it—they blamed everything on God or someone else who had it in for them.

"We must accept our fate. It is our god, the master of all things, who does what he wants. But with prayer, donations, charity, it will all work out. Keep praying, give everything you own, obey, you will see, our god knows what he is doing."

It was the others, the small gods, the frustrated and frigid gods, the new prophets, the lecherous false muqaddams—masturbating with words, with images—who were putting themselves in the place of their god and telling people stories, another apprentice philosopher would say. And laughing, the apprentice philosopher would add that they were the ones out doing the worst things! Instead of encouraging people to be responsible and to take charge of their lives and their relationships with God, these false muqaddams would drive them into the most extreme turmoil. That way, they could better manipulate them and play out their self-serving roles. These false muqaddams and others were irresponsible with their own lives, with their own existences. And to justify themselves, they would recruit ignorant or aimless men and women and keep them that way for as long as possible. Muezzin understood all of this, but was obliged to behave like everyone else, for survival. For survival, people would pretend. However, this did not suit Muezzin at all. Muezzin had secret desires, but he did not want to act on them. Otherwise, he stood to lose the privilege of being the one who made the morning call to prayer. For that privilege, he chose hypocrisy, lying, while telling himself that God would forgive him.

Who can hurt God?

God is in us!

And God knows no evil!

Muezzin's secret desires were that he wanted to be an integral part of Felix Faure Street. Muezzin wanted to be a Felix Faure Street resident. With his two wives, he was fumbling around in the dark. He would try to imagine things that he had never seen. Whereas with Felix Faure Street girls, those things were nearly exposed with an all-the-more arousing coyness. His penis, whenever it found itself on Felix Faure Street, would perk up in his pants. Since Muezzin did not know that wearing underwear could keep it in check, his penis would do its own thing—free and erect, ready to fire. Heaven forbid anyone brush past him in that state. Or even the wind! But whenever desire reached its pinnacle, whenever a girl burst out laughing, out in front of a doorway, he would ejaculate violently, his eyes closed, squeezing his prayer beads so tightly that they groaned under the intense pressure. Almost every night, Muezzin would get off like that, when he could no longer contain himself. That, too, was Felix Faure Street. A light street, light like the girls' panties offered up at the whim of a breeze!

At his present location, Muezzin sensed that he had not collapsed onto the body of one of the Felix Faure Street girls. Which he would have really loved, especially at that time of morning when love was so delicious. Muezzin got up in a hurry and noticed, upon bending back down, that he had fallen onto a chopped-up body. Muezzin did not know that this chopped-up body was that of a leper, a large leper with a bulging belly, whose eyes were laughing.

Muezzin did not notice that the large leper's eyes were laughing. The lights from the wicks of the four lanterns placed at the four cardinal points all around the large leper's chopped-up body were growing increasingly bold. Muezzin raised his head toward the few remaining stars, which were lingering to take in the spectacle. He scanned the sky to see if God was there and if He was watching him and if He was witnessing the spectacle. In the meantime, the large leper's eyes were laughing and his bulging belly was shaking in spasms from such asphyxiating laughter. And Muezzin was still not paying any attention to the large leper's eyes, which were convulsing in laughter. Muezzin was scared. It was chilly outside. Felix Faure Street was calm, nearly deserted at that hour. A few night owls were still hanging around in dark corners, held back by invisible but alluring muses. Those stragglers were searching the dark corners of Felix Faure Street for partners-in-crime in order to quench their burning desire to surrender to Felix Faure Street oblivion, that dizzying oblivion, to which resistance was futile. Muezzin was panic-stricken. He was turning his head every which way. He seemed to be looking for help. At that hour, aside from the last disciples of Bacchus, Epicurious, and Eros, there was no one else on Felix Faure Street and it was completely silent. Except for a piercing violin music in the background, oozing out from the shuttered hair salon, Chez Tonio. Muezzin opened his eyes wide to make out something else or someone else on the street. In the nerve-racking silence, he thought he heard noises. The noises were not coming from far away. Muezzin let the noises guide him and ended up in an interminable, torturous, winding passageway, with puddles of water that his feet—squeezed into his babouche slippers—kept sinking into disgustingly. Muezzin was caught in the passageway, which was winding around him like a whirlpool. Intoxicated, he plunged deeper and deeper into the passageway and suddenly found himself within a small courtyard. That was Felix Faure Street. Behind the daytime facades, there was a universe of courts and courtyards, through a labyrinth of passageways. These courts and courtyards were surrounded by little cottages with red-tiled roofs. There were sturdy cottages, wooden cottages, cardboard cottages, but they all had red tiles. Red tiles were part of Felix Faure Street. Young trees were growing among centenarian trees in those courts and courtyards. Sheep, goats, pigs were sometimes there tied to makeshift stakes or tree trunks. There were colorful basins with water from the previous day's wash. Little windows faced each other, turning their backs, giving the cold shoulder, opening up, laughing like magical frames. Those little cottages looked like magic boxes! That, too, was Felix Faure Street. It was a magical street! But very soon perhaps, Felix Faure Street was about to lose its magic, with the new monsters of real estate planning to tear everything down in order to burst forth horrors in concrete and glass. And then, Felix Faure Street will rise up to heaven with God. For the time being, Muezzin was staying in one of those rear lots on Felix Faure Street. He had found a studio apartment, so as to not be too far away from the mosque where he was charged with making the morning call to prayer. It was dark in that courtyard where Muezzin now found himself. Everything was silent, aside from some strange noises. The noises were late-night noises. Noises of ending and beginning anew. As if thousands of lives were about to bloom and the nighttime vampires were about to hide away from the light of Felix Faure Street. Muezzin heard some furtive noises and almost ran away. He realized that it was just some big rats. Those big rats would take advantage of those silences, nibbling up the crumbs dropped from the hands and mouths of people who—unsure of the immediate future—devoured life voraciously. Muezzin's eyes were getting used to the darkness and were seeing a bit more clearly. What was he to do? The time for the last call to prayer was imminent. Why was he worrying about the last call to morning prayer, since there had not been a first call? He wondered. The mosque was located a short ways away, just past the turn at the top of Felix Faure Street. He still needed to walk up the street a bit before reaching it. And at that moment, he was in a labyrinth of passageways and courtyards, with a chopped-up body waiting for him out on the sidewalk! Was the Imam even worried after not hearing the first call? Whereas Muezzin would get up early for the first call to prayer, the Imam leading the prayer would take his time and get there just a few minutes or even a few seconds beforehand. Maybe the Imam would think that there had been a power outage? Muezzin did not know what to think and did not want to think anymore.

He was stuck.

He could not back out.

He was doomed.

He had to move forward.

He had to keep pushing through those passageways.

What was he going to find deep inside those passageways, courts, and courtyards?

Muezzin did not know that he was already part of the story that the large chopped-up leper's eyes were telling out on the sidewalk! Muezzin saw a door leading to another passageway. He rushed through it, swept along, carried away by an invisible guide. He found himself once again in another silent courtyard, numbed by the coolness of that morning. Just a few big rats were running for cover. He was unable to discern everything around him. He opened his eyes wide in that labyrinth of courts and courtyards diverging in any and every direction. He thought he heard breathing, not far away. He directed his gaze toward the source of the breathing and caught sight of some figures on large wooden tables. And all around there were lanterns with feeble flames. As Muezzin drew closer to the figures, the breathing grew increasingly louder. The breathing was coming from the figures. Muezzin moved even closer and put a hesitant hand on one of the figures. He heard a grumbling and backed several meters away. Muezzin was able to make out the figures seated on large assorted tables and benches. He cried, "Help, Waloussilène!"

"Who's there?" a strange-sounding voice suddenly said.

He thought he was hearing a voice that had been asleep for a long time, a warm, strange-sounding voice. Muezzin was unable to locate the voice, but he felt it close by. He was trembling in fear, but he could not back out. As if he were hypnotized. He did not see a hand grab a nearby lantern and draw up its flame. An opaque light was bathing the courtyard in a supernatural halo. The warm, strange-sounding voice belonged to a body, a body sitting on an old leather chair. The body was wrapped in a big blanket. Behind the voice and the body, a door opened slightly and suddenly flew off its hinges, striking the wooden wall of the cottage. A lantern's flame was glowing in the back of the room and the silhouette of a girl was standing at the entrance.

"Go back to bed, it's nothing," the warm, strange-sounding voice said and the silhouette disappeared into the back of the room, chanting the blues. And her shadow, cast by the lantern, faded from view. After a moment of silence lasting only a few seconds, the warm, strange-sounding voice cried:

"What's the matter?"

"There's a dead man, here, in front of your house!" Muezzin said.

"A dead man?

"In front of my house?

"Where did you see a dead man here?"

The warm, strange, deliberately sleepy-sounding voice mumbled something incomprehensible. Suddenly, four veiled figures, which seemed to be multiplying in the darkness, rose up from a space in the courtyard, like a macabre symphony orchestra. The four veiled figures, which seemed to be multiplying, lined up in single file, running the length of one small passageway. They were each holding a lantern. Suddenly, they disappeared around a corner. Muezzin caught sight of them just as they were disappearing from view. Muezzin stopped talking to the warm, strange, deliberately sleepy-sounding voice—which was now completely awake. Muezzin wanted to know which way the four veiled figures, which seemed to be in two places at once, had gone. He was turning his head every which way, when the warm, strange-sounding voice said to him:

"Are you talking to me or are you looking for someone?"

The body from which the strange voice was coming lifted itself slightly and was surprised to see Muezzin standing before it:

"But aren't you Muezzin?

"What are you doing here at this hour?

"Didn't you go to call your people to prayer?"

Muezzin felt somewhat relieved. At least the voice recognized him, even if he himself did not recognize the voice:

"I was going to the mosque when I stumbled upon a chopped-up body. I thought it best to look for help.

"There's hardly anyone in the street, aside from the last few vampires.

"I wanted to look for help and I went through the first doorway, right in front of me. I found myself lost in the labyrinth of passageways, courts, and courtyards, until, suddenly, I heard breathing noises and I saw strange figures on the tables over there."

Muezzin pointed toward a space not far from the courtyard in which he found himself with the warm, strange-sounding voice.

"I think they are veiled figures.

"They just left in a single file.

"They disappeared over there. They were each holding a lantern.

"Didn't you see them?

"They were there when I got here!

"I am sure that I saw them, those veiled figures.

"But just what were those four veiled figures?"

The warm, strange-sounding voice replied:

"Listen, mind your own business. First you talk about strange figures, now you talk about four veiled figures."

Muezzin was casting glances all around.

"Did you come to talk about a dead man, or did you come to deal with old ghosts?" the deliberately sleepy-sounding voice asked him.

"Old ghosts?" Muezzin exclaimed, in a panicked voice. "Don't scare me. I really did see those veiled figures.

"I thought I saw four of them, but it seemed like they were in two places at once. I know that anything goes in your cottages and courtyards, but don't talk about old ghosts. And what do you mean by *old ghosts*? A ghost is a ghost!"

It was starting to get a little bit lighter. The light from the lantern, next to the leather chair, was glowing increasingly bright. The warm, strange-sounding voice softened. That strange, deliberately sleepy-sounding voice had woken up completely and had become a face.

A woman's face.

A small-statured woman.

A curvy woman.

A light-skinned woman.

This woman was Driankė.

"Driankė, is that you?" Muezzin exclaimed, surprised.

"I didn't even realize that I was at your place!

"With these courtyards and passageways, I never know where I am.

"I didn't know I was at your place.

"Well, Driankė, what are you doing here?

"Are you sleeping outside or what?

"I didn't even recognize you."

Everyone on Felix Faure Street knew Drianké. She belonged to Felix Faure Street. Although her cottage was located deep among the courtyards and passageways, Drianké lived on Felix Faure Street. Drianké was a lifelong pillar of Felix Faure Street, the street's residents had tacitly decreed when she came here a few years ago, limping along.

"You don't recognize my house?

"And yet, you've taken these passageways hundreds of times.

"Stop telling tales!

"A dead man, you said?"

"Yes, a dead man!"

"A dead-dead man?"

"Yes, a dead-dead man!"

"A dead man in front of which house?"

"Well, not in front of a house!

"In the street, on the sidewalk, across from Chez Tonio!"

Silence fell between Drianké and Muezzin. The only sound was the blues emanating from the inside of the cottage. A blues as piercing as the violin music oozing out of the shuttered hair salon, Chez Tonio. The silence between Drianké and Muezzin lingered and Muezzin wondered if had been dreaming.

Ultimately, there was no dead man. There was just a body chopped up into big pieces! Ultimately, nothing had happened. There were just four lanterns placed at the four cardinal points!

It was all beyond Muezzin.

"Everyone will finish their insane journey one day!" Drianké suddenly said.

With this silence broken, Muezzin realized that he was not dreaming.

Ultimately, there definitely was a chopped-up body outside, on the sidewalk.

Muezzin was at his wits' end. Maybe the chopped-up body was not that of a dead man!

Still monologuing, Drianké got up.

"In this life, everything has a price, everything is for sale, everything is bought and paid for.

"Even the slightest thought, even the slightest action.

"There is no other world, no other life.

"Everything happens here and nowhere else.

"Everyone reaps what they sow, and God has nothing to do with it. God doesn't reward those who deem themselves worthy. Everyone sets their own price. God has been done with us since Creation, since the reflection. God left Eden with His magi—Adam, Eve, and Satan. We are all in the same boat, now and forever. And in this boat we are all mixed up together. Anyone can be God or Satan, Adam or Eve, as they wish."

Drianké got up, grabbed the cane lying next to her and, leaning on it (but not limping), headed to the entryway. Muezzin followed her, glancing all around, and he thought that Drianké, who was talking nonstop, was saying a prayer of requiem for the large chopped-up leper. And Muezzin was saying, "Amen, amen, amen" and did notice that Drianké—who he had always seen limping ever since her arrival on Felix Faure Street—was not limping. Despite his amens, Muezzin kept turning his head every which way. He was scared and he was trembling. He even tried to latch on to Drianké and she stopped, leaned on her cane, and said to him:

"Are you a man or what? What is up with you trembling like that?"

Drianké headed toward the entryway through the labyrinth of passageways, with no hesitation. It was at this very moment that the Felix Faure Street Philosopher crossed the threshold of that entryway, perhaps in search of the four multiplying veiled figures. Which for the Philosopher could prove difficult. This multitude of cottages, courts, courtyards, passageways all accessed Felix Faure

Street through a single entryway. As soon as you crossed the threshold, it was like being snatched up by a multi-tentacled monster. Muezzin was still trailing Drianké, latched on to her like a little boy. The door that opened up onto the street was made of wood and it swung back and forth at the whim of whichever hand was pushing it. When the Philosopher caught sight of Drianké and Muezzin, he retraced his steps. Four seemingly multiplying veiled figures had passed through the same passageways some time before the Philosopher, and had been out on Felix Faure Street. The four multiplying veiled figures had not even glanced at the onlookers, or the apprentice philosophers, or the large leper's chopped-up body. And the large leper's eyes were begging the four veiled figures, each one holding a lantern, not to leave like that. The large leper's eyes saw the four veiled figures as soon as they reached the street, and the large chopped-up leper's eyes were crying. The large chopped-up leper's eyes had recognized the four veiled figures. With his tiny genitals stuffed deep into his mouth, the large chopped-up leper's eyes knew the four veiled figures. Lying in a pool of indescribably red blood, the large leper's eyes were begging the four veiled figures to stay and listen to them. The large leper's eyes did not understand why the four veiled figures did not stop. Surrounded by onlookers and apprentice philosophers, the large leper's eyes did not understand why the four veiled figures were leaving without looking at them. The large leper's eyes did not understand why the four veiled figures were moving away so calmly, as if nothing had happened. The large leper's eyes wanted the four veiled figures to stop, so they could tell them the story.

The four veiled figures left peacefully and disappeared around the first corner, onto Felix Faure Street, holding their lanterns, the flames of which kept rising higher and higher. Just as the four veiled figures were fading from view, the two fat policemen arrived.

Who had alerted the two fat policemen?

Who had told them that there was this spectacle on Felix Faure Street?

The two fat policemen were trying to push back the onlookers and the apprentice philosophers who were gathering in droves around them, but they were unable to do so.

On Felix Faure Street?

Somewhere else, it was possible! Anywhere else, it was possible! But on Felix Faure Street, it was impossible!

The street belonged to the onlookers.

Who were these onlookers?

Well, the proprietors and co-proprietors of Felix Faure Street! The Felix Faure Street residents themselves.

There were also those who did not live on Felix Faure Street, but were part of Felix Faure Street. Like the great young man, the filmmaker Djib, to whom the story that the large leper's eyes were telling had to be told to make into a film!

The Felix Faure Street proprietors were not the ones who had alerted the two fat policemen. No one had alerted the two fat policemen. The two fat policemen had been making the rounds of this hot and cold Plateau neighborhood, because they liked it there (and with good reason)!

Girl kebabs!

Meat kebabs!

Cash-money kebabs!

Pleasure kebabs!

Bottles of Gazelle Coumba beer kebabs!

Glasses of Kiravi Valpierre wine kebabs!

They had not done anything since finding themselves in front of the large leper's chopped-up body, with his tiny genitals stuffed deep into his month. The apprentice philosophers were making deductions, analyses, hypotheses, postulates. But the two fat policemen, who had found every excuse to be on Felix Faure Street—on rounds, on tour, for canvassing, for safety—were still standing there with their legs spread wide and still not saying anything. Felix Faure Street had never needed any policemen on rounds, any policemen for canvassing, any policemen for safety. Felix Faure Street had its own rules and its own law. There were no traitors on Felix Faure Street. There was an honor code for residing, living, passing through, passing away on that street. If that leper was found chopped up into big pieces on Felix Faure Street, there was a good reason for it. That was what they needed to find. And the reason was not far away. It was on Felix Faure Street, somewhere or another. But the reason, the large chopped-up leper's eyes were giving it away and no one was paying any attention to them!

3

FELIX FAURE STREET was located in a neighborhood in the heart of this great city nearly surrounded by ocean. The neighborhood was called the Plateau. It was the neighborhood of the occupiers, the neighborhood of the collaborators. It became the neighborhood of the bourgeois, the neighborhood of people with means, the neighborhood of people with influence, the neighborhood of cedars and sabers. It was the neighborhood of people with recognized ancestries and lineages, the neighborhood of people appointed to office, citizens. The neighborhood was a residential neighborhood. There were large buildings. There were administrative buildings, the governor's palace—which has since become the Palace—with its numerous annexes. There were also buildings with chic apartments for those who had the means and for foreigners hailing from afar who generally, at the time, always had the means. There were haute couture boutiques for those who lived there. There were tea rooms for those who had the time and the means. This neighborhood was not for everyday people, who had neither the time nor the means. This was not the neighborhood of those who had been appointed to "indigenous" offices. This was the neighborhood of the occupiers, the well-to-do, and the citizens. The citizens were most often well-to-do. For these citizens had education, training, and all of the associated privileges, as well as all of the opportunities with all of the requisite compromises. The people lived farther away, in the Medina. Between the Plateau and the Medina, there was a mid-range neighborhood, which began a little ways away, down Madeleine Street, toward Reims Street and l'Abattoir Street. This neighborhood, called Niayes Thioker, was occupied by the Aristocrats, the ancestors of Bouna, the Trotskyist older brother of the Felix Faure Street Philosopher. These Aristocrats had refused to lower themselves and live alongside the uncircumcised who occupied the Plateau with their collaborators, compatriots, neighbors, and friends. When the people started to receive education and training, in order to serve as subordinates—salaried intermediate or middle managers—other neighborhoods were created by a large real estate firm dating back to the time of the occupation. The first housing lots were pompously named Baobab and Liberty. Baobab I, Baobab II, Liberty I, Liberty II, Liberty III, Liberty IV, Liberty V, Liberty VI. With the decline of the occupation and the advent of the liberation era, other housing lots started having local names. Dieuppeul I, Dieuppeul II, Dieuppeul III, Dieuppeul IV. Sacré-Coeur I, II, III. And, for everyday people, housing projects were built, with most of them modeled—whether out of contempt or a lack of imagination—after pigeon cages. With liberation and liberalization, new real estate businesses were established and housing lots began to have increasingly common names or the names of developers who did not plant trees. The city was sprawling and did not stop sprawling, like a pandemic. Years of drought propelled millions of people toward the city, which brought about gigantic suburban neighborhoods with increasingly exotic names. Diamegueune, Guédiawaye, Yeumbeul! And the city became increasingly vast, sprawling from the far side of the Plateau neighborhood, over to the sea running the length of the country, and inward. The Plateau neighborhood had not moved. Some of its former occupants had cleared out and gone elsewhere, farther away, which left room for the Cape Verdean immigrants, the Felix Faure Street Philosopher, and the Felix Faure Street apprentice philosophers. The Plateau neighborhood was backed up by its ramparts, buried deep in the ocean, and had thus maintained its exclusive neighborhood character. And Felix Faure Street was in this exclusive neighborhood with its well-established bars, its dive bars, its gambling dens, its Chinese-Vietnamese restaurants, its French restaurants, its hair salons. On Felix Faure Street, an entire community treated by others like scum, misfits, degenerates, was taking shape. And yet, Felix Faure Street residents lived with God! Felix Faure Street residents were a community that lived with honor codes! A community where one part would work days and the other nights. This community was primarily comprised of nationals and Cape Verdean immigrants. There were Cape Verdeans throughout this Plateau neighborhood. On Blanchot Street, Raffenel Street, Bayeux Street, Carnot Street, Malenfant Street, Thiers Street, Denain Street, Jules Ferry Street, Doctor Thèse Street, Escarfait Street, Tolbiac Street, Grammont Street, Paul Holle Street! But the Felix Faure Street Cape Verdeans were different, because they were on Felix Faure Street. The Cape Verdeans were generally discreet and, at the time, did not often mix with the local population, but they lived together harmoniously. They had not managed to get any farther away than right across from their islands. They had stopped on a peninsula. Maybe that was why! They had wanted to go much farther away, to America like other people. Alas! Their boat had washed ashore right across from their islands! The Cape Verdeans had come with their families. They had come with women, children, guitars, and violins. They were bronze-complected and—if not for their occupations as hairdressers, seamstresses, their Western style of dress, the language they spoke, the violin and the morna—they would be easily taken for Kabylians, Berbers, or Greeks. When it was hot, the men would be in undershirts and shorts and the women would wear strappy floral dresses! Felix Faure Street had a reputation for being a hot street in every sense of the word. Yet, the Cape Verdeans did not run any gambling dens or dive bars on Felix Faure Street. Cape Verdeans were merely part of the decor.

Like the violin music!

Like the caramel-toned girls in halter tops!

Like the hair salons!

Like the fashion!

The Cape Verdean women would sew in their little dining room salons, with pedal machines. Fittings would take place in a corner of a bedroom or dining/living room, next to a table sometimes featuring a platter of cakes that smelled so good, they made you want to have one or two. Definitely two! The Cape Verdean women were good seamstresses. They would add special finishes and charge more than the local seamstresses, which was standard. On Felix Faure Street, there were also Moorish jewelers who sold silver treasures. Chains, bracelets, engraved spoons, pipes, for those who delighted in unique objects. There were a few stores, a few shops for essentials where one could buy a delicious pain-thon sandwich. But these few shops on Felix Faure Street went unnoticed. Felix Faure Street was Cape Verdean hair salons. Felix Faure Street was restaurants, bars, and one hotel-restaurant—which technically did not belong to Felix Faure Street residents, but Felix Faure Street residents could work there. During the daytime, all of this appeared normal. Felix Faure Street was a masked street, a veiled street. Nighttime was when Felix Faure Street truly revealed itself.

Every night there would be one or two policemen in the vicinity, on pretext. "It's a hot street!" they would say.

Felix Faure Street was not a hot street, as was implied. Felix Faure Street had the reputation for being what it was not. Other people badmouthed this street without knowing it. Felix Faure

Street was the street of life, of hope and patience combined, God's street. But there were no temples for praying to God. The street was there for living with God. Felix Faure Street residents did not pray to God. They lived God with God. And that was something that ordinary people—rather abundant in this day and age—could not understand. Those two fat policemen did not need to be there, plain and simple, an apprentice philosopher would say. But the two fat policemen were there, for the Felix Faure Street reputation.

Everyone wanted to be on Felix Faure Street

Everyone had to be on Felix Faure Street.

Day and night.

The daytime was another life. The same life as the nighttime one, with the difference being that Felix Faure Street residents wore masks during the day and costumes at night. During the daytime, some of the street's residents hid their faces under hats, parasols, scarves; under hands shading eyes; behind window shutters. They did not want to be exposed. They had to keep others from seeing their true faces. Their true faces were impossible to imagine. Their faces were not the faces of mere mortals. Their faces were supra-terrestrial faces, divine faces. Felix Faure Street residents were supra-people. They did not see what we ourselves saw. Whereas we saw shit, misery, gunk, stupidity, nastiness, ugliness, violence, evil everywhere—and that all was written on our faces. We saw hopelessness, jealousy, yearning, hypocrisy—and that was written on our faces. As for Felix Faure Street residents, they saw what no one thought to see on Felix Faure Street. They saw God face-to-face and he saw them. They looked God in the eyes.

Felix Faure Street residents were different from all this city's other residents. Whenever night fell on Felix Faure Street, you had to see how they were dressed! Such magnificent costumes! They would don the apparel of people from very far away places. Shimmering, daring apparel, in bright colors. There were also frills, ribbons, straps, bows in every color. Their faces were radiant and harkened back to some of the mystical faces of Velasquez. And so the first part of night on Felix Faure Street was left to its community. Those who could not do without the street would come later. Those who badmouthed Felix Faure Street, who denigrated it, slandered it, did not go there at night. Only the audacious, the fellow non-conformists dared to come to Felix Faure Street. Most people in this city, especially in this exclusive neighborhood, thought that Felix Faure Street was the street of disorder, rampant disarray, debauchery. Self-proclaimed good people, coming home in the early evening and having to pass through Felix Faure Street, would pick up the pace. They did not want to linger, for Felix Faure Street people were about to inundate their street with their magnificent costumes. It was hard to distinguish men from women, young from old, as the costumes gave everyone a completely different look, different air, different attitude. They were like guests at a ball. A ball to which God would have invited them—and vice versa. They would walk slowly, stop, look each other over; admire, embrace, love one another. And as soon as night moved into its second phase, they would go home after breathing in just about all of the fresh air on the street. They would thereby leave the street to the audacious and the non-conformists. They were the ones who occupied Felix Faure Street during this other phase of night, while the residents were at home resting with God.

Everyone on Felix Faure Street knew each other. And everyone knew Drianké. And as with the other Felix Faure Street residents, everyone knew her, but no one knew her story. On Felix Faure Street, people did not go looking for stories, but everyone had their own story. Felix Faure Street camouflaged everyone's stories and made up new stories for them, with hope and patience combined, with God. Drianké—the curvy, small-statured woman—was walking with a slight limp when she arrived one day on Felix Faure

Street. And no one asked her any questions. She arrived with the blues on her lips.

Muezzin and Drianké—the curvy, small-statured woman—arrived at the scene of the spectacle together, along with the Philosopher (who had done a one-eighty and perhaps not yet noticed that Drianké was not limping). At the sight of the two fat policemen, Drianké—the curvy, small-statured, no-longer-limping woman—pouted in disdain. One of the two fat policemen immediately shouted:

"Drianké, you know this street like the fingers of your hand, can you tell us what happened here?"

Drianké shot them an ever scornful look.

"Is that how you talk to people?

"Who are you talking to?

"Even with dogs, you greet them first!"

(Especially! an apprentice philosopher would say.)

"And why me?

"Muezzin is the one who came to tell me," she said.

"Yes, I'm the one who went to tell her that there was a dead man, I mean, a body chopped up into big pieces in the street," Muezzin confirmed, erratic.

"I found Drianké outside in her courtyard, sitting in her old armchair . . ."

No one was listening to Muezzin.

Drianké did not look at the large leper's chopped-up body with his tiny genitals stuffed deep into his mouth. She yawned with an extraordinary serenity, wrapped up in a big blanket, the colors of which complemented her skin tone.

"Did you see that?" one of the two fat policemen said, pointing out the leper's chopped-up body.

Drianké drew a little closer and then immediately backed away, staggering, like in a tragic scene from a Latin American soap opera.

(Drianké had gotten the chance to display her acting talents in several films and plays.) A moment passed and, with everything completely silent, she softly said:

"That's my leper!"

"What, that's your leper?" one of the two fat policemen said.

"That's my leper, that's my leper," Drianké chanted.

And then, Drianké suddenly fell silent.

After a few disorienting moments in space and time, she started to sing. From Drianké's throat emerged one of the most beautiful blues songs ever heard since the Cotton Club. A song unleashed from desert dunes, carried along by sandy winds, to oceans near and far! Drianké's song came back trembling over the large leper's chopped-up body whose bulging belly had taken on even more gigantic proportions. When Drianké's voice rang out on Felix Faure Street, the Felix Faure Street sparrows, the Felix Faure Street pigeons were happy, the people too, the swallows too. Drianké's voice was the voice of Felix Faure Street. From her voice emerged the guts of Felix Faure Street. The guts of the lives of these thousands of people, descendants of families, former proprietors of the premises, scattered throughout hundreds of cottages, courts, and courtyards. With the problems of inheritance, legitimacy, illegitimacy, incest, everything had been chopped up into small pieces, by hand. Everyone was clinging to their little piece of property, like to a rampart before the great maelstrom. In this community of rear courtyards, there was everything, but then again, there was very little education, very little training, very few opportunities. Some people worked, everyone else scraped by with odd jobs. Only the Cape Verdean immigrants who lived there were doing whatever it took because they had to. They were obliged. They did not leave their islands across the way for nothing. They had not been able to go any farther, but still dreamed, hoped. As for their daughters, as soon as they reached the age of consent, they immediately tried to get jobs somewhere, outside of this milieu. They were not about to find work, a husband, set up a home, have children on Felix Faure Street. They did not want to stay on Felix Faure Street forever. All they wanted was to escape from this place, which, for them, represented immigration, overcrowding, hairdressing, dressmaking, violins, and nostalgic desserts. They had lived in narrow cottages or in small rooms with hairdresser fathers, dressmaker mothers, shared among everyone. They wanted to break that chain. They had been educated in their new country and had an easier time fitting in than their parents. As such, most of them got married to locals. And others got married to people from their country of origin who had moved on with them in this new life.

The overcrowding, the close quarters on Felix Faure Street were indescribable. So many things were happening behind Felix Faure Street facades! People would brush their teeth at their windows. People would shave in front of the doors to their rooms. And people were constantly coming and going. There was movement on Felix Faure Street. At night, residents would go to bed late due to the heat left behind by those passing through Felix Faure Street without stopping, because they looked down on this street. With windows rolled up, they would speed down the street in their cars, leaving in their wake their disdain for this street that they trash-talked, along with the heat from their hearts and their vehicles, with their engines running at full throttle. Most Felix Faure Street residents would stay out in the street, sitting on benches, chairs, standing, walking, coming and going, until nighttime fell and everyone would get ready for the grand masked ball. Not only were people seeking fresh air, but they were also meeting up with God. God loved nightfall on Felix Faure Street. Did He still exist? Would He keep His promises to the last of us? Why not? If that was what the last of us wanted, instead of being the first of us right now. God's promises to the last of us were to all victims of injustice and arbitrariness and to everyone not living in hope and patience with God. Because those who had committed those injustices and those arbitrary acts would all pay sooner or later, here on earth. If the justice of men did not make things right, their conscience would torture them until their last breath, and if they did not have a conscience, a never-ending feeling of resentment would hound them all the days of their lives. They will never know the serenity of those who are in complete harmony with their conscience. Good men. Fair men. Men of virtue. Men of God. Like the Felix Faure Street residents! As for the Felix Faure Street residents, they did not have any doubts. They were not concerned with promises. They were in God in every moment.

"I am closer to you than your jugular vein.

"When you take one step toward me, I take ten steps toward you," God has said.

The Felix Faure Street residents had God and they had the violin! The violin was a divine instrument, an apprentice philosopher would say whenever he heard a violin playing. That was the instrument that the angels played around God, he would add.

On those mornings, like this morning, some people were also looking for ways to get a bite to eat. The local shopkeeper's list of debtors was already so long that he refused to add anyone else. At times, it would take tremendous powers of seduction, persuasion of an imminent cash influx, for him to add a few pieces of sugar, a bag of coffee, two or three cigarettes for smokers, a little oil, some eggs, some pain-thon, some buttered bread, some Chocolega pain au chocolat, some plain and simple bread to the long list. With all that overcrowding, the inheritors of Felix Faure Street were finding ways to sublet halves of rooms, sometimes even quarters of rooms. Owners, inheritors, and immigrant renters managed to get by, to dream, to hope, in the wake of frequent yet quickly quashed arguments and fights. Felix Faure Street had an honor code, everyone knew that. Not everyone had the privilege of living on a divine street, a street soothed by violins, in the heart of the city, in the Plateau neighborhood, the exclusive neighborhood. On Felix Faure Street, everything was toned down, as was God in their lives! There were no explosions on Felix Faure Street. Felix Faure Street was a well-situated street, in that exclusive neighborhood!

Felix Faure Street was steps away from the presidential Palace!

Felix Faure Street was steps away from the Great Church!

Felix Faure Street was steps away from the Bureau of radio and television!

Felix Faure Street was steps away from the National Theater!

It was in that theater that Drianké, the small-statured woman, would work from time to time. But what Drianké knew best was singing the blues. She wanted to use her acting talents as a gateway for a grand blues singing career. She was not there yet, but she will get there, the Felix Faure Street Philosopher and the Felix Faure Street apprentice philosophers would always say.

Felix Faure Street overlooked Independence Square!

Felix Faure Street was not far from the French cultural center.

Felix Faure Street was not far from the Central Market.

Certain privileged occupants of the Plateau neighborhood had left, after the departure of the occupiers who had granted them their privileges. Some collaborators had followed them. The bourgeois and the wealthy had left to settle elsewhere, farther along toward the outermost point. They had created residential neighborhoods, far from the immigrants, far from all the people who were starting to move up into the neighborhood that had once been reserved for them. But since the street was strategically located, there were some big law offices, some big medical offices and consulting firms, owned by people who did not live on Felix Faure Street. All of those chic and precious offices abutted the Cape

Verdean hair salons, with music oozing out every minute of the day. Morna, biguine. A piercing, captivating, enchanting, nostalgic music, a music from the islands, not far away. As soon as night fell, the Felix Faure Street residents who had been hiding away from the heat of the asphalt, of luxury cars, of people dressed to the nines, would go back into their street with another world, another kind. This other world, this other kind would take over the street until daybreak, even after the Felix Faure Street residents had gone back home with God in the middle of the night, to fall asleep with Him, to the sound of the morna.

Drianké carried on with her plaintive blues lament, in front of the spectacle unfolding on the Felix Faure Street sidewalk across from the shuttered hair salon, Chez Tonio. The two fat policemen did not seem to appreciate Drianké's voice.

"We're not at the theater here," one of the two fat policemen said to her.

"Do you know this leper?"

Drianké was still chanting the blues. She was turning her head back and forth as if to say No! No! No! I can't believe it.

"I know him.

"He is my leper.

"He was sleeping at my place.

"I was the one who let him.

"I found him one night on Maginot Avenue.

"I told him he could sleep at night, in a corner of my courtyard."

Drianké stopped whispering the blues. She looked at the large leper's chopped-up body, and got back to her blues, now chanting them.

"He is your leper, and this morning, he is here on the sidewalk, chopped up into big pieces, with his tiny genitals stuffed deep into his mouth! What do you have to say for yourself?"

The fat policeman who was talking like that was practically yelling at Drianké. He was still standing like the other one, with his legs spread wide.

"Leave her alone!" one of the apprentice philosophers said.

"That's what you get for doing something good!" Muezzin added.

The two fat policemen were still trying to make the apprentice philosophers and the growing number of onlookers move back, in vain. That morning, no one was worrying about how they were going to charm the local shopkeeper. The spectacle had stopped everything in its tracks—every urge, every instinct, every desire, every craving. Drianké was still looking at the large leper's chopped-up body while chanting the blues. For those unable to make sense of it, her face, half-covered by a big blanket, called to mind the Madonna looking at her dead son. The Madonna's son was not dead. We are the Madonna's son! an apprentice philosopher would have said.

Drianké sat down on the curb, with her cane beside her, and was wiping her shining tears with part of her blanket. Muezzin, reinvigorated by Drianké's blues chanting, moved by Drianké's lyrics, upset by Drianké's tear drops, stepped toward the two fat policemen to explain how it had happened:

"I was going to the mosque, like usual, for the call to prayer when I saw this terrible thing.

"I didn't see anything at first.

"I fell onto a heap.

"It was when I got up that . . .

"I didn't even know he was a leper.

"I didn't even see the four lanterns . . ."

"It's okay, it's okay," one of the two fat policemen said, cutting Muezzin's explanation short.

"What do you mean, it's okay, it's okay?

"I'm the one who discovered the chopped-up body, this morning.

"When I happened upon him, you weren't here and now you won't even let me speak! This is unbelievable!

"Who better to provide you with information than me?

"It's always the same in this country!

"I'm the one who found the chopped-up body, I'm the one who went to call for help and now I'm being excluded, ignored, downplayed, cut out of everything! And you tell me, it's okay, it's okay.

"That's my chopped-up body, even if it is Drianké's leper!"

Muezzin was muttering. The apprentice philosophers agreed with him and some offered their support by patting him on the shoulder.

"Since it's your body, tell us how you ended up here, just by chance?" one of the two fat policemen fired back.

"You didn't have a problem with him?

"Couldn't you be the one who, how shall I say, chopped him up into pieces and who stuffed his tiny genitals into his mouth?"

Muezzin could barely breathe.

"But what are you saying?

"How could I end up here by chance?

"There was no chance here. Every morning, I take the same route to go to make the call to prayer.

"How could I kill a leper?

"How could I chop him up like that all alone?

"Are you the ones who helped me then?

"Listen, just stop with these insinuations. I don't like this one bit.

"I've never had a problem with anyone.

"God is my witness."

In the crowd, an apprentice philosopher broke away and drew closer to Muezzin and said:

"Muezzin, have you forgotten about the problem you had with that man who led your oldest daughter astray under the pretexts of religion, a religious path, days she had to go to prayer? That man abused your oldest daughter and, through her, has extorted every bit of your small savings. You said that, at first, he asked her to come to his place of work to counsel her. And he made her talk. At first, your oldest daughter did talk, telling him about her young life, and she didn't realize that the man was asking her to keep talking, because he was masturbating while watching her mouth. Up until the day when the man dragged her over to where he was staying and raped her while promising her purification and his god's good graces?

"Have you forgotten that story?"

"I could never forget that story," Muezzin said, with a strange gleam shining deep in his eyes.

"Never. That man called himself a man of God, when he was a pervert, a self-serving, sick, unstable person who, under the cover of religion and his path, took advantage of women in particular. But that man wasn't a leper. That man called himself a muqaddam."

Muezzin was now sweating. He was choking on a rage that was hard to hold back. A silence had set in. The violin music oozing out of the still-shuttered hair salon, Chez Tonio, alone pervaded. The large leper's chopped-up body with his tiny genitals stuffed deep into his mouth was lying on the sidewalk and his eyes were now dancing to the sound of the violin. At that early morning hour, Felix Faure Street still bore traces of the great masked ball. Little silk bows and ribbons in every color were lying all around. Star-shaped confetti fluttered along the sidewalk and roadway, waiting to be crushed under the insolent tires of cars driven by people who looked down on Felix Faure Street. The apprentice philosophers, all around the chopped-up body, were trying to think like the Felix Faure Street Philosopher would. With one hand on his mouth, the other hand in a pocket, sometimes on his forehead, on his neck, coming and going. The two fat, plump-bellied policemen, still standing with their two legs spread wide, were yawning. Drianké's blues had soared to new heights and ascended up to heaven. At that very moment, Muezzin remembered that his time of duty had long since passed. It was almost daytime. But the sun had still not risen.

Who could have gone to prayer?

On this so-called hot street in this exclusive neighborhood, praying in a temple was not the most commonly shared thing. On Felix Faure Street, prayer was life. Praying was living, it was moving forward! an apprentice philosopher would often say. God asked that the straight path be the one that every creature had to take to get to Him. Regardless, another apprentice philosopher would say, it was the shortest path. For Felix Faure Street residents, inevitably and undeniably, every creature was moving toward God, but they themselves had taken the shortest path, the straight path. It was simple math, another apprentice philosopher would have stated.

Muezzin was already considering the consequences of his dereliction of duty that morning. He had done a good deed nonetheless. He had discovered a chopped-up body very early that morning and he had gone to look for help. A good deed was worth as much as a call to prayer. It was a prayer even. It was prayer. Other people thought that they had done a good deed by praying in a temple. They were mistaken. Good deeds were in every moment. But would the Imam understand? That was the problem. God, He understood everything, along with the Felix Faure Street residents, but those who took themselves for intermediaries and messengers—the new prophets, the false muqaddams—did not understand a thing, and on earth, they made the rules and their gods let them do it. What are we waiting for to revolt against these monstrous intermediaries?

Muezzin thought that the Imam who led the prayer was thinking about replacing him. For quite some time, the Imam suspected him of being too friendly with the residents of this so-called hot street,

Muezzin thought. Yet, the Imam was not above all suspicion. All of the girls on Felix Faure Street knew it. The Imam often liked to come and stroll through Felix Faure Street even though he did not live in the area. And whenever the girls would call him Imam in a certain tone of voice, he would raise his prayer beads and make strange grunting noises. It was said that he also happened to be part of Felix Faure Street on some nights. And so he would become human, a simple human, but he was afraid of staying that way. No one could live in the vicinity of Felix Faure Street and not want to be part of it. Impossible. Muezzin instead thought that the Imam was jealous of him because he practically lived on Felix Faure Street, and not being an imam, he was a little more free. And Muezzin thought that he had found a compromise with God because he lived in a rear courtyard off of Felix Faure Street, God's street. On that street, God and the devil coexisted. That was the power of Felix Faure Street. Harmonious cohabitation! God was upstairs, the devil was downstairs. They were both stacked up evenly. That was how many intermediaries like the false muqaddams, the new prophets, believed they were with God because they believed they were aligned, even though they were in league with the devil. That was what being with God from below was like. A constant battle between good and evil was raging on. And with good reason. The neighbors, the overcrowding, the stifled resentment, the occasional conspicuous moment, survival. Sometimes, the moment would drag on. And the dreamers did not like moments that dragged on! They needed to live, enjoy life as it happened! It was true that, night and day, Felix Faure Street offered a wide range of options for every type of lifestyle. Soft prostitution. Hot prostitution.

House bars. Backstreet bars. Alley bars.

Window bars. Balcony bars.

Streetside food stands. Storefront food stands.

Courtyard food stands. Front-yard food stands.

Backyard food stands.

Yet, everything meshed together virtuously since Felix Faure Street residents had a virtue code. Vice was dissociated from virtue. Just like on Felix Faure Street where there were no temples, but where people truly believed in God and lived with Him all the time. An ambiance of alcohol, Cape Verdean music—biguine, morna—prevailed in the Felix Faure Street air. That was also part of God. Felix Faure Street residents were not the ones in the bars, the restaurants. Felix Faure Street residents did not do sex work on their street. Felix Faure Street residents did not binge drink on their street. They did not need to. Felix Faure Street residents got drunk with God. Felix Faure Street residents listened to violin music in God's company and that music lingered on that street like a boat run aground in a once feverish port.

Felix Faure Street was not far from the city's main port.

Felix Faure Street was across from the Cape Verde Islands!

The Cape Verdean women sewed to the sounds of violin.

The Cape Verdean men did hair to the sounds of violin.

The girls and the old folks beautified the street with their elegance, all of this in muted tones with violin and guitar!

The children born out of these violin and guitar sounds quite quickly integrated themselves into the local community, in order to escape Felix Faure Street, because they wanted to be ordinary people. The children wanted a change of scene, all while preserving Felix Faure Street. The women had a bad reputation. They aged poorly, one might say, and were frivolous. Such jealous locals! The Cape Verdeans were called "Poortooogays" or "Poortoo Nyanyas." Their complexions looked like caramel, pure honey, the color of their cakes. The Cape Verdean Islands were not far away. They were just across from the Continent. But the country was terribly dry. And whenever nostalgia took hold of the senses, the men would most often play violin and sometimes guitar. And the women would hum. On Felix Faure Street, life had sound and swing and everyone knew how to dance. And there was always music on Felix Faure Street. Felix Faure Street was also a nostalgic street, from the time of occupation when soldiers, sailors, adventurers, lovers of new worlds would walk up and down that street like a sacred place, like a place of pilgrimage, like a vital passage. The laughing girls, with their tiny waists, offered up bodies pulsing with life. Strong liquor, Gazelle Coumba beer, Kiravi Valpierre wine drenched all that life of debauchery—from good-natured coyness to little guilty pleasures.

Drianké, that small-statured woman, that curvy woman who walked with a slight limp when she first arrived, did not have a high-end bar. She welcomed men, women, girls in the company of artists, young liberated women, married women, people from other places to her spot. They would come to drink, smoke, and talk. In front of her cottage, she sold small plates that she cooked up for her client friends, fans of her voice, with blues on her lips. Everyone who wanted to be part of the progressive scene liked to go to Drianké's. It was even considered chic to be at her place. The front of her cottage, deep within the passageways, courts, and courtyards, was the coolest place on this street, in this neighborhood, even in this city. The great young man, the filmmaker Djib, to whom the story that the large chopped-up leper's eyes were telling had to be told, to make into a film, also went to Drianké's place. He really liked Drianké. He came more for Drianké than for her small plates. The great young man, the filmmaker Djib, was not a big eater. The great young man, the filmmaker Djib, did not eat. Drianké wondered, despite her friendship with the great young man, if she had ever seen him eat. The great young man, the filmmaker Djib, fed on other things. The great young man, the filmmaker Djib, fed on the food of those who were already beyond survival.

Drianké kept chanting her blues on Felix Faure Street, at that hour of morning when the call to prayer had not been heard, for the first time in a long time! The eyes of the large chopped-up leper with his tiny genitals stuffed deep into his mouth were not saying anything anymore. The large leper's eyes were not laughing anymore. The large chopped-up leper's eyes were listening to Drianké chant the blues, with bright flashes in their depths. It was as if the lanterns' flames were fluttering within them. At some point, an apprentice philosopher, who was trying to think, stopped trying to think and looked at one of the two fat policemen and said:

"By the way, I think I saw you at Drianké's place.

"Aren't you the one who sometimes comes with a coworker?

"Weren't you the one who had a potentially escalating problem with the shadowy mass who has been spending the night at Drianké's place?

"It's definitely you. I remember now."

The fat policeman was embarrassed. People all around were looking at him and looking at each other. The Philosopher was standing off to the side, ever pensive. Since returning with Drianké and Muezzin to the scene of the large leper's chopped-up body, he had not made any remarks. He listened to the two fat policemen when they made a rare comment. He listened to Drianké when she chanted the blues. He listened to Muezzin when he spoke. He listened to the apprentice philosophers when they spoke. He would come and go from time to time, with his hand on his forehead. Sometimes, he would mumble to himself:

"The leper spent nights at Drianké's place.

"He was Drianké's leper.

"Four veiled figures that seem to be multiplying show up on Felix Faure Street.

"No one knows them.

"No one knows where they are from.

"This morning, the leper's body is discovered on the sidewalk by Muezzin, chopped up into big pieces, with his tiny genitals stuffed deep into his mouth.

"There is a story, a terrible story behind all this.

"The leper's chopped-up body reveals nothing of interest.

"It is the story behind the story that is of interest."

Muezzin drew a little closer to the apprentice philosopher as if to support him in his revelations regarding one of the two fat policemen.

"If I have gone to Drianké's place once or twice, it was for my job," the policeman said, trying to pull himself together.

"I disagree," the apprentice philosopher fired back, buoyed by his refreshed memory.

"We, on Felix Faure Street—on the street or in the rear courtyards—don't need the police. Here, on Felix Faure Street, we don't ever have any problems with the police. The laws that govern the street are stricter than those of the police."

Drianké spoke up and started in on one of the two fat policemen:

"You have been to my place, I remember now.

"And you've come often. It isn't just one or two times.

"I remember you.

"One day . . . Oh! Wait . . .

"Yes, I remember. One night, you'd had a little too much Kiravi Valpierre and . . ."

The policeman tried to stop Drianké, gesticulating wildly. The apprentice philosopher was feeling increasingly confident. He nodded his head, bolstered by the surrounding onlookers and the other apprentice philosophers. The Felix Faure Street Philosopher smiled while watching Drianké and the apprentice philosopher speaking like that about one of the two fat policemen. The apprentice philosopher was fired up and picked up after Drianké:

"Yes, I remember now. That night, you were completely wasted. It was the first time I've seen a fat policeman so drunk. You started to dance the mayonnaise and the shadowy mass, settled in at the back of the courtyard, was laughing while watching you dance. At some point, you headed toward the shadowy mass, still dancing, and he got up to imitate you. And then, suddenly, no one knew what got into you, you pulled out a gun and threatened the shadowy mass. You called him every name in the book and you started saying outlandish things:

"'You don't know who I am.

"'I'm more than a policeman.

"'I'm a superman.

"'I'm big, fat, beautiful, strong, and I've got it going on.'

"You took off your clothes while saying:

"'I'm going to show you that I've got some muscle.'

"You kept on dancing the mayonnaise. One of the patrons grabbed hold of you and poured water on your head and helped you put your clothes back on. You were ridiculous, I felt ashamed for you. We've never seen such a spectacle on Felix Faure Street. Upon leaving, you said this:

"'I will get you, scumbag, you little scumbag, you filthy scumbag. I will.'"

The fat policeman targeted by the apprentice philosopher cried:

"But he wasn't a leper.

"He was a shadowy mass . . ."

Drianké stopped him right there:

"That shadowy mass, he is my leper who is right there, chopped up into big pieces."

The fat policeman was sweating and trying to explain himself.

"That's not it. I only went to Drianké's place one time, because an informant had told us that a lecherous leper was in the Felix Faure Street vicinity. He would beg out on the avenues but actually, under the cover of begging, he was skillfully trafficking young people. This leper would attract these youths, under the cover of the word of his god—whom he'd gotten close to when he was a false muqaddam in another life. He would then ask them to recount obscene sex scenes to him as he masturbated. That was why I went to Drianké's place, to find out if someone had heard about this and provide any information about that lecherous pedophile. I didn't even know that there was a leper at Drianké's place. Even after that incident, I didn't know that the shadowy mass was a leper."

Drianké, still sitting on the sidewalk, shouted at the embarrassed fat policeman, who was sweating all the more. Looking directly into his eyes, she said:

"You were so drunk that you don't remember anymore, but I remember, because you didn't pay for your drinks."

Drianké went back to chanting her blues, waiting for what the fat policeman would say. The fat policeman did not say anything.

"You owe me money," Drianké picked back up again.

"I can't forget you.

"I might give away everything I own, but I don't like it when anyone owes me a penny, be it a policeman or a chief of police. I will also report this to your Chief.

"Don't say that you only came here once. You've come many times. Even your Chief comes here. But he is decent. He drinks up, talks a little, pays what he owes and leaves. A decent policeman. You know, on Felix Faure Street, we know how to gauge quality people. Here, quality comes first."

Muezzin, not wanting to distance himself from the events, was trying to speak, but an apprentice philosopher had edged in a little closer to the fat policeman in question. All the while, the Philosopher kept coming and going, ever pensive, sometimes with a smile on his lips.

"Here, people don't commit crimes, regardless of whether they are villainous or not. Felix Faure Street has a code of ethics, of conduct, of attitude. Ever since its existence, there has never been a single crime reported! Whoever committed this crime is not from Felix Faure Street." the apprentice philosopher articulated.

The Philosopher stopped and solemnly said:

"Stop talking about crime.

"This is not a crime.

"This is a spectacle.

"This spectacle was staged here, on Felix Faure Street and nowhere else. Whoever staged it was helped by someone from Felix Faure Street or someone who was on Felix Faure Street. There is a story to this spectacle."

Muezzin seized the opportunity to step into the spotlight:

"Well, Mr. Fat Policeman, what do you have to say about this? Did you hear what the Philosopher just said?

"Things seem pretty obvious, I think.

"What do you have to say?"

Muezzin was wriggling around like an earthworm that someone would have stepped on. At some point, he went over to Drianké:

"Drianké, who on Felix Faure Street knew that you had a leper at your place? I come by every now and again to catch up, but I've never seen a leper there."

Drianké, without looking at Muezzin, said:

"I didn't know that the shadowy mass was a leper.

"He's been here for a little more than a year.

"That shadowy mass, I never really saw his face.

"He was always swaddled up in his big towel.

"He would come in late at night and leave early in the morning.

"Just yesterday, I learned some things about him.

"Just yesterday, I got to know him better.

"Just yesterday, I found out who he was.

"And this morning is when I found out that the shadowy mass was a leper."

Drianké fell silent, and a gleam flashed in her eyes.

The Philosopher watched Drianké curiously as she spoke. In the Philosopher's mind, the story of that leper discovered that morning, chopped up into big pieces on the sidewalk, with his tiny genitals stuffed deep into his mouth, would resolve itself. That leper had to be involved in the spectacle that he was staging that morning, on a Felix Faure Street sidewalk.

Drianké picked up her blues, to the rhythm of the violin music that was oozing out of the still-shuttered hair salon, Chez Tonio.

This morning was supernatural, but that was exciting.

Chopped-up leper, blues, violin, sidewalk, Chez Tonio.

And the sun still did not want to show its face.

The large leper's chopped-up body seemed to take up increasingly more space on the sidewalk. The large leper's eyes kept speaking and no one was paying attention to what they were saying. The leper's eyes were telling a story and no one was listening to them. The Felix Faure Street Philosopher was not looking at the leper's eyes. The Philosopher was avoiding the leper's eyes. All around the chopped-up body of the large leper whose eyes were speaking, there were increasingly more onlookers. The Felix Faure Street Philosopher was now smiling as if he had solved the enigma of the large leper's chopped-up body, with his tiny genitals stuffed deep into his mouth!

"Well, we are going to the station to inform the Chief and to send over an ambulance to transport the chopped-up body," one of the two fat policemen suddenly declared.

Felix Faure Street was not far from the city's two big hospitals. Felix Faure Street was not far from the Ministry of the Interior. Felix Faure Street was truly well-situated in this exclusive neighborhood.

Muezzin offered to accompany the two fat policemen. The suspect fat policeman refused, but the onlookers, the apprentice philosophers, and Drianké stood up to him:

"Why not?

"Muezzin was the one who discovered the chopped-up body and now you want to take it away!

"That is his chopped-up body, even if it is Drianké's leper! He also needs to go to see your Chief to explain how it all happened. If not, we'll all go to see your Chief and we'll all explain what happened."

The two fat policemen hesitated.

Drianké spoke:

"You wait here, we'll send for your Chief. This chopped-up body is Felix Faure Street's business."

The Felix Faure Street Philosopher—who was walking around with his head down, silent, pensive, sometimes smiling—was appointed to go to find the Chief of the two fat policemen.

Felix Faure Street was not far from the central police precinct.

During all that time, the leper's eyes were telling the story that had to be told to the great young man, the filmmaker Djib, to make into a film. The only thing missing from the story that had to be told to the great young man Djib, was the end of the story!

And the large leper's eyes were trying to tell the end of the story to the four veiled, seemingly multiplying figures, who had disappeared around the corner, holding lanterns!

4

IT WAS A MORNING just like this one, when the large leper's body was discovered, that a girl had come to Drianké's place on Felix Faure Street, one year ago, looking for work. But how did she get here on that morning, at such an early hour? An hour that might make an apprentice philosopher wonder where that girl had slept to be such an early bird. On this street, people had stopped asking questions a long time ago. There were so many people who came and went! People who came from everywhere, people who came from nowhere. People were there and that was that. The chubby, light-skinned young girl was solidly built. Her short hair appeared to have been cut recently. Her calf, poking out from under a gathered skirt, was resolute. She came to Drianké's place, saying that she was looking for domestic work. When Drianké, the small-statured woman, looked at her that morning, she did not say anything right away. She just asked her to sit down. The girl sat down on a nearby bench, her eyes staring straight ahead, and did not say anything either. Drianké kept looking at her. Somehow, they resembled each other slightly. They had almost the same complexion—a fine, light, but resilient complexion. They seemed to have a family resemblance. Drianké looked at the girl and still did not say anything. The girl, frozen in her demeanor, was still staring straight ahead. Sometimes, at neck-level, you could see her swallow her saliva and this slight movement would make her throat move with a muffled sound. This silence between the two women was sustained by some sort of undefinable complicity.

"Why did you get up so early to look for work?" Drianké suddenly said.

"I like to get up early," the girl replied without looking at Drianké.

Once again, silence fell between them.

"Do you know how to sweep, wash, iron, do the shopping?" Drianké asked her.

"Yes, I know how to do everything," the girl replied, still staring straight ahead.

"You know how do to everything or you can do everything?"

"I know how to do everything and I can do everything."

"When can you start?"

"Right away if you want!" the girl replied, suddenly excited.

"Where do you live?" Drianké then asked her.

"I just got to this city.

"I arrived last night. I haven't found where I can live yet. But don't worry, I'll manage. I will find a place somewhere."

The girl raised her head toward Drianké.

"Somewhere where?" Drianké replied.

"I am going to look," the girl said.

"On the street? How can you live on the street?" Drianké exclaimed.

"Where are your parents?"

"My parents aren't from here.

"I came to this city for my mother who is sick, with a serious illness."

Drianké paused and picked back up again:

"Where are you from?"

As if she did not hear Drianké, the girl did not reply. Drianké returned to the charge:

"I am speaking to you. What place are you from?"

"We're not originally from where we've been living for the past several years. The place is called Hogbo."

"Hogbo, Hogbo, Hogbo!" Drianké repeated, pensive, her gaze distant, with a sudden strange gleam in her eyes.

"Isn't there another name for that place?"

The girl did not respond. Drianké gave in, but Drianké seemed upset. She returned to the charge once again: "And where did you sleep after you got here yesterday?"

"I haven't slept," the girl replied.

"You haven't slept? How did you manage to hold out, after a such long journey?"

"I walked the streets," the girl replied.

"You walked the streets until daybreak?

"On Felix Faure Street?

"All night long?

"Well, then!

"Someone walking up and down the street a whole night through!

"And you aren't sleepy now?"

"No, I'm not sleepy!" the girl said.

"I went up and down the street and I wasn't alone.

"Other people were out walking the street too."

"They're used to it!" Drianké insisted.

"More and more people are out on the streets.

"But you, you shouldn't be used to it."

"I know how to get used to things. I can get used to anything.

"It's no problem. Don't worry about me.

"I'll figure something out if you hire me."

The girl spoke in a determined way. She did not let herself be pitied. She did not hesitate for a single moment while speaking.

"If you want, you can sleep here, that's fine with me. On that note, you can keep me company, I've been all alone for quite some time!" Drianké said.

"Well, then! That's perfect, I will hire you and you can start today. But you didn't say anything about pay.

"How much do you want to make per month?" Drianké asked.

"Whatever you give me," the girl replied.

"You don't have a salary in mind? So what if I don't give you anything?"

"You will pay me," the girl said in a confident tone.

Drianké was thrown off by that girl. A strange feeling came over her. A muddled feeling, between intrigue and fascination. Although Drianké had met women and girls of all kinds, colors, and characters, this one was truly different.

Struck by the determination, the confidence of that girl, Drianké eventually asked, "What's your name?"

"Muñ!"

"Muñ?

"That's not a common first name.

"And your last name?"

"Muñ!"

"Well then! So your name is Muñ Muñ!"

That was how Muñ started working on Felix Faure Street, for Drianké, the small-statured woman who walked with a slight limp and sang the blues.

Drianké's wooden cottage was located in the back of a courtyard made up of several small courtyards, like most of the cottages on the back side of Felix Faure Street. There was a series of scattered houses, joined together in the middle by courts and courtyards. It all made up one big house whose wooden, metal, or iron entryway opened onto Felix Faure Street. As soon as you passed through the entryway, you had to walk through endless passageways. In some spots, you had to jump to avoid a hole or puddles of dirty water. In the courtyard where Drianké's wooden cottage was located, one passageway housed some sort of empty lot with a few large tables and benches. In front of Drianké's cottage, there were some small benches, scattered here and there. These small benches were where people would sit, among which were married women, married men, girls, young women, men from other places. These men and women came to unwind at Drianké's place. These men and women came for the forbidden fruits. These men and women came to drink beer, rosé, red wine, sangara, Kiravi Valpierre, while talking and laughing.* Which was becoming increasingly taboo among so many other things. But fortunately, Kiravi Valpierre and company were there to serve as safeguards. Otherwise, the hospitals would be full of sick people whose only illness was not being allowed to talk and laugh. Kiravi Valpierre had baptized Felix Faure Street. Kiravi Valpierre was part of the Felix Faure Street archives! What secret bars, dive bars, house bars, courtyard bars, backyard bars didn't use Kiravi Valpierre to liberate people hailing from other places! Men, women, imams, muezzins, executives, artists, lepers (cured or not). Clients who came as mere visitors and became friends or even relatives! Those people came there to get their fill of vice or virtue (depending on their mood) to compensate for something, all under Drianké's amused, or sometimes not-the-least-bit-amused, gaze. What often caused the not-amused gaze was when the client was a nasty drunk and started to overstep the Felix Faure Street codes. But that was rare. Those on the fringes of society were generally good people, even when drunk, even when wasted, even when dead, as they often died anonymously.

Drianké, and everyone like her on this street, had been giving

* Sangara is a mix of alcohol and an herbal tea made with tobacco, pepper, and hot red peppers.

people what they had been asking of the gods, of the new prophets, and the false muqaddams for quite some time. Moments of escape, moments of joy, moments of pleasure, moments of freedom, far from that existence where most people were getting screwed over, mired as they were in inescapable moral, spiritual misery. For the most part, those women who came to her place were frustrated, beaten, abused, humiliated women. There were broken men and women, despised by social, political, religious systems that privileged some to the detriment of the greater majority. A privileged few had everything. Big families, beautiful houses, beautiful cars, everything beautiful, honors, compliments, everything, even if, most of the time, it was all a farce, a facade, an act, an imitation, a shitshow. But those privileged few liked that shit more than any other value in life, more than life itself. And so the vast majority of people would spend their time in churches, in mosques, in all kinds of temples and places of worship, to pray to a god who was deaf, blind to their requests. God was deaf to those requests because this was not what God had asked people to do. Prayer was not for God. God did not need prayers. God was self-sufficient. One had to find fulfillment with God in a dynamic. And this dynamic did not preclude action, commitment, and the struggle to survive. But some miscreants had used God as a scapegoat in order to carry out their dirty work. And under the cover of God, they were doing evil things. Those miscreants would tell themselves that in the last minutes of their lives, they could be forgiven by God. But God was not concerned with forgiveness. No one could harm God. He was impervious to lechers, evil-doers and twisted masterminds, hypocrites, perverts, amoral people, and people who did not listen to violins. So around the globe, new temples, new mosques, new churches, places of worship for meetings where manipulation was the prayer of choice were dotting the landscape. The people who needed to practice the notion of God, the idea of God through love would find themselves hoodwinked by miscreants who exploited them in their minds, in their spirits, in their pockets, in their private lives. Whereas people needed free clinics, hospitals for health care, schools for teaching and learning, homes for shelter, and a street like Felix Faure Street for being with God. Among those disheartened, those depressed—no longer certain of which way to turn in this absurd world with its multitudes of temples and false muqaddams—some jumped at the slightest pleasure, the slightest moment of forgetting their fate, and when they went to bed, they thanked God for creating beer, sangara, Kiravi Valpierre, and people like Drianké.

There was an honor code on Felix Faure Street—this can never be stressed enough for those who do not know it, do not want to know it, or do not care. Here, we did not want any trouble. Those who were looking for trouble had to go to the ordinary, run-of-the-mill streets, outside of Felix Faure Street. Despite the overcrowding, despite some raised voices, everyone was close-knit on Felix Faure Street. Here, we had to stick together. The only battle on the street was the one between God and the devil. Sometimes, you got the impression that there was a consensus in favor of this coexistence and that the street was enlightened. It might go on like that until the day a guru would come to town, promising hellfire and misery to those who do not start begging his god morning, noon, and night. Yet, this guru sometimes did come to Felix Faure Street, in disguise, to attend the great masked ball. If he was truly enlightened by the grace of Felix Faure Street, he would never leave. He would become a member of Felix Faure Street and throw away his fake prayer beads, fake books, and pretensions. This one would be lucky. On Felix Faure Street, this lucky false guru or false muqaddam (in a former life) would become God. While the others, caught up in their whirlwinds of gloom and doom, would continue along on their paths, spouting nonsense to people. The young women, the married women who came to Drianké's place were very attractive.

They were all beautiful. They were there, free, laid-back, at ease. All women were beautiful, the Felix Faure Street Philosopher would say. As soon as they recognized their own worth, they could show that they were divine creatures and not objects for consumption. Give women the time to make themselves beautiful and you will see God! Let them be free, let them be themselves, let them bloom! Those who tended to find some women old or ugly, had old age and ugliness in their own souls. On top of that, those people did not respect Creation. Nothing had been created out of ugliness. God had created creatures in his own image. Those who saw ugliness in Creation were insulting God. Women preferred for their beauty to bloom in the afternoon. As the sun set—over there toward the open sea—the ocher, red, yellow hues that painted the walls, the air, the sky, would give their skin and their eyes bronze shimmers, and whenever they smiled, gold would slip out from between their lips. At that time of day, for those who had already drunk a beer or a glass of rosé, their joyfulness made you want to draw close to them to catch hold of the life that was bursting from their eyes.

Muñ would sometimes sit next to them and watch them, unfeeling. She did not talk to them. Yet, Drianké had not told her not to. Muñ was not talkative. Drianké had noticed this the entire time she had been there. She took care of her work, applied herself in everything that she did. Muñ had been working at Drianké's place for one year to the day, when the event in question occurred that morning on Felix Faure Street. That morning, when Muezzin collapsed onto the large leper's chopped-up body, with his tiny genitals stuffed deep into his mouth! Muñ had already gotten used to the local scene and everyone seemed to like her without being able to say why. People could not say why because people did not know her at all. People saw her, that was all. Muñ did not talk to anyone. Deep down, Drianké thought that it was better to have such a neutral person in this kind of environment. In that house, every night, and for some time before Muñ's arrival, the large tables and benches thrown together in a space in Drianké's courtyard had been expecting a strange visitor. That visitor, no one saw him coming, perhaps no one saw him going either. Each night, that visitor, who looked like a shadowy mass, would slip into that lightless space and sit down noiselessly. Every morning, ever since she had been working at Drianké's place, Muñ swept that space that the shadowy mass occupied at night. There, she would find cigarette butts, roaches from joints, empty bottles of alcohol, leftover grilled meat, used and crumpled-up paper napkins. She carefully swept that space every day. That place attracted her, as did the shadowy mass who occupied it every night. The shadowy mass would leave very early in the morning. Drianké would also get up very early in the morning, regardless of what time she went to bed, and take a cold shower. She always got up long before Muñ did. She would silently come limping out of her room and sit down in her usual spot in front of her cottage, in front of the empty benches where, the night before, people had snatched life away from nothingness. She would sit down in her old leather armchair and set her cane down beside her. She would look out in front of her and sometimes whistle the blues, with a strange gleam flashing in her half-closed eyes. It was like that every morning, ever since the shadowy mass had started spending nights in that courtyard space. Before that, she had always gotten up early but would stay in her room after taking a cold shower. She would dress elegantly, and the fragrances of the perfumes that she wore and the incense that she burned would take flight with the songs of birds, happy to wake up on Felix Faure Street.

Muñ slept with one eye open and often observed Drianké through the open door. Muñ also woke up very early.

Drianké did not know that Muñ was not sleeping.

Drianké did not know that Muñ could not sleep.

And so every morning, Muñ would observe Drianké, unbeknownst to her. Drianké sometimes reminded her of her mother. Drianké sometimes looked like her mother. It was strange. Her mother, back home, sometimes had the same demeanor as Drianké. She liked Drianké. That woman had a strong personality and was beautiful. She had a beautiful mouth, a large mouth, with well-defined lips. She was struggling to make ends meet. Every day, she prepared small plates, replenished her stock of beers, rosé wine, Kiravi Valpierre. And sometimes she would sing the blues. And sometimes she would whisper the blues. And often she would whistle the blues. She had been whistling the blues more often since Muñ had been there. But in reality, Drianké had been whistling the blues ever since the shadowy mass began spending nights at her place. And each time the strange gleam would flash in her eyes. That strange gleam would vary depending on whether she was singing, whispering, or whistling the blues. And every time she heard Drianké sing, Muñ dreamed of singing the blues like her. Muñ had noticed that Drianké seemed relaxed when she was singing the blues, but in her eyes, always that strange gleam. A mysterious gleam, which made her eyes change colors. Those were also the rare times when Muñ would find respite from the fever that was burning inside of her. Muñ would have liked to sing the blues to free herself from that thing that was stuck inside of her chest. That thing was a violent hate. A hate born one day in her mother's presence. She had tried everything, but that hate was still there. She had prayed, begged God and the devil, the hate was still here. That hate was choking her. It made her suffer atrociously. But no one had any inkling or suspicion of this suffering, which hate was making her endure every moment of her life, in violent attacks.

What did Muñ come to find at Drianké's place?

She came to this city, for her sick mother, she said! She did not say anything else to Drianké, but she thought that Muñ had not come to this city and to Felix Faure Street just for that. Well, maybe no one was on Felix Faure Street just to be on Felix Faure Street. Not even Drianké. Those who were born on this street, in its labyrinths and its courtyards, dreamed of going somewhere far away. But those who moved to Felix Faure Street and frequented Felix Faure Street were looking for something else, but what? Felix Faure Street was like a springboard toward another somewhere. A somewhere here on Felix Faure Street or a somewhere, somewhere else. It was not precise in anyone's mind, but everyone was dreaming. All Felix Faure Street residents had ambitions, plans. Plans to be or to become someone else. Plans to achieve great ambitions. It was as if Felix Faure Street residents were in transit, even those who had died there, even those who had been there this whole time and knew nothing other than Felix Faure Street. They were full of ambitions and they dreamed. As long as you lived on Felix Faure Street, you had to hope. Hope to be One with God in a constant dynamic, a perpetual dynamic. Felix Faure Street was the street of hope and patience combined. People who were only rich in money looked down on Felix Faure Street. They thought that Felix Faure Street was the street of debauchery for the poor and the less fortunate. Luckily, the poor at least had the chance to access that Felix Faure Street debauchery! Debauchery was no longer the privilege of the rich. Felix Faure Street offered respectable debauchery to this world's less fortunate, this world's poor, with Kiravi Valpierre. This debauchery was a healthy debauchery, a hope-and-patience-combined kind of debauchery. Felix Faure Street was also the street of the mind, of thought. Felix Faure Street residents lived in a constant state of stimulation. They were always thinking. The street had a philosopher and many apprentice philosophers. One could even say that there was only one philosopher and some apprentice philosophers who lived on Felix Faure Street. But this philosopher and these apprentice philosophers were not cited in philosophy books and textbooks. The Felix Faure Street Philosopher and the apprentice philosophers also drew their strength and their originality from the sole fact that they had never read any other philosophers. That was what philosophy was, the Felix Faure Street Philosopher would say. Certain references sometimes twisted the minds of the small-minded. And that became indoctrination. And from there, all the derivatives. One needed to live, live in the moment, that was philosophy, the Felix Faure Street Philosopher would say.

Kierkegaard? Kant? Socrates? Bergson? Hegel?

Never heard of them! Except for Socrates!

Sartre? A little.

B. H. Lévy? A little too, through Sartre!

While people were thinking or dreaming, Muñ was stealthily observing the shadowy mass who came to spend the night at Drianké's place. She watched his every move. She tried to catch snippets of his life, through the grunts that he sometimes produced. The shadowy mass was a good ways away from the front of Drianké's cottage. Since Muñ had been working at Drianké's place, she had never seen the shadowy mass go beyond the space where he spent the night. Muñ tried to guess the shadowy mass's thoughts. While sleeping, she tried to unravel the shadowy mass's dreams in her own dreams.

Muñ had followed the shadowy mass one night, on the first day of her arrival in this city. And it was the shadowy mass who had led her to Felix Faure Street and to Drianké's place. Muñ was linked to that shadowy mass, that much was certain. But what was the link that tied her to that shadowy mass? Muñ herself did not know, but she felt deep down that there was a connection. Drianké also did not know that the shadowy mass was the one who had led Muñ to her door. No one could guess what Muñ had come to find on Felix Faure Street. Why Felix Faure Street? For finding a job as a domestic worker, the civil servants' neighborhoods were more appropriate than Felix Faure Street. There were not many civil servants on Felix

Faure Street, especially not many female civil servants. And it was the female civil servants, who no longer had the time to take care of their households, who were seeking employees for cooking and cleaning, albeit with a few risks. Whenever the domestic employee would do her job to a tee, that was enough for her to catch the husband's eye, and she would end up doing her job in the bedroom too.

Months passed that way, at Drianké's place. Muñ, still choking on fierce hatred, knew that she had to be patient since she had no other plan than to rid her blood of the hate that was boiling inside of her. Unlike Felix Faure Street residents, Muñ was not hoping. She did not live on hope. Muñ did not dream. Muñ had a single objective. It was clear in her mind. She did not know when she would achieve this objective, but she would achieve it—or else, that hate would choke her to death. And that hate was growing, every day, more and more, in her chest. She lived each moment in terrible suffering. In spite of everything, Muñ had something in common with Felix Faure Street residents. She knew how to be patient. Whenever the shadowy mass would leave very early in the morning, Muñ would get the urge to follow him. But she could not. She was working. She contented herself with the fact that the shadowy mass always spent the night at Drianké's place. She could say that she lived with the shadowy mass. She had all of the time in the world with the shadowy mass. She had a lifetime with the shadowy mass. As long as he did not leave here for good! If she had to do it, Muñ knew that she would follow him. She would not hesitate for a single moment. But how would she know? Why was Muñ latching on to this shadowy mass whom she had never approached? And if the shadowy mass decided to leave one day without letting Drianké know? Muñ got upset just thinking about that possibility. Something had to happen so she could put an end to this. She pushed away the idea that this shadowy mass could just up and leave one day.

One morning, while sweeping the space where the shadowy mass spent the night as usual, Muñ found a document in a yellow folder. The document was quite thick and looked like a typescript. Muñ looked at the document for a long time. It was a typescript. She stroked the yellow folder. After a while, she carefully placed the typescript on one of the large tables and went back to sweeping.

Muñ had gone to school through college level. Drianké did not know this either. She thought that Muñ had done a little schooling like most young people, and that she was one of those left-behind students, school dropout casualties, which were becoming widespread in this country. In the first plans for development, priority had been given to education, to training. At the start of the school year, there was great pride and joy in seeing all those young people going to school. Those young people were joyful, in those days! School was free, school supplies were free. For the poor, less fortunate children, there were academic scholarships, financial aid. There were libraries in schools, with books. There were professors, teachers, classrooms, tables, benches, doors and windows that closed. It was a pleasure to go to school. Administrators were trained. The standards were decent and competitive. By the 1980s, everything had collapsed. Fewer educational subsidies, successive withdrawals, lack of means for the less fortunate. Girls were pulled out first. And the regression began. How many young people had made it past primary school or high school since the 1980s? How many unemployed graduates, dating back to the 1970s? From the 1980s to the present day, there still have not been any more subsidies for education, nor more recruitment of civil servants. The great financiers of this world decided that we had to privatize, clean up, cut the workforce. The ensuing economic stagnation and impoverishment was starting to rear its head. The victims were numerous, the rancor profuse. Muñ had managed to escape this terrible educational crisis, the consequences of which were still palpable.

The consequences that this was going to have on the nation's development were not yet understood by the leaders. The country was going to face a major crisis. A population with no education, no teaching, no teachers. No more traditional education with the initiation system, with teachers playing a decisive role in the development of character, personality, and the transmission of values. No more modern education with teachers providing children with essential knowledge and open-mindedness. No more initiation, no more education. The egg was broken from the inside out. And children were taking to the streets and becoming street children. And that created jobs for the people who were taking care of the street children. At any rate, let's not digress, let's continue on our path. Muñ had managed to go to school through college level and she had pursued professional training abroad. Drianké did not know that either. It was during her last visit, during the summer break, that she decided not to go back. It was during this trip that she saw the state her mother was in. She decided to stop everything and to go out looking for the man who had put her mother in that state. Muñ knew that her mother was not just suffering from health problems. Her mother was suffering from another kind of pain. This other suffering had changed her. She had become unrecognizable. Her mother did not say much about her condition, but she was experiencing a great deal of suffering inside. Muñ could not bear to see her mother in decline like this toward death.

Her mother only said:

"It's him."

"Who?" Muñ asked.

"The tall, dark-skinned man with a big, scarred belly.

"The muqaddam."

And then, Muñ remembered.

That infamous muqaddam!

That muqaddam and all of the other new prophets and false gurus of his ilk were overrunning people's lives under the cover of their gods, and manipulating them to the point of collapse. More and more of the country was being overrun by these new gods. Each one of them wanted to create his own church, his own mosque, his own place of prayer, his temple. They would form associations—as friends of Moses, Mohamed, Jesus, the devil. The temples were popping up like mushrooms all over the country. While misery was gnawing away everywhere, temples kept sprouting up, bigger, more majestic. In places where people needed decent housing, temples, places of prayer were arrogantly rising up to the sky. And every Sunday, and Friday, and other days, and mornings, and evenings, people would rush into these places of prayer to call on a god who was not there. Instead of going to rest, to breathe in nature's fresh air, to gaze upon flowers, the great outdoors, to go and see friends, to read, to meditate, to travel, people would rush into those places of prayer, which God had not asked anyone to do. Whenever the repetition became mind-numbing and boredom set in, they would improvise prayers with music to revive lost causes. And from the music, they would move onto romantic problems and develop new types of neuroses. To inhibit these neuroses, they would recommend dressing in a particular way, and the poor babies who needed comfortable cotton clothing would find themselves turbaned, or decked out in long satin dresses with funny hats on their heads. These new disciples, barefooted, with babouches on their feet, with heads covered in veils, ridiculous hats, were growing in number in this country and others. It made you want to wish for a Christmas in Siberia for all of those barefooted people, except for the babies. Then, they would see if their gods would come to their rescue. For it was the false guru, the false muqaddam, the new prophet, the new messenger of god, who dressed that way, albeit with more expensive materials. For some little gods, it was immaculate white caftans with Emirati headdresses. For others, it was long, purple satin robes. And the flock of recruits was out there, in the presence of these men who would con them out of their money, their lives, their aspirations, their energy.

Muñ had come to this city where it was said that one could find anything and anyone. And it was the shadowy mass who she had met on a street, who had led her to Felix Faure Street, to Drianké's place. Muñ had found that shadowy mass out begging on a street, sitting on the ground, holding out a yellow plastic pot that he was using to collect coins tossed over by people who felt victimized, irritated, guilt-ridden, because they were different. As soon as Muñ saw the shadowy mass, she sensed that he would lead her to her objective! She looked at him and with just one look, her heart started racing. She immediately thought that this shadowy mass would be her guide toward the terrible fate that she was pursuing. This shadowy mass was unblocking something related to her fate, her objective, this hate which was completely engulfing her. In her pores, in her head, in her blood.

Drianké did not know much about Muñ. But since she did not speak very much, it was not easy to know what to make of her. She had only told Drianké that her mother was still alive, but sick, with a serious illness. She had also said that her mother was apparently terminally ill. Drianké was dismayed each time that Muñ spoke of her mother that way.

"But we can do something!

"There are hospitals!

"All illnesses are treatable today!

"Even AIDS, if people wanted, we could find a cure for it, even malaria, even the flu, even the Spanish flu!

"You have to bring your mother here.

"We will take her to the hospital."

"Yes, I will go and get her," Muñ would always say as a means of shutting down Drianké's words.

Drianké, the small-statured woman who walked with a slight limp, would accept Muñ's remarks with a doubt that she could not hide. Muñ knew that her mother would not come. Ever since she had been following the shadowy mass, Muñ had stopped taking care of her mother. Muñ was pursuing an objective and her mother was no longer part of that objective.

Muñ did not know anything about Drianké either. For the several months that she had been there, Drianké was a mystery to her. Behind her blues, in that strange gleam that flashed in her eyes, in the way that she limped, Muñ thought, felt, that there was something else.

Why did Drianké walk with a limp?

Since when had she been walking with a limp?

Did she really walk with a limp?

And why had she asked if Hogbo had another name? Muñ was intrigued by Drianké too. And Drianké oddly reminded her of her mother.

The document that Muñ had picked up while sweeping the shadowy mass's space was slightly crinkled, but legible. It was typed in a bold black ink. After finishing sweeping the shadowy mass's space, Muñ wondered what she was going to do with the typescript. Would she take it or would she leave it in its place or would she give it to Drianké? But ever since Muñ saw that typescript on the ground, she immediately knew that she was going to take it. That typescript, she had to take it, she had to grab it, she had to have it. Muñ felt that the typescript was not there by chance, because she no longer believed in chance. She had never believed in it anyway. Muñ was a very pragmatic and quick-thinking person. That typescript in the yellow folder, she had to take it. It was like a necessity. The sight of that document made her heart race. She did not hesitate any longer.

Muñ took the typescript and hid it under her clothes. She put everything back in order in the space reserved for the shadowy mass and went back to Drianké's cottage as if nothing had happened, as if nothing had ever happened, apart from her objective, which had completely taken over her mind. She was looking for how to hide that typescript. In any case, this was an unnecessary precaution. Drianké did not bother with paperwork. She would always say that she did not know anything about paperwork and that paperwork created problems. The less one knew, the better. Drianké did not know how to read or write, but she spoke very well and understood many things through a no-frills empirical logic. That was the most important thing. Understanding. Communicating. For that, she had the skills because she had an open mind, and she was receptive. Drianké knew how to listen, which was becoming increasingly rare.

Muñ started looking for a place to hide the typescript in Drianké's cottage. She was not looking to hide it from Drianké because of what Drianké might think, but because Drianké could ask her to put it back where she had picked it up. That was what Muñ thought, and for her, this was not an option. But maybe this typescript could also be of interest to Drianké. This idea had quickly crossed Muñ's mind. Muñ could not explain why she did not give the typescript to Drianké, nor why she did not leave it where she had found it. Whatever had driven her, she felt it deep down in her guts. In Muñ's guts, there was that indescribable hate that seemed to be guiding her like an invisible thread. A hate that made her suffer tremendously, but which was now her reason for living. She could no longer do without that hate. That yellow folder had also struck her when she saw it on the ground, in the space reserved for the shadowy mass. She could not explain what drew her to that yellow folder, but that yellow folder, like the shadowy mass that she had followed one night, was part of her hate and her objective.

She was excited.

She was shivering.

She was trembling.

She was practically feverish.

The yellow color of the folder containing the typescript was making her feverish. With a fever that was burning all over her body. And hate was rumbling in her heart, banging against it like a jackhammer. Held back for such a long time, the hate was now the same shade of yellow as the folder containing the document. She looked for a place in Drianké's room, where she herself slept too, but no corner inspired confidence. Drianké was in every corner. Drianké would set down her creams, her beauty products—which she could not get enough of—anywhere and everywhere. Pastel eyeliners over here, red nail polish over there. There were sleek wigs, braided wigs. There were also her pipes. Drianké smoked the Moorish tobacco of her ancestors. Drianké had everything it took to be a big star, a great blues singer. Why hadn't she become the big blues star that she could have been? Drianké did not talk about it. Drianké never talked about it. Muñ looked in the court and the courtyards. There were too many comings and goings in that multitude of cottages, courts, and courtyards. While thinking about the bathroom, she suddenly realized that it was the best place to stash and hide the typescript. In the bathroom, there was a shower area in the corner. It was a service bathroom as one might say. It was located at the back of the courtyard, and aside from Muñ, only the people who came to Drianké's place ever used it, and that was rare. Which made you wonder how those people managed with all of those liters of beer, rosé, or sangara that they were drinking! So one might say that this bathroom was Muñ's bathroom. Drianké had her own bathroom, where she spent a lot of time before taking her place in the courtyard, in front of her ovens. This service bathroom was the place where no one would think of looking for anything. There was an old-fashioned toilet. This type of toilet was only found in old houses. The toilet tank was located way up high with a chain hanging down, and you had to pull down on that chain to get the water to flow down from its reservoir over the Turkish squat toilet. There was a long pipe running from top to bottom. In order to access that toilet tank, you had to get up on top of something. Muñ had been able to reach it by climbing up the pipe. Like all materials from that time, the pipe was sturdy enough to support a girl as well-built as Muñ. The materials from that time were of better quality than those of today—made to deteriorate quite quickly in order to keep the infernal machine of production, consumption, and capitalism running. She carefully placed the typescript on top of the toilet tank and made sure that it was well in place and that there was no risk of it slipping off. What was drawing Muñ to this typescript? When she first found it in the shadowy space, she did not dare to pick it up right away. While sweeping, she had managed to read the title. On the yellow-colored folder, there was a title written in all caps: VENGEANCE. As soon as she saw that title, she was suddenly overcome with anxiety and she shuddered. Muñ could no longer take her eyes off that word. She was hung up on that word. The word had seeped into her veins, into her arteries. The word had traveled through her entire body through the circulation of her blood. The word had invaded her brain, swallowed it whole. The word had started out impure and had come back pure, loaded with oxygen. The word had become clean like oxygenated blood, rid of its impurities. The word had become her life's oxygen. "Vengeance" was the word that had pushed, told, urged, obliged, shoved, forced Muñ to take the typescript. The few lines that she had managed to read made her understand that this was definitely a story that had been told. This was the story that the eyes of the large chopped-up leper, with his tiny genitals stuffed deep into his mouth, would tell, one morning, on a Felix Faure Street sidewalk.

Ever since Muñ had found that document, she seemed more focused on her work, to such an extent that Drianké was worried.

"Muñ, why are you working so hard?

"Take your time, there is nothing urgent.

"And everything you're doing right now is not important.

"Everything you're doing right now is not urgent.

"Come sit down or else go for a walk down the street.

"You are not like girls your age!"

Ever since Muñ had been working at Drianké's place, she had never gone anywhere on her own! If she went out, it was because Drianké had sent her. She would go out to run errands and come back right away. She did not hang out, did not have any friends, but everyone seemed to like her. She was not particularly sweet, but was not particularly unpleasant either. She had a neutral personality that bordered on indifference and yet, she left no one indifferent. There was something undefinable about that girl, something disturbing.

At Drianké's place, she mainly took care of the cleaning and the errands. She swept the only room in the cottage, made the two twin beds, cleaned Drianké's bathroom, washed the clothes. Muñ did not cook. Drianké was the one who cooked. Drianké liked to cook. The only thing that made her happy, besides the blues, was when she had her pots in front of her with sauces simmering, steeped in aromas of grilled onions, garlic, fragrant peppers. In these moments, Drianké seemed happy and she would hum the blues. Drianké would cook out in front of her cottage. She would not leave her post. She had everything she needed brought out to her. Whenever she did get up from there, it meant that she had finished. She would go take a cold shower and relax with an iron pipe stuffed with Moorish tobacco. In between two long drags, she would whisper or hum the blues. Muñ knew this ritual by heart.

So, every day around ten or eleven in the morning, after doing the shopping, Muñ would get the stoves and the pots ready and make sure that the cats that roamed the courts and courtyards did not get away with any of the all-too-tempting little fish. Seeing Muñ like that, no one could ever imagine how much she was dying to start reading the typescript in the yellow folder, titled "Vengeance." That word fascinated her.

Vengeance!

A terrible word.

Vengeance!

The sound of it alone was enough to take hold of all of her senses.

Vengeance!

Its rhythm alone made her want to dance a dance of death.

Vengeance!

A word that shook, disturbed, sent shivers and waves of ecstasy.

Vengeance!

The word that every being had felt or wished for and repressed out of fear. Fear of what? Of someone else's god? The new prophets, the false muqaddams, and gurus would say that their god had a dreadful hell for those who sought vengeance. For Felix Faure Street residents, God—so good, so merciful, so forgiving—did not have a hell and He did not seek vengeance. For no one could harm God, since God knew no evil. Everyone built their own hell, their own personal hell, and locked themselves up inside of it all alone for eternity, unless they repented, and repentance was what people had understood the least. It was not confession; it was not the act of distributing bags of flour, feeding people who often were not even poor, sending people on pilgrimages; it was not asking God for forgiveness night after night. No one could harm God! the Felix Faure Street Philosopher would say. We had been advised to forgive, to suppress our urges because they were not right, according to moral standards, according to the Ten Commandments. No, this was not in the Ten Commandments. But maybe we needed to double-check! Most people asked God to avenge them. God did not harm anyone. Many expected this divine justice to be the solution to their problems. God does not sleep, God is not blind, they would say at every turn. It would be enough for something to happen to the person that they had it in for—and obviously something bad—for them to feel satisfied. God showed us! God took matters into His own hands, they would say at every turn! They did not need to get God mixed up in every situation that they cooked up. Especially since God knew no evil and he was inaccessible.

Vengeance!

The syllables of the word "vengeance" hissed like an attack from a rattlesnake, coiled up after someone had stepped on it. The rattlesnake would coil itself up to gather all of its forces and project itself like a missile.

Vengeance!

The ambiguity, between God and devil!

Morality imposed things on us that were so difficult to uphold! We had to forgive. But how do you forgive someone who has hurt you deliberately, with no regrets? As if hurting was the most mundane thing a person could do to someone else, and yet, one would say that we had to forgive!

God loves people who forgive!

Who said that?

God, He said: "Do no harm."

And what does God do with those who harm others?

He takes care of them too, some will say.

He does not have the time, others will say.

This is all speculation, an apprentice philosopher would say.

The harm done, it was there—concrete, visible, palpable. The person subjected to the harm would suffer, everyone knew it, everyone saw it, everyone talked about it. And we had to forgive. Such circumstances could not meet the moment. Unless you only lived in the moment, abandoned yourself to it. You had to be on top of the Himalayas, or in a monastery perched high above the clouds. Muñ did not live above the clouds. Her mother did not live above the clouds either. She lived beneath the clouds where there were many monstrous monsters. The moment that Muñ was experiencing right now was the moment of vengeance, beneath the clouds. It was the first time that she felt a reduction in the violent suffering boiling inside of her chest. As for Muñ, what mattered to her most was her objective. Whether it would be in the moment, or in time, or in an eternity, she did not care. Those were concepts that did not concern her. In her mind, they all canceled each other out. There was only her objective in her mind. For that matter, Muñ no longer had a mind. Muñ only had an objective. And the word "vengeance," written on a typescript in a yellow folder, had come along to set things straight.

When Drianké had finished cooking, Muñ would wash the plates, the utensils. Then she would clear off the stoves, put away the bowls in which Drianké had put the premade dishes. Drianké did not sell her food, one might say. She liked to cook to see the food all around her. She would eat a little, giving away more than she sold, to all kinds of visitors. Clients, relatives, allies, and friends. Muñ ate with Drianké, but did not eat very much. Often Drianké reproached her.

"What's wrong?

"Why aren't you eating?

"Isn't what I made good?

"You should be the wife of the great young man, the filmmaker Djib!

"Do you know Djib?"

"Yes, I know Djib," Muñ replied.

Drianké was once again disconcerted by the assuredness with

which she spoke. Muñ said she knew Djib, with no further comment.

"How can you say that you know Djib?

"I've never seen you talk to him. I've never seen you go up to him.

"It is true that you don't go up to anyone.

"Well, with you, I should expect some surprises."

"I don't need to talk to Djib to know him," Muñ said quietly.

"I know Djib and I'm getting to know him better and better," she added, in a way that left Drianké feeling even more stupefied. Drianké was confused. This girl was really something else. How did she know the filmmaker Djib when she had never seen her speak to him? And she said that she was getting to know him better and better. What did that mean?

"My present concern is that you are not eating enough for my taste," Drianké said after a moment, just to say something, anything, to dispel her disconcertment in front of this strange girl.

"You're young, you need to eat. I don't want you getting sick."

"I won't get sick," Muñ said, pulling away.

Drianké did not know that Muñ was hungry for something else. Every day in the early afternoon, Drianké would take a nap, after her cold shower. She would go to her room, smoke a pipe, with its tobacco smell drifting all the way into the courtyard. She would rest and there would not be any visitors just yet. The visitors would not start to come until mid-afternoon, people who did not work or had flexible schedules. The others would come in the late afternoon. Otherwise, there was just Muezzin, who would sometimes pop in, claiming to have lost his cock (and he did not have one) in order to make a quick stop at Drianké's place.

"I'm coming to check in," he said each time he walked into Drianké's place.

"Check in on what?" Drianké asked, laughing.

"Say what you want to say and don't beat around the bush.

"I'm resting. I don't have time for you."

Muezzin laughed and quickly downed one or two glasses of Kiravi Valpierre while looking all around. Upon leaving, he popped a strong mint candy into his mouth and took out his prayer beads for survival. Muñ was observing his charade and when he realized this, he tried to find something to say and greeted Muñ in passing:

"So, Drianké's girl, how are you?

"Still stuck in your mother's house?

"Don't you want to get out a little and talk with girls your age on the street?

"You're really too well-behaved for your age, but maybe you're right to be.

"That reminds me, Drianké asked me if I knew a place called Hogbo. Are you from there?

"Is there another name for that place?"

Muñ looked Muezzin in the eyes and said: "We're not from there originally!

"But there are other names.

"Every ethnic group might have a different name for that place.

"Some call it Chada, others Hogbo."

Muñ did not expect Muezzin's reaction. She pulled away. At that time of the day, with the few glasses of Kiravi Valpierre that he had just gulped down, Muezzin also had other plans in mind. Maybe he had not even heard Muñ's last few words. He was slightly drunk and he was feeling fickle. He found himself in the street, happy. The sound of his prayer beads set the beat for bursts of laughter from young Cape Verdean girls in short shorts and espadrilles who, at that time of day, had gone out to stroll on Felix Faure Street.

Felix Faure Street was a mystical street. You had to believe in something to live there. The street was a stone's throw away from the Great Church, however. The Great Church was a big white building where all of the believers and nonbelievers would gather on Christmas. Muslims, Christians, Jews, animists, fetishists, atheists, Felix Faure Street residents would all gather at the Great Church on Christmas Eve. People sang, danced, and asked nothing of God. The Great Church was God's temple, on Christmas. All of the other temples wanted to break God up into little pieces even though God was One. And on Christmas, the Great Church next to Felix Faure Street served God. Every day should be like Christmas in the Great Church!

At that time of early afternoon when Drianké was taking her nap, young Cape Verdean girls in short shorts and bare backs were outside, laughing out loud. Upon leaving Drianké's place, Muezzin saw them and, underneath his baggy pants, something moved. At that time of day, the heat was bearable and the smell of the sea would rush into your nostrils. It was a good time for love too. Coolness and light sweat. Arousing moments. It was on this same day, at this same time, that Muñ had started to read the typescript retrieved in the shadowy mass's space. The typescript in the yellow folder! It was the beginning of November. Muñ had been working at Drianké's place for almost a year. It was also on this same day that the great young man, the filmmaker Djib, came to Drianké's place, all worked up. Drianké was in her room, but as soon as she found out that it was Djib, she asked him to come in. Djib knew that he could come to Drianké's place at any time of day. Drianké would also welcome Djib at any time of day. When Djib stopped by a place, he was always well-received. Djib was not some weirdo who was trying too hard to be liked. Djib was liked for who he was, and Djib was himself. Drianké was lying on her metal bed, in her eclectic room where there were always one or two lanterns lit, night and day. She had that strange gleam in her eyes. And she was whistling the blues. The arrival of the great young man, the filmmaker Djib, pulled her out of that state and her face lit up. The room was filled with photos. Photos of Drianké at the theater. Photos of Drianké singing. Photos of the National Ballet on tour. Photos of Drianké striking a pose. Photos of her children and grandchildren. As soon as Djib came into her room, Drianké stopped whistling the blues and the gleam in her eyes vanished. She welcomed Djib with a laugh and a skeptical look. Drianké's laugh was a loud laugh, but lacked sincerity. The filmmaker Djib did not normally come to her place at that time of day.

"Djib, what's the matter?

"You seem strange.

"Do you want something to drink?"

Djib was in the middle of Drianké's room. He was looking all around. He stopped in front of a photo of Drianké and gazed at it for a long time.

"This photo, do you know where it was taken?"

"It was during the tour with the National Ballet in Tougal!

"What a tour! Unforgettable!" Drianké said.

Still standing there, looking at the photo, Djib smiled with his trademark sweetness and suddenly said: "I lost my story!"

"What story?

"How can you lose a story?" Drianké said, inviting Djib to sit down on the bed across from her. It was the bed where Muñ slept. Djib remained standing and kept looking at the photos all around.

"You know, you can't lose a story.

"And which story is it?

"You have a headful of stories.

"If you lose one, you'll find another one.

"And besides, you can't lose a story.

"You live so much with your stories that they're always inside of you.

"The story that you think you've lost is inside of you, in your blood, in your brain."

Still looking at the photos on the walls and atop a red wooden sideboard, Djib said, as if talking to himself:

"No, I didn't lose a story. I lost my story.

"I have to find that story, I can't lose it.

"It isn't a story. It's a story that has to be told. It's a story that the shadowy mass has to tell me. But he is unable to tell it. So I wanted to tell that story in his place and I lost it."

Drianké cast Djib an affectionate gaze and said:

"You know, Djib, you're going to find your story.

"You're a poet, you are an artist, you are with God, like all of your friends, like all of your loved ones, like the people of Felix Faure Street. I'm not worried about you.

"In any case, the shadowy mass is here every night. Come see him and you'll find your story."

One night, a few months earlier, at Drianké's place—where he had been coming as of late with a short-haired, light-skinned young woman with a sexy kind of beauty—Djib had met the shadowy mass. Djib was touched by Drianké's gesture of offering to let the shadowy mass spend the night in a space in her courtyard. Djib would have done as much if he could have, but he did not have the space. Djib was his own space. Djib did not have a place. He was his own place. But Djib liked the misfits, the marginalized, the dregs of society. Djib liked everyday people. So, on the night of that same day, with a glass of rosé in hand, he got up from out in front of Drianké's cottage and headed over to the space where the shadowy mass was staying. He had not yet arrived and Djib was pacing back and forth in the space, with his glass of rosé still in hand, his eyes fixed on the ground. From time to time, he would stop and then resume his rounds. The short-haired, light-skinned young woman, who had gotten up at the same time as him and followed him, sat down on the edge of one of the large tables located in the space. She had a glass of red wine in hand and was watching Djib move around the space. A little later, after nightfall, the shadowy mass appeared at the end of the passageway. He was walking awkwardly. It looked like he was dragging his feet. The shadowy mass was large and it was difficult to make out his face. He had covered his head with a large cloth that concealed his entire face. When he reached the great young man, the filmmaker Djib, and the short-haired, light-skinned young woman, he let out a strange noise and sat down, exhaling loudly. Djib greeted him and introduced himself, extending his hand. The shadowy mass replied to his greeting in a nasal tone, but did not offer his own hand to shake Djib's outstretched one. Djib did not insist. The hands of the shadowy mass were wrapped in old rags. Djib immediately initiated a conversation with him, about mystical plants, movies. This was how Djib got to know and established a relationship with the shadowy mass. The short-haired, light-skinned young woman—who did not say anything—was the witness to the destiny that had just been sealed, the outcome of which no one could ever imagine. And every night the great young man, the filmmaker Djib, would come to wait for the shadowy mass. And ever since his first visit with the shadowy mass, he had been intrigued. He wondered why Drianké had invited this shadowy mass to spend nights in a space in the courtyard of her cottage. And ever since that shadowy mass had been there, Drianké had started to get that increasingly strange gleam flashing in her eyes. Ever since that shadowy mass began spending the night there, Drianké whistled the blues more often than she hummed them. Ever since that shadowy mass had been there, Drianké had put even more lanterns out in her cottage, in her courts and courtyards. They were everywhere, except in the space reserved for the shadowy mass. Some were lit night and day. Some were not lit, but were ready to be. The great young man, the filmmaker Djib, asked Drianké the question:

"Why all of these lanterns?

"You have electricity here!"

"The lanterns remind me of my childhood. And besides, I need these lanterns," Drianké replied.

"You need them to do what?"

Without waiting for Drianké's response, Djib followed up with another question that was weighing on his mind.

"By the way, Drianké, how did you meet this shadowy mass?"

"Djib, you ask too many questions!" Drianké said, laughing.

As for that shadowy mass, Drianké had found him one night during a rare walk. It was one of those rare nights when Drianké would walk a bit on Felix Faure Street up to Maginot Avenue. She said that her doctor, a Felix Faure Street resident, had told her that she needed to walk a bit from time to time, or else with age, she would have problems.

"Walking is good for you, Drianké.

"If you want to live a long life, you need to walk.

"Walking is a release."

"The blues are my release," Drianké replied.

"That's possible. But add walking. You will see.

"You'll feel even better and you'll sing the blues even better.

"You will see," her doctor concluded.

Her doctor in question was a state-licensed nurse, but everyone called him doctor. On Felix Faure Street, promotions were quickly assigned. That nurse provided more services than a doctor from the big hospital, which was not far from Felix Faure Street. The nurse did community healthcare. On his way home from his job at the hospital, he would pass through many courts and courtyards, to get updates on elderly people, children, to take people's blood pressure, to give advice, to provide care—and everyone was happy with him. That, too, was Felix Faure Street. So, on that night, during her walk, Drianké almost collapsed onto a heap on the sidewalk.

"What are you doing there on the sidewalk?

"You are in the way!

"You almost made me fall!

"What's wrong with you?"

The shadowy mass was curled up like a ball, because at that time of year, in the month of November, it was chilly. It was even cold.

"I am trying to sleep," the shadowy mass replied.

"You have no place to go?"

"I don't know where to go anymore, so I'm looking for God."

"You're looking for God because you don't know where to go anymore?

"What happened to you?"

Drianké noticed that the shadowy mass was a man, a large one.

"How long have you been sleeping here?"

"For some time."

"What happened to you with God?"

Drianké said to herself that she had never noticed this shadowy mass before. This shadowy mass had not been here for long. Nothing escaped Felix Faure Street. And no one could escape Felix Faure Street. If this shadowy mass was out on Maginot Avenue, it was surely not by chance. Felix Faure Street intersected Maginot Avenue. And the shadowy mass reminded her of something. That shadowy mass reminded her of someone, someone familiar. He was wrapped in a big cloth, like a mummy. He was wearing socks on his feet. With the light from the Maginot Avenue streetlamps, she was unable to make out the shadowy mass's face. But Drianké sensed something familiar about that shadowy mass. Even under his big cloth, Drianké thought that she recognized someone. But that someone—she did not want to think about him, she did not want to remember him anymore. She would think about that someone sometimes, in spite of herself, and each time, she would whistle the blues to let go of that memory. A painful memory. A memory she was running from, a memory she was trying to escape, and that memory weighed down on her, and she walked with a limp. She had fled her hometown where she had experienced an ordeal, an ordeal that made being there unbearable. This shadowy mass, had he lived in the great North where she was from? She did not want to ask him any questions in this vein. She did not dare to either. And she did not want to remember that painful period anymore. A strange feeling came over Drianké. She whistled the blues. Drianké would whistle the blues whenever the painful memories of a time would flood in and give her strange urges.

"I've never noticed you here," Drianké said, after a moment.

The shadowy mass, adjusting his large cloth with his elbows, with his head lowered, started offering explanations to Drianké.

"When I arrived here, looking for God, I stopped and haven't moved since. Well, I move during the daytime but I'm here every night. Right now, even if it's cold, this avenue has warm nooks, because it's sheltered. There are many adjoining buildings, so there aren't any air pockets or empty spaces and it's warm enough for me. You know, when I was young, I suffered a fall during a basketball game and I injured my spine.

"Ever since, when it's cold out, I feel a little pain."

"Be careful, you could be paralyzed for life!" Drianké said.

"And do you live here?" the shadowy mass asked, gently raising his head as if trying to look at Drianké.

"Have you always lived here?

"Didn't you live somewhere else before coming here?

"Do you know . . .

"No, forget it."

The shadowy mass fell silent and lowered his head again. Drianké had the impression that she also reminded the shadowy mass of someone. The furtive way that he looked at her from time to time gave her the impression that this shadowy mass knew her, Drianké. Maybe from television. Drianké sometimes appeared on television with the National Ballet. But the shadowy mass, in his quest for a certain god, did not reveal his love of television to Drianké. The shadowy mass did not want to talk about his love of television either, because this love of television was another story altogether. Drianké would have liked it if the shadowy mass had recognized her from television. The idea that it could be from somewhere else and under different circumstances was making her a nervous wreck.

"Where did you live before coming here?" Drianké finally dared to ask.

"It's a long story that I need to tell, but . . ."

The shadowy mass fell silent mid-sentence, and Drianké sensed that he was crying. Drianké imagined the tears welling up in what one might call eyes, but she could not see them very well. The shadowy mass picked back up as if talking to himself:

"I want to see God!"

"What is all of this?" Drianké asked.

"I can help you out if you want," she added. "I don't live far from here, over there on that street . . ."

Drianké was mid-sentence when the shadowy mass said:

"Is that the street where I might see God?"

"You're funny. Is that how you're trying to see God? I don't know if you'll see God there, but I can give you a space for the night, while you're waiting to see God.

"It's better than here. Come with me.

"You can sleep in that space in the back of the courtyard, provided that you don't make any noise and leave early in the morning.

"I hope I've made myself clear.

"Come with me."

The shadowy mass immediately got up. Drianké noticed that the shadowy mass was large but she could not make out his face under the big cloth, which must have been white originally. Upon seeing him walk clumsily, dragging his feet, Drianké was convinced that there was something familiar about that shadowy mass. Drianké also noticed that, beneath the large cloth in which he was wrapped, the shadowy mass had a big belly.

"No, it can't be!" she said to herself.

Drianké, who had seen and experienced so much, did not want to ask him certain questions. Everyone on Felix Faure Street was masked by day, in costume at night. This shadowy mass wrapped in a large cloth, with his feet in socks, his hands in old rags, would not fit in with the Felix Faure Street scene, one might think. But this shadowy mass had a place there, even if Drianké did not know where. In her mind, the feeling of knowing the shadowy mass was bothering her. And Drianké did not know that Felix Faure Street was the street that the shadowy mass was trying to find in order to see God and to tell a story. And Drianké also did not know that Felix Faure Street was where the shadowy mass would see God and tell a story. Drianké also did not know that she lived on God's street. Drianké also did not know that she had something divine about her.

Drianké did not know that she was God.

That was how the shadowy mass came to Drianké's place. That shadowy mass, which no one ever saw coming or going. But early in the morning when he did go out, some eyes were trained on him, eyes from which strange gleams were bursting forth. The shadowy mass would spend the day in the streets of the capital. He did not stay on Felix Faure Street. Felix Faure Street was not a street for shadows. It was a street of lights, a street of blues, a divine street. A street of violins and guitars! The shadowy mass would come to Drianké's place at night, count the change that people had given to him in the street. Sometimes, the shadowy mass would let out a cry and Drianké would shudder. The cry that the shadowy mass let out seemed to come from deep inside of himself. A cry let out as if to expel something. A cry as if to shout at death. A strange cry. A cry that reminded Drianké of something. A cry that she had already heard before. A cry that she knew.

And ever since that night when he first met the shadowy mass (and for all the nights that followed), the great young man, the filmmaker Djib, would sit alongside the shadowy mass and not move for a large part of the night. Now, whenever the great young man, the filmmaker Djib, came over, he would shout a loud greeting to Drianké from afar. Whenever she complained that she no longer got to see him as much as she wanted, he would stop by for a quick kiss while telling her:

"I'm immersing myself in a story that has to be told to me. The story's originality is that the shadowy mass who wants to tell it to me does not know how to tell it. The shadowy mass says that he has memory problems."

Drianké thought that surely, the great young man, the filmmaker Djib, wanted to feature the shadowy mass in one of his films. The great young man, the filmmaker Djib, liked strange, unusual people, misfits, and it was surely for this reason that the great young man, the filmmaker Djib, was so interested in the shadowy mass. Djib was one of the greatest filmmakers of his time. An artist, the real deal, as Drianké would say. Djib had cast Drianké in a few of his films and was considering her for a big role. Whenever he came to see the shadowy mass, Djib would smoke some aphrodisiac herbs with him. The shadowy mass told him that it was good for one's health. The shadowy mass told Djib that in a past life, he was an apothecary.

"To get by," he said to Djib.

What really interested him, was knowing the secrets of plants, plants that made you read other people's thoughts, plants that gave supernatural powers, the shadowy mass had confided to Djib. He had also revealed to Djib that he had frequented many astrologers, many seers, many sorcerers, many witch doctors. He said that he also knew someone who used computers to analyze people's destinies. He also said that he'd had to make use of many of these beliefs.

"To do what?

"Why do you want to read other people's thoughts?

"Why do you want supernatural powers?

"To do what?" Djib asked him.

And the shadowy mass, laughing, said:

"For potency! For power!"

"What potency? What power?" Djib asked him again, a bit worried.

"I'm just kidding," he said.

On that day, the great young man, the filmmaker Djib, realized that the shadowy mass had a story to tell. Djib would always come over with the short-haired, light-skinned young woman. The short-haired, light-skinned young woman had that natural kind of beauty, a pure beauty, without artifice. People would say that this woman was not beautiful in makeup, in layers of powder, rolling their eyes. She had something authentic, something real. She was alluring in a way that was impossible to explain. She had a beautiful smile, but behind that smile, she exuded a type of sadness that was difficult to contain. Whenever she smiled, the corners of her lips would tremble. Something about her face seemed out of place. She gave the impression of someone who contained a great suffering. A suffering that sometimes gave her urges, which she did not dare to admit, and every now and then, a strange gleam would flash in her eyes. So then the great young man, the filmmaker Djib, would go each night to see the shadowy mass with the short-haired, light-skinned young woman. The young woman would also smoke aphrodisiac herbs with them. Djib had explained to the shadowy mass that this young woman was his girlfriend. Some nights, they would stay there, for a long time. The young woman had not told

Djib about the effect that seeing the shadowy mass had had on her. But she did not dare. She had the feeling that this shadowy mass reminded her of someone or something. From the first time she saw him, she was sure that she knew this shadowy mass. She could not make sense of it, but the feeling she had was there and growing stronger, up until the day when she asked Djib some questions:

"Why does he stay in the dark?

"Why doesn't he move from here?

"Why is he confined to this space?

"Before, you would come here to see Drianké. But ever since you met this shadowy mass, you're only interested in him!" the short-haired, light-skinned young woman with a sexy kind of beauty added.

Djib smiled sweetly at the young woman and, taking her affectionately by the hand, said:

"I'm so interested in him that I'd like to ask you something, and please, don't say no.

"It's not for today.

"It'll be for another time.

"But I'm telling you once again, this shadowy mass interests me. This shadowy mass wants to tell me a story, his story. He thought that it might be of interest to me. I have to spend more time with him, because the shadowy mass doesn't know how to tell the story. The shadowy mass is incapable of telling the story even though the story is his life, his own life. He says that he practically has to invent the story of this story. He says that he has memory problems or brain fog. This brain fog, he says, comes from emotional problems. You see, right now, I'm in the process of imagining how I might construct this story that he wants to tell me. I'm in the process of imagining how I'm going to tell this story in his place. The story of the story is what's missing. I have to find the story of the story. I must also find the end that this story deserves. I'll explain it to you.

But no questions, is that understood? You're my girlfriend, don't say anything more."

The great young man, the filmmaker Djib, and the short-haired, light-skinned young woman with a sexy kind of beauty had been living together for some time. Maybe six months. They were not conventional lovers. They did not talk about love on the day that they met. But they loved each other with an endearing love, a friendly love, a tender love. True love, an apprentice philosopher would have said. And they had not left each other's side since that day. They had met in a bar-restaurant where the short-haired, light-skinned young woman had been several times. The great young, the filmmaker Djib, was also a regular at that bar-restaurant. He was friends with the gay couple who owned it. The two gay men were tall, light-skinned, handsome, and they were always smiling. They were very elegant and would wear similar clothing, often in the same colors. They really liked the great young man, the filmmaker Djib, and were always happy to see him. The gay couple had lived abroad for a long time and, upon returning to the country, had opened this bar-restaurant located near the port. The clientele was a diverse but select group. The same regulars met there, almost tacitly, every day and a good ambiance prevailed. There were bigwig executives, businessmen, politicians, artists. The food was refined and the place was relaxed, despite the proximity to the city's large port. The short-haired, light-skinned young woman had been invited there once by an important local political official with ties to her family, and ever since that day, she had been coming back often. The young woman had come to this city to get away, to run away from herself, to escape the memory of a painful episode in her life. Although she thought she would never be able to, one day, she confided in the two gay men who had become her friends. They always told her that everything would work out in the end, that it was just a question of time. Time erased everything, time healed all wounds, they added. One day, the great young man came to that bar-restaurant and the two gay men introduced him to the short-haired, light-skinned young woman with a sexy kind of beauty. Upon leaving, the great young man took her with him, and ever since that day, they have been inseparable. The great young man, the filmmaker Djib, had been living in a room in a hotel for several months. He was working on a text that he wanted to adapt for the cinema. That was the filmmaker Djib's way. He liked to isolate himself in order to work. He liked to change his environment, setting, circumstances, location in order to think. And hotels offered that shift, that change of scene, that anonymity. But ever since the encounter with the shadowy mass, he had put that text aside. He was thinking about the story that the shadowy mass wanted to tell him and did not know how to tell. Djib was trying to type out the story of the shadowy mass in his mind. Djib had thought a great deal about the subject. From now on, all of his walks in the city, all of the hours spent in bars and bistros were completely devoted to this story that he was constructing in his head, which was intriguing him increasingly. One night, he went back to the hotel with the light-skinned young woman. They made love. After lovemaking, Djib asked her to tell him a story, any story. Any story that came to her mind. So began the story that the great young man, the filmmaker Djib, wanted to tell in the shadowy mass's place. And every night after lovemaking, the short-haired, light-skinned young woman would tell a story to Djib. The young woman would tell the story of a short-haired, light-skinned young woman with a man who made her suffer, a man who despised her, a man who made her do terrible things. A man who exploited her. A man who humiliated her. A man who hurt her a great deal. The short-haired, light-skinned young woman recounted how this young woman (who looked just like her) had met that man one day. While telling this young woman's story, the short-haired, light-skinned young woman seemed to identify with her. The story that the short-haired, light-skinned young woman was telling the great young man, the filmmaker Djib, seemed to be her story. The short-haired, light-skinned young woman and the young woman in the story that she was telling were the very same person.

"It was the month of November, I don't remember the exact date anymore, when I met that man. We met through an animal-man who had a terrible life story. The story of the animal-man must also be told one day. The animal-man was afraid of women, wasn't married, and didn't have kids. The animal-man lived alone but liked to introduce people to each other. The animal-man liked to be the go-between. He liked to play the pimp. I was on assignment on behalf of my government, and one day, at the hotel, the animal-man—who I knew from my home country—introduced me to that man. The man was tall, dark-skinned, and seemed kind. He immediately started hitting on me. He was a seducer and he seduced me. He would come to see me at the hotel and we would stay together until late in the night. Shortly after, he began making marriage proposals to me. I came from another country and I was of a different religious persuasion than the one to which he adhered. He even asked me to renounce my religion for his religion because, or so he said, he was a muqaddam of a religious sect and he was the leader of a prayer group. I started making plans to convert to his religion. I had some money and I was allied with an important political family who, at the time, were running my country. I didn't realize that he was only interested in me for my political and social position. I was wrapped up in his large stature and his kind and pious demeanor. He said that my astrological sign paired well with his sign. He said that we were made for each other. I believed him and I was happy to have found the love of my life. It was getting increasingly difficult for women of my position and status to meet their soulmates. Men were afraid of women who were educated, who had a position, who had responsibilities, women who made decisions, women who thought, women who spoke their minds. This type of woman often served as mistresses to married men with wives whom they possessed, dominated, wives who depended on them in every way, wives who did not think. Months passed like this, every time I came on assignment, I stayed with him. He started introducing me to people and I met most of the members of his family. He ended up asking me not to stay at the hotel anymore when I came on assignment. I could come to his place, to his house where he had just moved in, but which wasn't finished. I didn't know at the time that he'd built that house with the tithes taken from his siblings' fortune. He played the part of the great lord and began taking advantage of me without me actually realizing it. He made me buy a luxury car, a red one, which I would use when I was there and he would use when I was back home."

At times, the short-haired, light-skinned young woman would take a break from her story. She had a strange gleam in her eyes.

"I can't, I'm choking on hate," she said.

"Hatred for whom?" Djib asked.

"The story that you're telling me, is it your own story?"

"It could have been my story if I'd been able to relegate it to the darkest depths of my memory. I'm not telling you my story since it's not over yet. I'm telling you a story, that's all."

Whenever she would stop telling the story, she would go to bed and, late into the night, sob in her sleep. And Djib would immerse himself in the story in place of the shadowy mass who did not know how to tell it and simultaneously immerse himself in the story that the short-haired, light-skinned young woman was telling him. He was already really far along, but he was missing the end of the story. He was searching for the end of the story. The short-haired, light-skinned young woman seemed to be telling a never-ending story. That story that the shadowy mass wanted to tell him deserved a worthy ending. Djib wandered through the city streets in search of the end of the story. But he did not manage to find that ending. He told himself that this story would find its own ending. And that was the story, and the end of the story, that the eyes of the large chopped-up leper, with his tiny genitals stuffed deep into his mouth, would tell one morning, on a Felix Faure Street sidewalk. In front of the hair salon, Chez Tonio. And every night, the short-haired, light-skinned young woman would pick back up with the story that she was telling to Djib and to herself.

"I spent my money on him, without keeping track. I spent it on his kids, without keeping track. That man had kids with several different women. And I still didn't realize who this man truly was, he, who under the cover of his god, was a sicko, a psycho. His problem, or rather his sickness, was the desire for potency, the desire for power. He wanted to be rich, to be highly regarded, at all costs. He wanted to prove his worth to others but not to himself. I still refused to realize that he wasn't fitting the bill. In my mind, everything was done, all set for our wedding. I'd talked about it with my friends, my family. I was happy. I'd started giving up many things and I was doing everything to please him. He spent his time praying and invoking his god's name at every turn. I started to notice that this man was mentally unstable. He was superficial and he talked enviously about others. I tried to convince myself that he was just a bit strange. One day, he suggested something terrible to me. He told me that I had impurity problems and that I had to find money, a lot of money, which he had to give to an astrophysicist who was going to change my life by adjusting my astrological sign. I collected everything I had, sold one of my houses, took money from my family, even took a loan from the bank. He said that I would get everything back many times over because my life was about to change. I gave him everything. I already saw myself as his wife—well, with my adjusted astrological sign, thus with my new destiny. I was going to become rich, beautiful, famous. I was going to have the smartest, most beautiful children with him. The whole world would be talking about us. I got carried away and had my head in the clouds over my new destiny.

"'I am a man of my God, you'll see, you are lucky to have met me. You'll be the happiest woman in the world,' he said, adding that another ritual nonetheless remained. In order to get rid of all of my impurities, I had to receive the Holy Spirit within me. This seemed a bit strange to me, but at the point I was at, in that moment when my destiny was about to change dramatically, I trusted him completely. He even told me that a physical change was already happening inside of me, because the astrophysicist had started the work. I scrutinized every mirror and believed I was seeing that I had changed for the better. What he was now suggesting was for me to prepare myself to receive the Holy Spirit within me. So, one night, at his place, he asked me to take a shower, to get ready by putting a perfume—which he'd brought back from a great, mystical journey to the East—all over my body. He said that for the ritual, all of the lights had to be turned off. The only lights illuminating the room on the second floor of his house, which overlooked a river, were those of the night. At one point, he crept into the room. He was wrapped in a large, white cloth. I also got the impression that there was someone else with him. He didn't speak and I had received instructions not to speak until I felt something inside of me, in other words, the moment when the Holy Spirit was entering me. He'd asked me to get into a position where I would be on my knees. All of the sudden, I felt a small, slightly limp penis inside of me, which I recognized as his own. Very softly, he whispered in my ear:

"'Do you feel the Holy Spirit entering you?

"'Say that you feel it.

"'Say that you really feel it.

"'Say that you feel purified, say that you feel yourself born again.

"'Say it loud.

"'Don't stop.

"'Speak, shout, scream!'

"I heard him come and I got the impression that someone else was in the room. He pulled out and the penis that was now inside of me was different from his. This penis was more virile. Maybe this was the real Holy Spirit. When the second penis pulled out, I heard what sounded like two people breathing at different rhythms, in addition to my own breath, and I waited for instructions. He came up to me and took my head in his two hands. His eyes were gleaming, he was naked. Next to him stood a young man that I had never seen. I watched the young man who looked a little bit like him. The young man left quickly, he himself wrapped in a large white cloth, and I found myself alone with him. He solemnly proclaimed that I had received the Holy Spirit, that I was purified, saved, and that I was about to experience and enjoy a new era. We went down to the living room and he served me a strange-tasting tea, but I felt good. My destiny was about to change. At one point, he said that there was also something else. Would the Holy Spirit come back? He only said:

"'We must not see each other for two lunar months, until the whole process of adjusting your astrological sign is complete. That's what the astrophysicist said.'

"When I went back to my country, having completed my assignment, he asked the animal-man, while passing through, to tell me that we weren't made for each other and to stop trying to see him again, because I brought him bad luck, according to the astrophysicist. Even so, I wanted to know who the young man I'd met at his place was. I was unable to tell the animal-man, who he had sent, everything that had happened. I gave him a description of the young man, and the animal-man revealed that this young man was one of his sons, a son that he was hiding. I was stunned. I felt a shiver of horror run down my spine. I felt shaky and felt like throwing up. And when the animal-man asked me what was wrong, I didn't answer."

The short-haired, light-skinned young woman buried her head in the pillow and burst into tears. The great young man, the filmmaker Djib, remained silent. He looked solemn, even though, for those who really knew him, he was not someone who let his feelings show, especially when he was upset. The story that the shadowy mass needed to tell him had been stuck inside of his head for a few months now. And he was writing it along with the never-ending story that the light-skinned young woman was telling him every night after lovemaking. The great young man, the filmmaker Djib, had been engulfed in the shadowy mass's story for months. The day after the short-haired, light-skinned young woman told him this part of the story, the filmmaker Djib left the hotel unexpectedly. He had been quiet since waking up. He was quieter than usual. The hotel that he had moved into was located in a calm neighborhood, at night. It was in a neighborhood located not far from the city center. A great market known for its architecture, called the Kermel market, was also not far from there. The short-haired, light-skinned young woman with a sexy kind of beauty, rushed out of the hotel room to follow him, just like every other day since they had been together. She took a quick shower and did not take long to get dressed and do her hair. Since she kept her hair very short, this saved her a lot of time. The light-skinned young woman followed the great young man, the filmmaker Djib, everywhere. She did not do anything other than follow him around. To the hotel, bars, bistros, Drianké's place, sometimes his parents' place. The young woman picked up the pace to catch up with Djib, with whom she shared her days and nights, no questions asked. Djib did not walk fast. One might even say that he walked slowly, but his long legs made him take big steps. As usual, she caught up with him at the end of the street before it forked to the left, onto Dagorne Street. As usual, they walked together like those old couples who still loved each other! Softly, slowly, at a steady pace, and in silence. That morning, the short-haired, light-skinned young woman had a strange gleam in her eyes.

Dagorne Street was one of the oldest streets in the city. It was a colonial street and it had stayed that way after independence. It was a narrow street. Its roadway was narrow, its sidewalk too. Beautiful colonial buildings lined both sides of the street. They were small, multi-story houses with stylish wrought iron balconies. The great young man, the filmmaker Djib, liked to pass through there before making the rounds of the Kermel market. On Dagorne Street, there were restaurants and bistros, also from the colonial era. Bistros open from the morning onward. Bistros where one could spend the day. There were always regulars there. Colonial regulars. Regulars of an era, a way of life. There were the same owners, the same clients, and the same whores. Classic whores, colonial whores. A little time-worn, but classic whores. Classy whores, one might say, since they were so elegant! Whores who had lived through every chapter of the colonial period, whores who had seen it all. Whores who had things to tell. But no one gave them the mic. The mic was for the demagogic speeches of political leaders, dissidents, party switchers, false gurus, and false muqaddams, modern-day monsters. No one gave the mic to the whores who had lived through and knew things about the colonial period. Things that would have helped to better understand many other things! Too bad! The great young man, the filmmaker Djib, was very friendly with these whores. Djib loved whores and everyday people alike. Yet, Djib was not a womanizer. He did not chase girls. He did not go out looking for girls. He did not try to seduce girls. And yet, he was so handsome, so elegant, so refined! But Djib was chasing something else. Djib was chasing himself, chasing God. The God who was not in temples to be adored. The God who did not need intermediaries to speak in His place. The God who did not need false muqaddams to make Himself known. The short-haired, light-skinned young woman, with whom he was sharing his hotel room, was not a whore. But when she saw how Djib behaved around whores, she wanted to be a whore like these whores. A classy whore, a classic whore, a colonial whore. The short-haired, light-skinned young woman with a sexy kind of beauty had followed Djib around one day like a whore, and it had now been almost six months since they had spent any time apart. They did not say anything. They did not make any promises to each other. They did not talk about love but they made love every day.

On Dagorne Street, Djib went into a bar-restaurant, next to an old building with "Lacoste and Co." written up top. There, he found some friends who were also still in the area. On that day, there was the tall and beautiful Woré, in the company of Bousso, a sublime young woman. Bousso, in her splendor, brought to mind a Nubian princess, escaped from a Pharaonic palace. They talked for a while and then Djib left them to head over to the bar. With his beautiful smile, Djib kissed a whore leaning up against the bar. He stayed beside her, wrapping her in his big arms. He then took the short-haired, light-skinned young woman by the hand, keeping her near him while speaking to the whore who was leaning up against the bar. The light-skinned young woman always smiled at the girls that Djib hung out with. Tacitly, Djib did not introduce the young woman with a sexy kind of beauty. But everyone saw her there and knew that she was with him. Djib did not have a drink like he usually did, a glass of red as he liked. After exchanging a few words with the whore at the bar, she got off her stool and collected her little bag from the bar, a small shoulder bag that looked like a toiletry kit. The whore waved to the owner of the place and he raised a big hand and got back to his glasses. All three of them left and walked around the Kermel market, not far from there. The Kermel market was a place that Djib liked a lot. These days, Djib had been showing a special interest in the Kermel market. He was always making the rounds. There was a bar located inside of the market, Chez Kamu, and he could stay there for hours, sometimes until the market closed. This was the bar where he was heading in the company of the short-haired, light-skinned young woman and the whore with the shoulder bag. There, the two young women drank pastis. Djib did not have anything. The place was nice. People would come and go in that covered market, with its colonial-era architecture. People would do their shopping, their voices filled with delight. Vendors of vegetables, seafood, fruits all had their own way of attracting clients. Some would dance, others would sing. Everyone sold their goods with their most enticing vocabularies. All of this in a crowd with plenty of new settlers. The Kermel market was a market that would remain colonial, for a long time to come. When the market closed, it was already afternoon. Outside, flower peddlers were walking around with bouquets in every color on their heads, and more in their arms. They were the flower-women of the Kermel market! Was Djib searching for the end of the shadowy mass's story in the market? When he sat down in that market-bar, he did not move for quite some time. He smiled, laughed, smoked. But in his feverish gaze, he was searching. Djib did not talk very much. Even though, these days, people—especially the false gurus, false muqaddams, new prophets—would talk a lot to justify themselves, explain themselves, impose themselves, annoy others. There were so many chit-chatters, who loved to talk to impress, to fill the time, to fill themselves.

"Oh, if you only knew, if you only knew!

"My god who speaks to me, tells me things!

"Oh, if you only knew!"

As for Djib, he could be there without talking. He occupied the space. In the presence of Djib, people were admiring and impressed. While others were impressed with him, as always, Djib himself was searching for something in the market. Djib had been searching for something in that market ever since the day when he had glimpsed four veiled figures in the four corners of the market. Strange figures who did not seem to know each other but who were identical. That intrigued him. Who were those four veiled figures in this market? Who were those four veiled figures that he had glimpsed, in the four corners of this market? He had gotten up as soon as he caught sight of them. But he lost track of them in the crowd. Those four veiled figures did not come into the market. They had made an appearance in the market. When the market closed, he got up and left with the whore and the light-skinned young woman with a sexy kind of beauty. Djib went back up toward Independence Square with the two young women, with one on each arm. Djib had the elegance of a nobleman. Djib did not say that he was a nobleman to anyone and everyone. Djib never talked about himself. Djib was a nobleman, and he behaved, walked, lived, maintained relationships with others nobly. With the two young women, Djib crossed Independence Square and took Roume Avenue, also a colonial avenue, despite its attempts at independence. It was a calm avenue, especially in that time of early November when it was a bit cool by the end of afternoon, once the sun had started to give the city the slip, in order to go and take its chances with the ocean. Djib, with the two young women hanging on his arms, then took Felix Faure Street and headed toward Drianké's place. At that time of afternoon, the shadowy mass was not there yet. The shadowy mass would only come at night. The shadowy mass would come once the shadows of day and of evening had dispersed. Djib settled in near the front of Drianké's cottage, after kissing her affectionately, as usual. Drianké was happy. That great young man, the filmmaker Djib, was a light in her life. She was sure that he was the only person who sincerely loved her for herself. It was rare, to be loved quite simply for oneself. He immediately poured a drink for himself, as well as for the two young women. He talked with Drianké, asked her for updates on her health, her business. Drianké liked to hum the blues whenever Djib was there. But this blues was different from the blues that she would whistle whenever the strange gleam flashed in her eyes. And smiling, Djib teased her by saying that she had a new repertoire! She took out her iron pipe and took a few puffs. Drianké was so happy when Djib was there.

The end of the afternoon stretched on with these simple pleasures in life. Most of the people who came to Drianké's place knew Djib and liked him a lot. Djib was also famous. The films that he had already directed were cinema classics. People appreciated his talent but also his grace, his elegance, and his kindness. Djib never shouted. He always spoke softly. Djib was truly divine. And yet, there were people like the new prophets, the false gurus, and the false muqaddams, who, lacking convictions, would shout at others. They shouted at just about everyone. They shouted at their watchmen, their employees, their children. They vented at people who had not done anything to them. They shouted because they were no match for those who were fighting to make ends meet. They shouted because they were no match for those who got up early every morning to face existence, to earn their keep. They shouted at those everyday people working their fingers to the bone to make ends meet. Unsatisfied with their own lives, in which they spent their time playing the part of great lords (which they were not, which they could not be), they shouted at everyday people and everyone else too. And neither the people, nor their children, nor anyone else respected them. They would talk behind their backs and doubt them, their faith, their convictions. Those false muqaddams and false gurus, who took themselves for lords, buried their heads in the sand, and—since they had trouble convincing, because they themselves were not convinced—they would shout at others.

As soon as it started to get dark, the great young man, the filmmaker Djib, got up and went to settle into the space reserved for the shadowy mass who was not there yet.

"But Djib, the shadowy mass isn't here yet, stay a while with me," Drianké said. But she knew that whenever Djib got up, he would not be sitting back down again. The whore and the short-haired, light-skinned young woman followed him. They stayed there smoking aphrodisiac herbs, drinking rosé. Night had completely fallen and the shadowy mass arrived clumsily, dragging his stockinged feet. That night was very dark. It was so dark that it was impossible to imagine that any light was capable of illuminating that night. And yet, later on, a ball of violent brightness would shower the night and intensify its mysteriousness, because that brightness would seem supernatural. The shadowy mass settled in as usual at one of the large tables. He started smoking the aphrodisiac herbs with the two young women and Djib. They were drinking rosé and not saying much. There was something mysterious about that night. Djib pushed the whore toward the shadowy mass. The whore did as he said and pressed herself against the shadowy mass. They were still there smoking when Djib asked the light-skinned young woman to do the same, but she refused. Djib gently told her to do as he said and the young woman shouted:

"No, it's out of the question."

Drianké called out to Djib.

"Djib, what's the matter?

"You know, I don't like hearing noise here."

"No, it's nothing."

Djib grabbed the light-skinned young woman and pulled her toward him.

"Offer him a little pleasure, please. That's what I wanted to ask you the other day. He's my friend and he told me that he has a hard time coming normally. And this has been for quite some time. I think he's blocked up. He begged me to find him some girls. Why do other people come normally and not him? It's unfair. Everyone has the right to pleasure. These furtive little pleasures that we steal from life. This absurd life where some are ruthlessly crushed. Life doesn't give a damn about us. Life knows that death is waiting for us somewhere and it laughs in our face. Let him fondle you. Let him masturbate on you. Make him come just a little, please."

The light-skinned young woman did as she was told, moving forward. It was when she found herself very close to the shadowy mass's breath and when he tried to grab her to kiss her that she realized in horror that the shadowy mass was a leper. His hands were just stumps. The light-skinned young woman tried to run away. She was so disgusted, she was on the verge of passing out. The shadowy mass cornered her and overpowered her and masturbated against her until he came. A stifled orgasm. The short-haired, light-skinned young woman was struggling with all her might.

Suddenly, a scream tore through the air.

"What is going on?" Drianké forcefully exclaimed.

The scream faded and a terrible silence set in. Everyone was waiting for another scream to break the silence. Nothing happened. The space was in turmoil. Djib jumped up from one of the large tables where he was seated. The shadowy mass cursed:

"Slut!"

"It can't be, it can't be, it can't be," the light-skinned young woman said, backing up.

Djib drew close to the short-haired, light-skinned young woman and took her in his arms.

"What are you talking about?"

"It's him!"

"Him who?"

"I recognize him, I'm sure that it's him.

"I recognized him by the scar that he has on his big belly, when he was trying to hold me against him as I struggled. I touched his belly and the long scar was there.

"And his smell. He has an odd smell."

As she ran away through the passageways, courts, and courtyards, the echo of her scream came back even louder. One of Drianké's clients got up and started to speak.

"Does someone want to commit a murder here on this street?

"We cannot let it happen.

"This street is the street of dreams and not despair.

"Everyone here dreams.

"And then, there is hope and patience combined.

"There is God. As for us, we live with God."

This incident happened a few days before the discovery of the large leper's chopped-up body, with his tiny genitals stuffed deep into his mouth. That large leper's tiny genitals showed that he had not enjoyed a great virility. Perhaps for that large leper, discovered in that month of November, disease is what had eaten away at his penis. No! Generally speaking, tall people who used that height advantage to show off (because they did not have anything else to show off) always had small penises, an apprentice philosopher would say, laughing.

It was on the day of that altercation with the short-haired, light-skinned young woman that the typescript in the yellow folder had fallen into the space reserved for the shadowy mass. It was in the month of November.

5

MUÑ WAS SHUT away in the bathroom and had just started reading the typescript, on the very day that she had found it, picked it up, and taken it. She had gone into the bathroom with a bath mitt, a bar of soap, and a yellow towel. It was the only towel that she owned, and she washed it every day. Driankė had given it to her when she found out that she did not have one. Muñ had come to Driankė's place empty-handed, but with a burning heart. The whole time she had been there, Muñ had not touched any of her wages. She had asked Driankė to keep them for her. The few purchases that she did make were so rare that Driankė had stopped keeping track of them. A little dress, a bar of soap, a pair of underwear. Muñ was clearly not a girl of her time, to Driankė and to everyone else. As for Muñ, what now interested her was the typescript. The typescript carefully placed atop the water tank hanging over the Turkish squat toilet, in a bathroom area where you could also take a shower!

That day, on that November afternoon—when Muñ grabbed her bath mitt, her towel, her soap, and stepped into the bathroom—would leave a mark on Felix Faure Street, one fateful morning. As soon as she locked the bathroom door, she climbed up the pipe and grabbed the typescript in the yellow folder. She carefully removed the typescript and slowly slid down the pipe. Muñ was already beside herself. She closed her eyes and hugged the typescript tightly against her chest. She looked for somewhere to sit down, but there was nothing to sit on. She remained standing, and placed her things in a corner. With her eyes shining, excited by the title of the typescript, she anxiously opened it to the first page. The typescript appeared to be in the form of a letter. Muñ then started to read the story that the eyes of the large chopped-up leper, with his tiny genitals stuffed deep into his mouth, were going to tell, one morning that November, on a Felix Faure Street sidewalk.

I am writing you this letter today, on November 29.

I met you one day, one day in the month of August. That day was the day of the tenth anniversary of my husband's death. The ceremony took place in the house where my daughter and I were living. It was a very big house. It had many rooms, and it was a good place to live. You came over with one of your nephews whom you'd befriended, since you didn't have any friends of your own. As for your nephew, I can't say that I knew him very well, but I did know him. And yet, for so many years, he'd been coming to see me and I'd had to talk to him about things in life, in a superficial way.

I'm writing you this letter to refresh your memory and your conscience, if you have one. You yourself have told me that you have memory problems, which stem from emotional problems. Fortunately for you, because otherwise you would realize how many mistakes you've made and how often you've made a fool of yourself in front of others. Unfortunately too, because you don't realize how much harm you're doing to people. You go through this life like a ghost, because you claim to have memory problems. You go through this life in ignorant bliss, yet strangely, you never ignore yourself.

So, on that day in August, near mid-August—at that time

of year when this country was a good place to live, and especially this city located in the heart of a fertile valley—there was this ceremony. There were many relatives and friends, many onlookers, people who didn't know what else to do that day, people with no plans, like you. There were also people who were making the rounds of ceremonies for the food. Prayers were said by people appointed for the occasion. These people, by virtue of being appointed for the occasion, had made it into a profession. And what a profession! From the morning on, they were there, with their respective, well-organized prayer groups. Their attire was fit for the occasion. Special prayer apparel, which as a general rule, should have been understated, but in this case, was not. Instead, the apparel that these prayer professionals showed up in was extravagant, with ribbons on their heads, babouche slippers on their feet, long boubous, big books, and prayer beads galore. Seeing them had to have commanded respect, alas! These prayer professionals, in ceremonies, had a thriving business. They spoke of their god as if he were a villain, who made everyone pay. A god who had a terrible hell. These prayer professionals would make people cry. These prayer professionals would strike fear into people's hearts. And after their preaching, people, panic-stricken, would fork everything they owned over to these prayer professionals. They had found an optimal way to make these people give them everything they owned. Whenever someone would make a contribution, they would have to say the amount out loud into a mic. And so the next person was obligated to give just as much, if not more. People would go into debt, lie, steal, cheat, to give them money. Whereas in their homes, the children weren't getting enough to eat. Whereas in their homes, people were sick, and when their sick would die from lack of care, the prayer professionals would come to give sermons and preach and finagle everything that these people had or had left. And these prayer specialists, who were robbing anyone and everyone blind (especially the poor who wanted to act like they too were rich), were building beautiful villas, driving around in chauffeured cars, marrying several wives, sometimes even other people's wives (who would get divorced just to be in the inner circle of their completely made-up god). And more and more young people were choosing this occupation as prayer professional.

I had been living in my husband's big house with our only daughter ever since his death. I was born in another country, but I'd left it behind a long time ago. I was in a family and in a city that loved and accepted me. That's what I believed. Later on, I realized that the city had accepted me, but not all of the people had, especially a certain sister-in-law whose jealousy and nastiness were eating away at her like a cancer. But that was another story. Ultimately, in this life, all we had were stories, all of which had to be told. The prayer professionals talked about their god, and made sure to thank people, especially the designated head of the family who had managed, so lovingly, to preserve all of the dearly departed's possessions. The prayer professionals said that when they passed by the deceased person's home, they thought that it had been sold or rented out (but would have never imagined that people were living there), and that it had been so well maintained. The prayers offered for the person taking care of the property were never conveyed to her, because she didn't understand their language. The prayers were reclaimed by others. I was starting to get a little bored by this and wanted to call it a day, when I was told that someone wanted to see me. I gave up on my plan to leave and went over to see the person in question. That person was your nephew, one of those people lost in a life that was no longer his own. A nice person who had brilliant ideas, life plans, but who had never been able to live as he wanted. He was torn between the desire to act like everyone else and the urge to simply be himself, but the desire to look, to act like everyone else had won out and he had given into it. His life was now just one long lament. Despite all this, he was quite friendly. I met you on that day. You were sitting down, but you seemed tall, and you gave the impression of being a good man. Good! How many crimes have been committed in the name of that impression and that word? How much pain has been inflicted because of that word? People would always say that this word led to heaven, but would forget to say that it led to hell too, the hottest hell, which has yet to be described in any book! I have always wondered how one could believe that God, who was so merciful, so forgiving, could create so many hells, each one as horrible as the next, to punish people. God could not burn the ones that He had created in His own image. It was senseless. Hell was inside of us; it was us, an apprentice philosopher would say. Hell was other people, another apprentice philosopher would have paraphrased.

I talked to you about social disintegration, about collective transgression. You seemed interested in what I had to say, and I gave you a book on rehabilitation, a book that you drank up in one night like whey. You had been to school, but you weren't an intellectual in the true sense of the word, in the noble sense of the word. You knew how to read and write, but you didn't have a sense of discernment (based on the comments that you would later make about the book). Two or three days later, you started to pursue me relentlessly.

You would come morning, noon, and night, every day, even on Sundays. And yet, Sunday was the day when you would lead a prayer. You would come over with a god on your lips and prayer beads in your hands. You would talk to me about the religious path that you were leading. You told me that you were the one who had met the guide of this religious path and that he had appointed you muqaddam for the entire country. You met the members of this path some time after a psychoanalytic course of treatment, which you underwent for a personality complex disorder, I would later learn. In the beginning, I was not very taken by the big, large-statured person that you were, because you lacked charisma. There was something emanating from you, hard to explain, but something toxic. You presented well, but at the same time, a short conversation with you was enough to realize that something was not right. A kind of low intellectual level or low moral level. In any case, something you could feel, like an uneasiness. The relentlessness of the courtship drove me toward other feelings. The feeling of being desired by a man, feeling loved. I was so alone. I wasn't really looking for a man's company. I was looking without looking. I said that I was looking for someone well-rounded. You came under the cover of your god, and I gave in to your religious harassment. You would recite verses, psalms with such zeal that I fell into the trap. My housekeeper, she too charmed by your voice when you would recite verses, said to me:

"This is a good man. You should give him a room here."

As soon as you would step into our home, the housekeeper would run to get a prayer rug, prayer beads, and water for ablutions. She and I were both swept away. You came along, large in stature, and I refused to see the small mind beneath that large stature, and I didn't pay any attention to your big belly, which contained all of the vices that I would only later find out about. You completely monopolized us. I did everything I could to welcome you like the lord that you wanted to be. The housekeeper and I displayed all of our culinary talents to make you the best dishes, spent all of our small savings to buy you the best there was. One day, you came in shivering with fever, and you said that you didn't feel well. I covered you with an old blanket, an ancestral heirloom blanket. You stayed there, in this kind of touching fragility, and I gave in to it. When I took back the ancestral heirloom blanket and covered myself with it—as if to be one with you, in your fragility, which was accentuated by a religious fever that manifested every time you came over to see me—I caught the virus!

"May God bless you!" you said.

"Muñ, where are you?" It was the voice of Drianké.

Muñ climbed up the pipe, put the typescript in the yellow folder back on top of the water tank, and came out.

Muñ showed herself to Drianké, feverish, and said: "Here I am, I was in the bathroom!"

"You spent a long time in the bathroom!" Drianké said.

And every day, and sometimes several times throughout the day, whenever Drianké would retire to her room, Muñ would rush back over to the bathroom and get her hands on the typescript once again.

And so I caught the virus without even realizing it. You kept coming to see me morning, noon, and night. You created the dependency. I would wait every day for your arrival or your phone call. When you didn't come, I would call you, often, constantly, until my telephone got shut off because I hadn't paid the bill. I spent everything I had for your enjoyment. Ruin was gently starting to knock on my door. I got a cell phone and would call you just to hear your voice. The game was fun at first, but becoming increasingly dangerous. You let me know that you were interested in me and that you even wanted to marry me. I was hesitant. The match seemed promising, but I was still hesitant. How could such a good-looking, gainfully employed, seemingly pious man just get divorced again for the umpteenth time? How could a man who bragged about being desired by women, both young and old, still be single at his age, with children from several different mothers?

"You know, there are high school girls who come to my work to profess their love to me. You know, there is a very rich woman who wants me to marry her. My sisters are trying to set everything up, but me, what I'm looking for is a virtuous woman, a peaceable woman, a woman of God! Because I, what I want is not wealth, it's God!"

With each of my questions, you would find a way to sidestep my concerns.

"I still haven't had any luck in finding what I am looking for. I am looking for a peaceable woman," you said.

As for me, I told you that I was looking for a good man, but that I was also looking for a father for my little girl. My little girl needed a father figure. You came into our home, with the word of your god on your lips, with prayer beads ever in your hands. I told myself that with a man like you, there would be nothing to worry about ever again. This man who had a god with him didn't need anyone to tell him anything. His god had already told him everything. And if not, his god would tell him everything that he needed to do. I was swept off my feet. I had always been looking for God. I did not question His existence. For me, God had to exist. I needed Him. When you presented yourself in this way, I thought that every prayer had been answered. This was how I let my reassured self get dragged into this unbelievable affair. I thought I had found God, but I had met the devil. That is how you seduced me. I was almost the same age as you. I was at that age when a woman might doubt her youthfulness, but you managed to convince me that what interested you wasn't age, it was personality. While saying such things, you alluded to the prophet who had married a woman fifteen years older than himself. You kept coming to see me several times a day and I was growing increasingly attached to you. You would always come with a god on your lips. I wanted to believe in God, so I was content. You tried to convince me that in order to get to your god, I had to go through a path. You said that your god had granted certain people a power and that other people had to connect to these people, in order to get to him. I, who believed that every creature was a path toward God, started asking myself some questions, putting my knowledge to the test. When I tried to tell you that I was born into a family in which I had always been told that everyone had to find God on their own, you made it clear that I was on the path, but not on the best one. I had to join your path. And then, you solemnly proclaimed that you were the representative for the entire national region, and that you were its muqaddam. You told me that I was loved by your god by virtue of having met you. If you were interested in me, it was because your god loved me. You were going to put me on the path that would lead me directly to your god, but by going through you. I was skeptical, but at the same time, you were so relentless that I was unable to resist. I could always try this path out. As someone who had always had a somewhat liberal lifestyle, I began covering my head and monitoring my clothing on your instructions. You said that I shouldn't let my body be seen. That your god did not like that! You were really passing yourself off as the one who was going to guide me on the right path. You would bring me quotations from the Holy Scriptures, ask me to do certain prayers. I had embarked upon the path of salvation with you, you said. You said that every woman who had left you was unlucky. But I, I was the lucky one and I had to thank your god for putting a man like you on my path. You asked me to call my family to tell them about your desire to marry me. I, who was no longer expecting a man of my age to leave so many young, beautiful, and rich women behind to marry me! I didn't pay it any mind when you told me that high school girls were making dates with you to profess their love for you. You who had a daughter who could practically be the mother of these high school girls! If I had been vigilant, I would have realized that you had problems. Because your words were different from your behavior. You were passing yourself off as a holy man, but you would only talk about young girls who wanted to sleep with you and rich women who wanted to marry you. I would sometimes ask you why you didn't marry those very rich and very beautiful women who wanted you. You said that you, you were on God's path, on the spiritual path, and not on the material path. You insisted that what you wanted was a virtuous woman. I let your words intoxicate me. Little by little, you made me cut off relations with the people I associated with, saying that they weren't the type of people with whom I should be associating. You told me that your god would show you the people with whom I should associate. I was swept up and gave in increasingly. You expressed your desire to marry me, and said that the only person you could not fight, if she did not approve, was your mother. When you spoke to her about it, she showed no reluctance. You asked her to have the "visioning" done in order to see if this marriage was good, and she told you that it was a good one. You asked her to have another "visioning" done, because you didn't want to commit to yet another marriage that was destined to fail. Your mother assured you that this was a good one. You went to find one of your father's childhood friends to talk to him about me, about your desire to marry me, and to do another "visioning." When you went out to get the results two days later, you told me that your father's friend had been so dazzled by what he had seen that he got up in the middle of the night to offer two prayers of thanks to God! You told me to ask my family to do a "visioning" too. You pestered me every day until I called a family friend. As for me, I had lost my parents a long time ago. Two days later, I called back to get the results. Here too, everything was wonderful. I didn't understand why your god did not have anything to say on this matter. So then, you rushed our marriage, one October. The first few days were crazy. We were made for each other. You seemed really caring, affectionate, sensitive, and every night, I would leave my primary residence to go to spend the night at your place, with you, my now husband, in the presence of your god, which you were always talking about. I had stopped paying attention to my daughter in this relationship. She had been reluctant from the beginning. She didn't say anything to me, but I sensed that she wasn't happy with this relationship. As for me, I realized soon enough that you, who extolled kindness, love, mercy, you were paying no attention to my little girl, who was an orphan. I reread the sura from the Book about the poor and the orphans and did not comprehend how your god failed to inspire you in that regard. It seemed a little strange to me and I even talked to you about it. You told me that you were studying my little girl in order to know how to approach her, how to establish a relationship with her. It was strange. You told me this, but you didn't do anything to advance your study of my little girl. My little fourteen-year-old girl was abandoned by a mother who only had eyes and ears for her dead husband's infamous cousin, the muqaddam. A large-statured, dark-skinned muqaddam who loved to play the seducer and talk about his exploits with little high school girls.

I was a woman who had traveled, both through herself and around the world. I was trying to find myself and I had tried to find myself everywhere I went. This is how I had learned many things, done many things, seen many things. I hadn't lived the life of everyone else in my age group, in my generation, in my family, in my friend group. I had my life. A life that I loved. My friends considered me as someone special; people of my generation as someone unique; my family as someone abnormal. And yet, I was clearly just like everyone else. I talked, ate, slept, laughed, cried too. I was attached to fundamental values like friendship, justice. The only thing that one might reproach me for, which I fully owned, was my passion for freedom. I had another idea of freedom. For me, freedom wasn't about doing whatever you wanted, but about seeing whether or not you really wanted to do everything that you were doing, for yourself, without causing harm to others, of course. In any case, all of these wild ideas did not keep me from being liked by some. In the end, I didn't feel too bad about it. The last moments that I spent with my dying husband had also toughened me up. My husband was terminally ill and yet we were both looking after each other. One of us was looking after someone who was going to die and who knew it. And the other was looking after someone who had to keep living and who knew it. Both of us were facing death, and yet, we only talked about life. In the beginning, I would cry, but as life and death became increasingly intertwined, I stopped paying attention to either one. Sometimes, I even got the impression that death was like a journey and that, upon his arrival at his destination, he would write to me, or give me a sign, or even possibly come back. Death came as expected and I found myself at age forty-four with a little girl of barely four years old and a large house to keep up. Work in a neighboring country had me going back and forth for two more years and it wasn't until after that that I settled into a new life with my little girl. A new life, in a small colonial city, but with people from every colony. Portuguese, French, Afro-Brazilian, and other colonizers that I didn't know, but who had all left behind traces, in the beautiful blue eyes of our neighbors across the way. This small city (I remember the first time that I'd come here, many years before) had charmed me. What first appealed to me was that you had to cross a bridge in order to get there. A city of water, surrounded by a calm, serene river, and the city, with its ocher hues and colonial architecture, which reminded me of other cities in my home country. This also made my adjustment easier, because I adapted to this city rather quickly. I had come for the first time in a professional capacity, a few years before. I had made a date with the future man of my life. We agreed upon meeting in this small city, because he was from there originally. He was born there, spent part of his childhood there, until the untimely death of his mother. He was attached to it more than anywhere else. Completing his secondary and university studies abroad had only strengthened his attachment to this small city, perhaps out of nostalgia. The small city and the future man of my life were a lot alike. They were the same color. This is why, when I came here to settle down, years after his death, everything came rushing back into my mind. All of the experiences with this husband who died too young, alas! I also had the feeling that I hadn't just lost a husband, but an important being in my life. A being who had made me a woman, a wife, and a mother. So then, when you started relentlessly pursuing me, praying for my dead husband each time that you prayed, I said to myself here is someone who would surely be an ideal companion. What made me not play too hard to get was your look. You looked good, better than good. When I looked at you, I would tell myself that you had to be good, of sound mind, generous, and faithful. Especially faithful. Faith in a person always translated to me as someone balanced, someone honest, someone good. For God is good. Even if God does not exist, the notion of God is goodness. The idea of God is goodness. In my search, in my quest rather, for a better world, to achieve a harmony among beings and things through spirituality, with a non-dogmatic approach, you came along at just the right time. I identified you as someone who was deeply invested in the quest for God, and every day the conversation would revolve around the Creator. This approach suited me just fine. And I fell for it. I agreed to marry you. In my excitement and my happiness, I forgot about my little girl. It wasn't that I had physically forgotten about her. We lived together, I saw her every day. I had forgotten to include her in my life plan with you, the large-statured, big-bellied man. I was carefree. That's the tragedy of feelings that we believe to be love, when love should be all-encompassing. And you, the big man full of his god, but not the idea of God that you were selling me, you didn't take my little girl into account. You were only interested in yourself, and everything else mattered little to you. You put a spell on me. My little girl, the only child I had, how could I have imagined a life that didn't include her? You seduced me but you did not seduce my daughter. She didn't interest you yet. All that you wanted was to own me, without my daughter. She lived through this ordeal in a deep, hidden pain. The arrival of a friend from somewhere else occupied her for a while, but a mother was irreplaceable, especially at her age at the time, between thirteen and fourteen. My little girl was suffering, and I did not even realize it. You had completely overrun me. As soon as you came into our home, I only had eyes, ears, for you. And my little girl was suffering in silence. Days went by. I was still caught up in your whirlwind, and I wanted to trust you. I was completely delusional. And my little girl was suffering all the more. My little girl didn't criticize me. She didn't say anything to me, but she was speaking to me. She wanted to tell me that maybe I needed to be careful around you, the large-statured, big-bellied man. She was telling me that maybe I needed to not give in so easily. My little girl no longer had access to me. Whereas for her entire life, she had only ever known life with me, and then, all the more, after her father's death. My little girl had only known me. All of the feelings she could have for a father and a mother, she completely poured out to me. The arrival of a little friend from somewhere else seemed to distract her. But gradually, another feeling set in. My little girl saw the friend from somewhere else as a role model, since her mother figure wasn't around anymore. And the big-bellied man who had overrun her mother's life was not a father figure to her. She was captivated by the friend from somewhere else whose ways of dressing, behaving, and especially her freedom to go out, to talk to boys, had lured her in, as an alternative to her cultural foundations and our life at home. I abandoned my little girl because I only had eyes for you, the big-bellied man. My little girl followed the friend from somewhere else like a shadow and wanted to imitate everything that she did and said.

How could I have been so blind?

You then fast-tracked our wedding to that October, just before the dry season. I didn't want to marry you right away, because everything seemed too rushed and an inner voice was trying to warn me, but I was already head over heels in love. You, who championed the virtues of chastity in line with the path for which you were the muqaddam, you had even tried to make love with me before the wedding. I didn't want to because I was afraid. It had been a long time since I'd had sex with anyone, and then, what would you think of me, if I made love with you before the wedding? You were so fervent in your beliefs. In all of the sermons that you gave me, you always said that we must only do lawful things in God's presence, and that making love before the holy union in God's presence was an illicit act. I didn't really understand, because you often revealed to me that you had made love with past girlfriends. Immediately afterward, you would pull yourself together and you would tell me that this was a thing of the past and that you had sworn to God that you didn't want to engage in this kind of illicit behavior anymore. If need be, your penis would just have to remain calm, because you, you did not want to commit any more illicit acts. And listening to you, I said to myself: "This is the man who will lead me directly to God." The people from the small city who were still on speaking terms with me kept coming over to tell me that I had to be careful around you. People were saying that you were volatile, unstable, and that you didn't keep women around. People were saying that if you were as good as you tried to appear, I wouldn't have met you and gotten to know you in isolation. And yet, you had a professional position. You presented well, you were tall, you had style, but you did have a strange gleam that would flash in your eyes. I didn't want to listen to what people were telling me, I didn't want to hear people's warnings. For me, your god was the one who had sent you. This is what you ended up putting in my head. I was truly loved by your god, you would tell me time and again, and I ended up believing it, and I would thank your god in all of my prayers.

"You will be the happiest woman in the world!" you said to me. I wondered what I could have done to deserve all of this. Whenever you would say this to me, every single time, you would get an intense, distant look in your eyes. I was in heaven. All the while, my little girl was following the friend from somewhere else in outlandish ways. I was completely unaware. Days went by. I was now spending nights at your place, the great, big-bellied man. Divine nights of love, and you would say that love was part of the divine, and that pleasure was also God. I told myself: "Here is the ideal man." I began to detect little flaws, but I didn't want to pay them any mind. Those little flaws could take my illusion of happiness away. No, no, in any case, nothing was perfect, so I didn't want to dwell on small details. The first flaw that I detected was that you didn't get up early to say prayers. At first, you would do them, but after two or three times, that was it. You who had your god on your lips, you used to pray from dawn until noon. I tried to understand, telling myself that perhaps you were a man who had been pre-approved by his god. Increasingly, other details started to disillusion me, but I still didn't want to dwell on them. Except that, the small details were taking on increasingly gigantic proportions. And yet, your god was there in all that you said and did. But the contradictions had started springing up. I learned that you talked about people with means, successful people, as people who had eluded divine mercy. You said that these people had everything on earth but had nothing in the eyes of your god. I said to you: "Why not?" One can be rich and be close to God. I realized that you were a jealous and envious man. You were jealous of the people you talked about, especially of people who were well-to-do. You would make up incredible stories about them in this life and the next one too. You would console yourself with your god. These discoveries, these flaws, these contradictions were starting to get to me. You were large in size, but your mind seemed to be getting smaller, with each passing day. Sometimes you would make up for it and go through a period of great enlightenment and I would tell myself that I had quite simply been mistaken, and that in life, nothing is perfect. Except that I didn't want to be more perfect than you, because I was seeking perfection in you, or at least the pathway to perfection. From that point on, it became a little more difficult. I myself was starting to shoulder some of your weight. It was becoming awful for me. You were a man who I wanted to admire, who I wanted to behold, who I wanted to serve. I remember, when you would come over to badger me in my home, you would always tell me that you were looking for someone to serve you. Naively, I replied that I wanted to serve you. I told you that my ambition was to serve someone who served God. It wasn't until later that I understood that we didn't have the same interpretation of the word "serve." By the time I realized our two different notions of the word "serve," it was too late, so I told you that I had been mistaken in my understanding of the word. When we would sometimes talk about it, you always wanted to let me believe that my understanding was the same as yours, whereas, in reality, it wasn't. For you, serving you meant handing everything I had over to you. My money, my things. This was how I would get to your god on the quickest path. You had found us in our big house, and I had been traveling a lot, and you told yourself that I would fit the bill because I had to have had money. What you meant by serving you to get to your god, was that I had to rob myself, ruin myself for you. Another flaw that I detected about you was your bad faith. You would say something but then take it back later. When I noticed this about you, I became distraught. Now that I was in so deep, now that I had come so far, believing that I was going to God, I didn't know what to do. I was so disillusioned, and I was so terrified when I realized that I was headed toward the devil! But the devil I thought I saw was a just little demon, in comparison with your other sides, which I was about to discover! In spite of this all, I wanted to keep fighting and trying through prayer, conversation, to get you refocused on God's path, but increasingly, I kept discovering your hidden sides. When you would talk to me about the women you had been with, and in the way you would describe your relationships, I realized the obvious. Although you were large in size, you were a small man, and you were not the one for me. First of all, I have never liked men who badmouth the women they have been with. You said so many terrible things about the first woman you lived with and had your first child with, a daughter, who was thirty years old when we met! You had met this woman long before finishing high school, and you wanted to continue your studies at the university. After you left for college, the woman, who was already pregnant, gave birth to a daughter one month later, almost to the day! The woman had also wanted to continue her own studies and had dreams of going to college. Maybe she believed that this daughter would only make your relationship, which had lasted for several years, stronger. A relationship that your family had supported, your friends, even your enemies. No one could have imagined that this was not the woman you were going to marry. As soon as you set foot abroad for your studies, you fell for another woman. This woman, who you had met and who wasn't all that beautiful (to you, who talked about beauty at every turn), was in the same program as you and was quite well-off from her parents, so on that side of things, you were set. It was easy to fall for her. When the woman who had just given birth to your daughter came to join you later on, she found you in your dorm room in the other woman's company. That was how you ended your relationship, leaving her to sleep in your room on your bed that first night, while you slept on the floor, on the rug. The next morning, you got rid of her by going to ask some friends to take care of her, to push her away from you, so that she would enroll in another city. So the woman who had given you your first child, a daughter, packed her bags and left the next day. Once full of hope, promises, and now laden with great disappointment and bitterness. This first instance, which you yourself told me about, without regret, without remorse, made me doubt your righteousness all the more. You told me all of this while laughing at her, making fun of her. You wouldn't stop telling me that you couldn't live with her, because she was stagnant water, and you would say it so derisively. How long had you known this for? That woman, I imagined her suffering, her disappointment, for herself, for her family, for her community, because you both belonged to the same community. The entire community was disappointed. Your mother even threatened to disown you, and that didn't rattle you. You were already in with another group, another community. Little by little, with all of the stories you were telling me, I realized that you were a player. All that interested you were new self-serving conquests. You would only look where you might find a financial interest. You revealed yourself to be a player and a pervert too. You talked about the woman with the suitcase, practically gloating.

"I told her to find someone else. I told her that she was young, that she could even find someone better than me! I pray that she finds someone better than me if need be. She has slept around. I heard that she dated a guy from the North. I also heard that she was even expecting a child, but that she'd had an abortion. Maybe she was still hoping that it might work out one day, between us. You know, two years ago when I separated from my umpteenth wife, she called me. When I went to her office, she suggested that we start over again. I laughed, and I told her that I wasn't the same person anymore. That there was no way!"

And I watched you, lying on your bed, laughing, satisfied with yourself.

"And then, you know, she and her mother now spend their time attacking me. They consult every kind of charlatan to create problems for me. I learned this all from one of my security guards."

You were badmouthing the mother of your child, with so much rage!

"Oh my God," I said to myself. "Who have I fallen for?"

And with each passing day, I was getting increasingly bogged down. I did everything to satisfy you. I did everything to serve you, for I was still seeking God, and you were another god's salesman.

So you then ended up marrying the young woman from a different ethnic group, a different community, to enjoy an easy life. And so you went off to live with her several years later, in her country of origin. At the time, the woman was not of the same religious persuasion as you. You put up with it provided that she embrace your religion one day. But what really attracted you was the financial aspect. The woman belonged to a well-to-do family. The wedding was performed in both religions and took place shortly after you had met the people who were about to put you on a religious path. You, who had undergone psychoanalysis in order to find some balance, you thought that through this path, you would find absolute happiness, especially through money, which was the only thing that interested you, other than sex.

"Muñ, where are you?

"Are you still in the bathroom?

"Who can say what you are doing in the bathroom?"

It was Drianké calling for Muñ.

Muñ came out and showed herself to Drianké, who was staring at her exasperatedly. And as soon as it was possible, Muñ rushed back over to the typescript.

You are still searching, and you are searching in disarray, because from the time that I met you up until today, your faith has been shaky. You are always wavering. But if that's what faith is, then I don't understand anything anymore. In any case, I kept searching for God to unravel the mystery of disorder. Everything had been created with its opposite. Without its opposite, the thing did not exist, could not exist.

But what was there to do?

Abandon ourselves to disorder and become disordered ourselves?

But then, why morality?

Why insist on doing good and not on doing evil? Was I to understand that I was already in evil, and that I had to manage to do only good?

But who had created me?

It was God!

Why had He made me this way?

So that I would spend my life in this inner battle between good and evil, with uncertainties to boot! Spend my life battling myself, instead of spending time like the angels adoring God, glorifying Him with violins!

Only God knows who is going to hell and who is going to heaven. He forbids us from even saying that someone is good or that someone is bad. God has said that He only knows. But then, why still morality?

I had always feared that this disorder had led to a nonbelief in God. Maybe that was what God was seeking too? As for Him, He didn't need any of His creatures. He was powerful, omnipotent, He had created Himself. And all He had to do was say "*kun*" for a thing to be designed, and all He had to do was say "*fa yakun*" for the thing to exist, once and for all.*

In between *kun* and *fa yakun*, human beings had the

* *Kun fa yakun* is a Quranic phrase that translates to "Be, and it is," or "Be, and it becomes." *Kun* is the imperative *Be* and *fa yakun* is the indicative phrase that follows.

chance to change the face of the world. But very few human beings had fully grasped this moment, between *kun* and *fa yakun*. At this stage, the spirit was at work. The conscience was overridden.

As for me, none of this bothered me. I just wanted to be sure that I was the manifestation of God and that nothing would happen to me, regardless of whether I did good or evil! I wanted to be the expression of his will. It wouldn't be until much later that I would come to understand that his will could be my own!

"Muñ! Muñ! Where are you?

"In the bathroom?

"What are you still doing in the bathroom?"

It was Drianké calling for Muñ.

Muñ rushed out of the bathroom, she too exasperated. She hadn't even had the time to read many pages lately. Drianké made her come out of the bathroom, but she took the time to carefully place the typescript in the yellow folder back on top of the water tank.

"Ah, I would like to know what you're doing in the bathroom, Muñ! You spend hours in there washing yourself! Do you have diarrhea, or is it constipation? I don't even know what to say anymore!

"It's unbelievable!"

Whenever Drianké would speak this way, Muñ would not say anything. Muñ was no longer present with Drianké. Muñ had drowned herself in the typescript. And every day, each time that Drianké would finish cooking, take her cold shower, and retire to her room, smoking her pipe, while humming, whispering, or whistling the blues, Muñ would take off for the bathroom and get back to the typescript in the yellow folder.

So I wanted to see my relationship with you, the large-statured, big-bellied man, as God's will. By uncovering who you were little by little, I committed myself to a test that God had sent me. And I told myself that God was thinking of me. He only tested those who loved Him, as I had always been taught. In order to cope, I tried to see our relationship in that way. But why did God want to test me? Because He had something better in store for me? In order to arrive at this proof, I had to put myself to the test. Ah! Proof by fire! By nine or by three? By one? God's number was always an odd number. Ever since unity! In this hope, I had come to see the test as a single step, and its burden became less onerous. Only as time went on, your flaws kept piling up like dead leaves, and at this point, a shovel would no longer do the trick. I needed wheelbarrows, excavators, dumpsters, freight cars, cargo ships, container ships. You started to dazzle me less and less, for I was seeking God and you, you kept dragging me into your fantasies and your gods. For you, the best years in life seemed to be the ones spent in material wealth or in sex, from the way you would talk about your previous life, especially in that faraway country, which wasn't your own. You followed that woman there, the one that you had married and who had done the same studies as you. You would talk about that life like a paradise lost. You would talk about the house where you had lived like the kind you might find in the paradise lost. You would talk about the landscapes like the Eden that you would never see again, for you had been driven out by God. You would talk about the people you had met there as if they were Creation's finest specimens. You would talk about the cars that you'd had there as if no other auto company could ever make anything better. When we were together, I would go back into your past and your fantasies with you! You would drag me into your past and into your world. How your children had been born, the soup that your wife had consumed, in full detail. You were present at every childbirth. This is how I spent my days with you, the large-statured, big-bellied man, focused on your past. On the other hand, you didn't say much about your divorce. You, who liked to talk about your past, you never told me the reasons for your divorce. You, who liked to talk in full detail about your life with that woman from that other country, you only ever talked about the day when the divorce was finalized, and how despite everything bad that had been said about you in the courthouse, you insisted that your chauffeur drive your ex-wife home in your own car. You even said that your shared lawyer had been stunned by this. Yes, a gentleman until the very end, you fancied yourself. But then why not talk about the reasons for your divorce, since everything seemed to be paradise? And yet, you had not confessed that you also had a child, a son, with another woman from the same country as your ex-wife. A son who you were hiding. And I would just sit there watching you talk. You were nostalgic and seemed happy. You were a man of the past. You were quite simply the embodiment of Adam's fall from grace, but you were unable to rise back up like Adam, because you had not tasted God's grace like Adam had. And in this past, you disregarded everything that concerned you. You took advantage of that woman. You lived off of her back. You were a kept man. In addition, you were cheating on her and had a child, a boy, with another woman from the same community as her. You never talked to me about that. And yet, you were playing the part of the great believer. You would visit all of the religious officials that you had heard about. You would dress like an emir and recite verses, which you didn't understand a single word of, by heart. You didn't have the intellectual, moral, or spiritual capacities for it. You didn't have the ability to understand it because your mind was a tainted mind, twisted in nature. You didn't want to try to do better either. You delighted in vice. You were a member of a sorcerer's club, in which you experimented with every aspect of vice that a man could inflict on a fellow human. With men, you were driven by jealousy and envy, toward those who worked and achieved success. For women, it was what to do to have your way with them and, after indulging your vices, how to find others. For as long as there were women with material wealth or vices!

I had no life with you. You only had eyes for the young girls who were trying to get you and the rich women who wanted to marry you. You would also tell stories about couples coming to find you at your work to talk to you about their sex lives. You told the story of one woman would get too wet and whose husband was unable to come because her vagina wasn't tight enough. You even asked me if I knew a remedy for that. Stunned, my eyes widened in disbelief.

"But in what capacity are they coming to see you?" I asked.

"I'm a counselor, I give advice to people," you replied. But the advice that you could and did give always had something to do with sex. People needed to come to talk to you about their sex lives, their sexual relations, in great detail. And these were the moments when I could tell that you were feeling good about yourself. You would puff yourself up with your strengths as a seducer, a seducer that everyone wanted. When you were in these moments of jubilation, quite satisfied with yourself, you would have it in for everyone else. Why didn't others involve you in their businesses? You would say. You thought that people were nasty, that they had it in for you. You said that a lot of people owed you money. It was terrible to see a man who passed himself off as a man of God behaving in this way, by living only in his past, living his glory days on someone else's dime. But what about today? And this moment? Was it not said that God was in the moment? Why disregard the moment, and thus God? Live in the moment, that was the recommendation. And you, this man who was serving his god, you were only living in your past or in your fantasies. A glorious past in which you had been so glorious that you even left your ex-wife the house that you had built with her money, which also happened to be the house of paradise. So paradise was there, and a long time ago at that! A paradise built on lies, on that woman's exploitation. A paradise in which you were cheating on your wife with other women. A paradise in which you were taking advantage of a situation. But ever unstable, you have always needed and still need affairs. You have even called yourself a player or a hunter, a tiger according to your Chinese zodiac sign. Your role as a muqaddam now gave you the opportunity to attract women on the path to your god and to exploit them to the bone. A physical, material, moral exploitation. This last exploitation was, after everything else, the final phase of your method. You would tear women to shreds physically, morally, materially, and then, you would use this situation as a pretext to get rid of them. And then, you would move on to a new female conquest!

Increasingly, I felt like I had no life with you, I had no plans, I had no life experiences, because everything you ate, everything you heard, everything you saw, brought you back to your past and to your material and sexual fantasies. Nothing was new for you. Everything was related to your past and your fantasies. You compared everything to your past. You told me about a relationship that you'd had with one of your cousins. That girl, you said, was an intellectual. You were the one who had guided her on the path to your god. Her parents were believers but weren't practicing. She didn't know anything about her culture. You were the one who had initiated her, taught her many things that she didn't know, neither about her culture or nor about her religion. You spoke as if you were the messiah that this woman had been waiting for. You were the one who had taught her everything that she knew. It was thanks to you that she participated in televised debates. In all that you did and said, you were the one who was perfect. You had no faults. It was always other people. And the lord that you wanted to be never questioned himself!

What I found strange was that every day, you would only ever talk to me about your life. As if I myself didn't have a life! I had to listen to you talk. In any case, you couldn't stand me talking. I had to just sit there and listen to you talk. Whenever I would tell you that I couldn't get a word in edgewise, you would tell me that I didn't listen to other people speak! So I shut up. For good.

The path for which you were the muqaddam had two places for meeting and prayer. One was in the small city where we both lived, and the other was in another city not far from there. Every Sunday, you had to go to the community prayer with the other disciples. What surprised me, among other surprises, was that you would never get up early. In the beginning of our relationship, after I had started sleeping at your place, I realized that you could sleep until noon and that, sometimes, you wouldn't even pray. When you would talk about prayers in the presence of others, you would say that they were the link that connected believers to God. You would say that they needed to treat the first prayer of the day like a date with a beautiful woman. As if all believers were men! You only had women on your mind. "Who is going to miss a date with a beautiful woman?" you would say. But then, how were you able to miss your dates with God? Because God wasn't a beautiful woman? All that you said was not what you did. You would talk, but you didn't live by what you yourself were saying. I was so disappointed! But what could I do? You would speak bitterly to me about your brothers and sisters, who were more successful than you, and you had it in for a bunch of people. You would say that your brothers and sisters had achieved material success, but that this success was illicit. All of their activities were illicit in the eyes of your god. You would say that your god was enough for you. But your god was the dragged-down god.

You would say that this was because someone had obstructed you. And who had obstructed you? "My uncle!" you said. You said that your uncle had joined forces with the devil and that he was in a sorcerer's club, otherwise you would have been able to achieve success. You said that your uncle wanted to destroy you. You said that your uncle was even destroying his own children and that a hot hell was awaiting him. You would use all of these arguments to sensitize and recruit women into this path and to justify what you called your misfortune in life. Whereas your misfortune was your laziness. Your misfortune was wanting to take advantage of people at all costs, especially rich women, for the money and the sex. All while I believed that you had found success with your god, who was on your lips in the presence the Eternal!

If this relationship was proof, God would have to give me

the proof. The trial by fire had thus become another way for me to find God. Because I was seeking God through you, the large-statured, big-bellied man, whom I wanted to serve so that you could serve God and that I myself might get to God. But as I had come so far, I wanted to treat our relationship as a test. I consoled myself with this, and it gave me strength to bear my suffering. But what was becoming increasingly unbearable was realizing that you—the large-statured, big-bellied man—had other gods along with your own god. You really believed in geomancy, in visions (in your visions and those of others), in astrophysics, in books of dreams, in Chinese astrology, in sorcerers. In the beginning, I thought that I had found a cultivated man, but I quickly realized that your entire waking life was influenced by this alone. You liked to say that your father had given you one piece of advice:

"Don't be like other people, be careful, don't forget that you aren't like other people."

In your bathroom, the first time I went in there, it felt like I was entering a grand sorcerer's bathroom. There were soaps in every shade of black, dark brown, dark chocolate. Soaps in calabashes, plastic jars, pieces of calabash. There were all kinds of gloves and mystical fruits and vegetables. You would wash yourself with slimy, black fluids, with leaves mixed with animal fur. You said that you'd been hunted for several years by one or two people who wanted you dead. Especially your uncle. Among the people who wanted to harm you, there was also the woman you had your first child with, the woman with the suitcase, who you described as stagnant water. You also said that the last woman, the one you had a little girl with, the woman of easy virtue, was very involved in the chemistry of sorcery. You said that she had put you through hell. Ultimately, with you, everyone else was spending their time in black magic and in fetishes. You only ever had these words on your lips, along with your god who seemed unable to do anything for you. What was also strange was that you would spend most of your nights praying. At first, you reminded me of my father. You reminded me of all of the great mystics who would spend their nights praying, while other people slept. You would pray, but you did not pray with God. You prayed with your god. You prayed to get rich, to have beautiful houses, beautiful women with money, cars, especially SUVs with four-wheel drive, and Spaces, which were trending. I detected this all little by little. When you would talk about your brothers and sisters, you would always talk about them with envy and jealousy. Out of your entire family, apart from one brother, you said that you were the least well-off. And yet, you had gone to college, perhaps gotten some sort of diploma, were practicing a profession that could bring in enough to earn a decent living and to support your children from several different mothers. But this wasn't enough for you. You wanted to be like your brothers and sisters, like other people with material wealth, or preferably, to be above them. You were convinced that you could have achieved success if it wasn't for the evil forces that your family members were deploying all around you, especially your closest paternal uncle. I, who believed that you were a man of God, I was now discovering that you were a man of your gods. You told me that one of your brothers-in-law was using your name and your profession to get rich. You went so far as to say that your mother might even be in on it, but that she wouldn't say anything and that she would even find that normal. How could someone who was so jealous of others say that he believed only in God, that he left everything up to Him? When you would preach, you would say to your flock:

"What our god has in store for us is better than what other people have on earth.

"Ah! If you only knew!

"Ah! If other people only knew!

"What we are doing right now, reciting verses, is better than the people who are dealing with shipping containers and bank accounts!"

Whenever I heard you speak like this, I thought that you would end up convincing yourself of what you were saying! But no! As soon as you would get out of there, you would head directly over to see the charlatans and other magicians. You would tell me that it was just for fun. And yet, whenever your brothers and sisters and other people that you envied and denigrated would give you money, you did not refuse. You were bursting with contradictions, in this regard and many others. Whenever I would hear you talking like that about your family, I would get very worried. Because I was searching for God by serving you. And my little girl, who was my child, was being neglected. Abandoned, my little girl was out doing every stupid thing imaginable in the phase of adolescence that she was going through. First of all, since I wasn't sleeping at my place anymore, my little girl was staying there alone with a housekeeper and the much-talked-about little friend who had already been initiated into womanhood before coming to our place. And the housekeeper had only two passions in life, cigarettes and television. She didn't have enough strength of character to keep a close eye on my little girl, and she couldn't fill the void that I had left behind either. And my little girl gradually fell into delinquency. During this time, I was with a large-statured, big-bellied man, and wondering who he really was. The situation was painful. Each time I went back home, I felt so ashamed! I would go home very early in the morning, before sunrise. But there would always be a few early-riser neighbors who would see me sneaking back home, like a thief. I was ashamed, because I had left my house for a man who was becoming increasingly despicable, and whenever I would look at my house, it seemed to be reproaching me for having abandoned it, and I would feel even more ashamed. During this time, my little girl was learning about life with the little friend from somewhere else. She was smoking, drinking. She had even tried making love with a boy. I was not aware of any of this. I was absorbed by you, the large-statured, big-bellied man, who was starting to put me through hell. You still could not care less about my little girl. In fact, you didn't ask how she was doing, didn't ask about her studies. You were only there for me, rather for what you were expecting from me. First off, eating, because you were a big eater. So all of our small savings would go into shopping at the market. You liked to eat the best there was, but you did not like to spend money. All while I believed that the path you were boasting about—of being the great churchgoer and advocate and even the great vizier—would require a small-statured or a large-statured man to provide for the needs of his family in terms of food, shelter, and clothing. Not to mention, of course, all of the support and affection that his wife would need, especially when it came to making love. On this last point, you yourself said that it was a form of prayer. But you were bad at making love. I didn't know if it was because of your large size or your big belly, or your small penis, or your tiny testicles, or the numbness that you had been complaining about in your pelvic area for the past several years. Fortunately, since long before I met you!

I was seriously starting to worry because I failed to

realize that you were a self-involved and perverted man. You would indirectly ask me questions about my earnings, without me suspecting for a single moment that this was to find out whether or not I had money. One time, you looked at my fingernails and said:

"But you, normally, you should have money. You have spots on the tips of your fingernails. It's a sign of rich people."

Naively, I told you that I was indeed rich, rich with God, rich with everything that God had showed me in this life, rich with my health, rich with everything that I had compared to so many people suffering from hunger, illnesses. I didn't know that I was disappointing you. You, you were looking for money. And I, I was always in pursuit of God with you. Come to think of it, the first time I went to your place, you seemed worried. I found you on the balcony on the second floor of your house. The balcony overlooking a stream. Surely, it was the ideal spot in your home, to lure people into your god's net. Although the location was beautiful, it was uncomfortable because of the sun during the day and the mosquitos at night. In addition, the view was spoiled by the low edges of the roof which prevented us from standing upright to better enjoy it. You were in a bathrobe made from a local fabric. You welcomed me rather coldly and you asked me questions about my in-laws.

"Don't you have any in-laws who would want to marry you?" The question took me by surprise.

"No, you know, in the ten years since my husband's passing, if someone wanted me or if I wanted someone, you wouldn't have found me. Besides, these in-laws aren't my in-laws, they are my family now," I replied.

You looked at me strangely, your eyes narrowing. I think you were wondering if I fit the bill from a material perspective. This is the question you were asking yourself. But me,

I naively thought that you wanted to do things the right way and thus avoid any unpleasantness. I would later realize that the first flaws had appeared earlier on, but that I had been blinded by your god, which you were introducing me to, but which wasn't the God I was seeking. Increasingly, when I would sleep over at your place, I would have a hard time getting back to my place early, like I wanted. (My professional activity took place in my home.) Sometimes, I would spend almost the entire day there. One of the reasons was that you, the large-statured, big-bellied man, were a lazy man. You did not get up early and that surprised me. Because I thought that what you were flaunting as devotion was not what you were truly all about. You neglected the prayer times that you yourself championed as moments for important meetings with God. You instead adored Ra, the sun god. You would pray when the sun was out, clearly visible, clearly shining, clearly casting its rays. You would also sleep a lot, whereas a true believer should be an active person. It is said that true believers do not sleep very much. As for you, you would sleep and snore while farting loudly, as if your guts were about to unleash a torrent of shit. You would say that you were the tiger sign in Chinese astrology. You were a tiger, you would say, when you didn't even know which part of the world tigers were found in. You were a hunter, you would say, and you always had to be on the hunt.

What did any of this have to do with God?

And hunters had to get up early!

"Muñ! Muñ!" Drianké practically shouted at the top of her voice.

Muñ quickly closed the typescript, climbed up the pipe, and placed it on top of the water tank. She splashed herself with water and went out. Drianké looked at her, saying:

"Muñ, you really like spending time in the bathroom!

"You, who hardly eats a thing, what are you eating that is making you spend so much time in the bathroom?

"Huh? Answer me!

"Well, now, I've seen everything in this world.

"You're one of those people with a passion.

"And your passion, is for the bathroom."

Muñ was there in front of Drianké, but did not hear her. For Drianké, Muñ shutting herself away in the bathroom was now an everyday occurrence, but she still was unable to normalize it.

"Muñ, about your mother, don't you think we should consider going to get her, since we've been talking about it for some time now?

"What do you think?"

Muñ did not answer her.

She was still in the typescript. That woman's story was incredible, for it was strangely just like a story that she herself seemed to know. No, that was impossible. The story that she knew could not be being told in a typescript in a yellow folder, picked up in the courtyard of a cottage, on Felix Faure Street.

No, this was not the same story!

The story that Muñ wanted to know and understand was the one about a very beautiful woman who had a restaurant in a small city, in an inland part of the country. It was said that the woman was the most beautiful woman in that small city. Tall, shapely, and proportionate, she had an easy smile. She ran her restaurant next to the train station. This train station was very important in the region. It was a station with several connecting lines. Many travelers were routed through there. One day, a large-statured man with a big belly came in and ordered something to eat. This man came in holding prayer beads and repeating the name of a god at every turn. The man had eaten for free because the woman thought that she was doing a good deed by giving a man of God something to eat. Serve God and He will serve you. When the man finished eating, the woman suggested that he rest on a bed, which she had set up in a room in the back of the restaurant. She made the bed and invited the large-statured man to sit down. As soon as the man sat down on the bed, he brusquely pulled the woman by the arm and, looking her in the eyes, holding the prayer beads in front of her, said: "You are a good woman, but you have problems due to impurities, which are blocking your luck in this life. You are a woman who has a lot of luck, but impurities are blocking this luck. My god has shown them to me. I can help you, and I want to help you." The woman did not really understand what the man with the prayer beads was trying to say.

"For all that you have done for me, given that I'm on a mission in this world—I am a vested muqaddam—I'm going to help you. I'm going to purify you. Don't worry, you won't have to pay me anything. Everything I do, I do for my god."

And this is how the woman found herself in bed with the big-bellied man, for a purification that had to be performed through a sex act. Once he had fulfilled his fantasies by asking the woman to put herself into uncomfortable positions, he said to her, all while uttering gibberish:

"In order to rid you of your impurities, I am obliged to use this method, my god is the one who inspired it in me. For the impurities have gotten inside of you through equally tortuous paths. May my god bless you!"

After this purification ritual, the man asked where he could have his gabardine caftan washed. The woman offered to wash it for him as she still had some soap left. She took the large-statured, big-bellied man's gabardine caftan and washed it. When she had finished, she put it out to dry in the sun. The sun on that afternoon was hot and bright. It was a burning, hivernage sun, but this was a good thing, because the gabardine caftan was heavy and difficult to dry under normal conditions. A few hours later, the large-statured, big-bellied man put on his gabardine caftan, dried by that fiery sun, and after thanking the woman with some prayers, he left. She never saw him again. And then, one fine day she started to see spots on her skin. The spotted areas became numb. The woman had contracted leprosy. This leprosy, she had contracted it from the gabardine caftan of the large-statured, big-bellied man who had eaten in her restaurant. In her line of work, she had chapped fingers, nicked by the knives that she used to scale fish, to cut pieces of meat, which she bought in bulk. While washing the caftan, the leprosy had slipped in through her tiny wounds. She had contracted leprosy from a large-statured, big-bellied man, who had disappeared. A man with no name, no address, no destination. That large-statured, big-bellied man did not look like a leper. He had leprosy and maybe did not even know it yet himself. No one ever knew what became of that man. All that the woman recalled, was that he was a large-statured, dark-skinned, big-bellied man. And he said he was vested in a mission for his god. He said he was a muqaddam. And the beautiful waitress had not been able to get her illness treated. Gradually, she lost her toes, her fingers. The skin on her face had wrinkled, and her eyes had lost all of their lashes. Her heavy eyelids drooped like old rags. She would stay in a room in a part of their house, removed from public view, completely covered in veils. Before that, she'd had grown children, and one of her sisters had been staying with her since their own mother's death. The man was never found, and she just kept repeating that he was large-statured, dark-skinned, big-bellied, and that he called himself a muqaddam. Her relatives thought that one had to be careful these days. There were more and more sects and more and more temples with new gurus and muqaddams. The traditional temples for God, the one who has been recognized since Creation, have been abandoned for new temples with new gods, which were asking women (married to men who had not been chosen by their gods) to physically purify themselves by offering their so-called defiled bodies to these new prophets. The woman who had contracted leprosy from the big-bellied man's caftan was ashamed to say that he had a small penis, tiny testicles, and that he did not know how to make love. That was the story that Muñ wanted to know, not a different story, not the one that the large chopped-up leper's eyes would tell, one November morning, on a Felix Faure Street sidewalk.

"Muñ, I'm talking to you!" Drianké reprimanded.

"I'm sorry, I was thinking.

"I think that my mother won't want to come. Her illness is very advanced, and besides, we have tried everything to cure her, in vain."

"What do you mean, in vain?" Drianké exclaimed.

"What illness is untreatable in hospitals, clinics?

"You know we can do everything here, even on this street.

"Muñ, listen, if you don't want to go, I can send someone to get her.

"What do you say?

"Remind me of the name of the place.

"Hogbo? Is that it?

"Is it far from here? Isn't there another name for that place?

"You're so secretive that no one knows anything about you!

"You don't have any friends, you don't have any family here, nothing.

"Work. Bathroom, bathroom, bathroom, bathroom, bathroom.

"Why do you like the bathroom?

"Wouldn't you rather have friends instead of shutting yourself away in the bathroom?

"Or, are you the one who is sick?

"If you're having problems, you have to tell someone.

"We're in a big city here. There are good hospitals.

"Muñ, do you understand me?"

"Nothing is wrong with me!" Muñ said.

"Admit that you like the bathroom then," Drianké said.

"Well, getting back to your mother, I would really like for her to come.

"What do you think?"

Muñ stood there, silent, looking Drianké in the eyes, without blinking. Muñ was staring so hard at her that it made Drianké wince. Muñ kept looking at Drianké, and yet, upon closer examination, she was not looking at Drianké, but beyond Drianké. She saw her mother there, sitting in the back of the courtyard of their house, in the scorching heat. Her mother would come out of the room, completely covered in veils. She would slowly walk toward the back of the courtyard where an old rattan armchair awaited her, and there, she would sit for a long while. She could stay there until nightfall.

Drianké did not dare to say anything more to Muñ, as her look was not the kind of look that left any room for questions. Drianké was worried. This look was a hateful look, a violent look, a look whose origin and cause or reason she did not want to know. And in this look, a strange gleam flashed.

Drianké was the first to lower her eyes.

"Well, think about it.

"When you want, we'll have your mother brought here for treatment."

Drianké, the small-statured woman who walked with a slight limp, was the first to turn her back and head over to the front of her cottage where she would stay for a good part of the day.

Muñ kept staring off in the distance. Her mother had been such a lively, such a beautiful, such an elegant, such a joyful woman! Everyone liked her for her charm, her kindness, and her vitality. She loved children, respected people, and had a kind word or a smile for everyone. She was someone who had lived life and who was the type of person that Muñ wanted to be like when she got older. Her mother, usually so full of life, was now this figure covered in veils who, each afternoon, would slowly walk over to the back of the courtyard of their home and sit down in her armchair, that old rattan armchair upon which she had rocked so many times, before ruining her life with a big-bellied muqaddam. Her mother could not be that figure, that shadow. No, that was not possible! Muñ had been born when her mother was truly in the prime of life. Mature, balanced, cultured, passionate. She breathed in life and exuded it. She was a joy to behold. She grew proud of this mother as she started getting older. She loved to be seen in her mother's company. She loved her mother. She admired her mother. Muñ had not really known her father, who had died several years before, when she was just four years old. Around the age of eight, she would take photos of her father and isolate herself somewhere with them. Sometimes, while going around the house, one might find, somewhere or another, a rug, a book, and a photo of her father. She missed her father, that much was certain. Perhaps she was wondering what life would be like with her father and her mother together? What relationship might she have with her father? When she would hear her friends talking about their fathers, perhaps this had an effect on her. She was trying to get to know this father that she had never known. She tried to get to know him by asking her mother all sorts of questions.

"How did you meet?

"What did he give you for your wedding?

"Which dress did you wear on your wedding day?

"Show me your wedding photos.

"Didn't you take any photos?

"Didn't you plan a reception for your friends?

"What was his name?

"Did you have a honeymoon somewhere?

"What did he call me when I was little?

"Did he hold me in his arms?

"Did he sing for me?

"When I cried, what would he say?"

And her mother's responses would make her laugh. She was happy to have this mystery father that her mother would talk to her about. Although the mother had tried to play the roles of mother and father, a father was essential. Upon her father's death, her mother continued to work and travel a great deal until the day when she stopped everything to dedicate herself to her passions and to her little girl. But the father was still missing. In the very beginning, she had tried to start a new life, but she thought that the child should be given the opportunity to grow up in her birthplace, in her father's homeland, close to his family, to build her character in her father's birthplace. For her mother, starting a new life might mean abandoning all of that and adapting to a different environment. Perhaps it was better to live with the paternal side of the family, and this is what led her and her mother to settle in her father's homeland. Starting a new life did not necessarily mean getting remarried either. For her mother, starting a new life could also mean going back to her homeland or going somewhere else. Going back to her homeland would not be a problem for her. But for the child, what might such a long-distance move entail? She and her own mother had lived all over the place, in several countries. So they had lived alone, far from the father, far from the mother's country of origin, culturally isolated, and they had tried to overcome these drawbacks by creating a way of life on their own terms. This is why the mother wanted to stay in the father's homeland, so that her child would be immersed in his way of life, with his blood, with his ethnic group. And that would last forever, it would be indelible. Her mother also indirectly benefited from this environment to integrate herself into a culture, close to that of her own family, for which she was also nostalgic. And this had been going on for several years. Muñ had grown up this way, but no one could ever figure out what was going on in her head. She was a quiet, modest, rather withdrawn little girl. Her mother thought that this was the lot of orphans. Her mother did everything to give her a good life without a father, and sometimes, she came to forget that a father was essential.

"Muñ, Muñ, what's wrong?

"What are you doing standing there in the middle of the courtyard?" Drianké shouted, sitting in her old leather armchair.

"I was thinking about my mother," Muñ replied.

Muñ did not want to believe that the story contained in the typescript was about to become her story. Muñ had been trying for many years to forget that story. She had never talked about it, never. She wanted that story to have never existed. The typescript retrieved in the courtyard where the shadowy mass spent the night contained a story, identical to a story that she knew, and now she was afraid that it would become her own story. As for her story, she did not want anyone to talk about it, not in a typescript or anywhere else.

Drianké did not know that Muñ would not be present anymore, at least not until she had finished reading the typescript. Drianké seemed a bit more comfortable with Muñ after she told her that she was thinking about her mother.

"Ah! At last!

"Maybe you will make up your mind.

"This is good. Well, come and get the dishes and glasses for me.

"Get the lanterns ready too. Friends will be arriving soon."

Muñ did not understand why Drianké had so many lanterns and why they were particularly important to her. Every day, she had to clean them, add fuel, and light some of them. And lighted lanterns were constantly burning. Whenever the people who came to her place would talk to her about her lanterns, they would say, laughing, that she resembled her lanterns because she was always radiant. People did not really understand Drianké's connection to these many lanterns. Perhaps she was using these lanterns for some sort of mysterious protection or for success one day, as a blues singer. Drianké was not into these kinds of beliefs and superstitions. Drianké had her small business, with rosé wine, beer, Kiravi Valpierre, and simple but succulent small plates. After the clients had had a bit to drink, they would buy Drianké's small plates, spicy little dishes recommended for drunkenness. These were dishes consisting of little fried fish with a very hot, very spicy sauce. It was always said that people who drank a lot of alcohol liked spices. Tongues assailed by tannins liked spices and tobacco too. Sometimes, Drianké would make meat kebabs, or cow foot soup, also very popular. By late afternoon, you would hear laughter and exclamations of joy all around Drianké. Muñ would wash the glasses and plates along the way, but did not get involved in conversations. When a client would call her over, it would be to ask for a glass of water, but no one was ever aggressive with her or made any type of proposition. Muñ did not have a propensity for such propositions. Muñ was an enigma to all those people who came to Drianké's place—and all kinds of people came to Drianké's place. At Drianké's place, cases of beer, bottles of Kiravi Valpierre were stored inside, in Drianké's living quarters. But Drianké knew everyone's habits ever since she had been in this business. As soon as someone expressed the need for something to drink, without specifying what, Drianké would ask Muñ to go and get what they wanted. Drianké knew the habits of each of her regular clients. The drinks were served in dark glassware. That way, no one could tell what other people were drinking. Everything was served inside. Muñ had quickly learned to recognize all of the drinks that Drianké sold. Drianké really liked Muñ. She worked hard, was efficient, and was a fast learner. Her only problems with her were that she did not have any friends, that she had a secret life, and that she loved the bathroom. That passion for the bathroom puzzled her.

"Well, the important thing is that she does a good job, she is decent, discreet, and she hasn't caused any problems since she's been here. Ultimately, in this life, what are we trying to find?

"Peace! And she leaves everyone in peace."

Drianké did not work late into the night. The girls, young women, men, married women who came to her place would leave in the early evening, either to go back home or to stay out on Felix Faure Street, which would be getting ready for the grand ball. Before nightfall, the small crowd would empty out from the front of Drianké's cottage. Muñ would pick up the glasses, the plates left lying around here and there, clean, and put everything away. Drianké did not like for her to sweep at night, but Muñ would pick up everything that was lying around: paper napkins, cigarette butts, matchsticks. Drianké did not go to bed right away. She read through her accounts every night while humming the blues. From time to time, she would start singing, especially on moonlit nights. Drianké would sing nostalgic songs, songs that tugged at the deepest heartstrings. She sang like the great Afro-American songstresses. When she would sing for an aficionado, it would sometimes be like Billie Holiday! She had a magnificent voice, a voice whose Berber and Kabylian roots were perceptible. Upon hearing it, it made you wonder why she did not do concerts. One time, she told her clients, who had heard her talking about her nighttime blues, that she had sung with a band when she was young. But she had not been able to go any further because she'd had a problem in her life. She would always stop there. Drianké had a story to tell. Drianké had a story that was perhaps the reason why she had not been able to become a great blues singer. But Drianké's story, no one would tell it, not before one November morning. Drianké did not want to talk about that story. Drianké was this beautiful girl born in the great North where the hot sands would get swept up into swirling winds. She was very beautiful. She had met a man who hailed from afar. He called himself a muqaddam. She fell into his trap, as did her family, and agreed to marry him, believing that she was marrying a man of God. Those who knew her at the time said that this caused great disappointment and great suffering. This man who called himself a muqaddam scorned her, humiliated her, and ripped her to shreds in no time at all. The muqaddam had started to humiliate her, by cheating with her childhood friends at first, then with her sisters and cousins. He had no respect for anything and went so far as to try to sleep with Drianké's mother. This muqaddam, like most of those new gods, had two areas of interest: sex and money. Money to buy himself fine clothes like the others, cars like the others. Because what this muqaddam wanted was power. He wanted to dominate. He wanted to be noticed. He wanted to be powerful. This man was only ever curious about Drianké. He saw this beautiful woman and wanted to sleep with her, after getting wrapped up in her mouth when he saw her singing the blues. Once the curiosity was satisfied, he did not want anything more to do with her, because she was an artist and not a wealthy woman. He gave the excuse that a great astrologer had told him that she brought bad luck on the one hand, and on the other hand, his astrological sign did not match with Drianké's and that their wedding date had been poorly chosen. He had a pack of justifications, which he offered to anyone and everyone. And so Drianké was unable to stay in her hometown. She then left for the capital and found this small cottage on Felix Faure Street. With the blues still clenched between her teeth, she tried to bear her sufferings and pick herself back up. But the harm done was indelible. This was also why Drianké did not believe in that god used by those modern-day monsters anymore. She still wanted to believe in God, God as she imagined Him, but she did not pray anymore. She had given up on going to temples, to places of prayer, on giving her money to false gurus and false muqaddams. Drianké had chosen Felix Faure Street, for she felt like she was going to find some hope there. And there, she found hope and patience combined. She found God. The Only One. Drianké had gotten remarried to a man and had children with him. A man who understood her, a man who had rescued her in her great disillusionment, but the open wound was still there—hot, palpitating, bloody—and she walked with a limp. So whenever she would retire to her room, her blues sometimes traveling all the way into the street, you knew that Drianké had finished for the day and that she would not be hosting anymore. For Muñ, this was a godsend, for at night she could continue reading the typescript until Drianké would call her over to close the door. They slept in the only room of the cottage. But Drianké did not have her close the door right away. It was hot out and she did not like electric fans. She would let the fresh air pass through the screen door. When she had finished doing her bookkeeping, she would keep humming the blues while smoking her small iron pipe, seated on her metal bed, with a lantern lit to one side, among several other lanterns. Muñ would stay in the courtyard for a while to observe the shadowy mass clumsily entering the courtyard of the home. The shadowy mass would hoist himself up onto one of the big tables or sometimes he would use one of the big benches like a tripod to hoist himself up. Muñ could not make out his face, because it was dark in that part of the courtyard. The light from the lanterns glowing in front of Drianké's cottage did not reach that far. What had sparked Muñ's interest in the shadowy mass was the typescript that she had retrieved in that space, one morning that November. It was with the help of the shadowy mass that Muñ had found Drianké's cottage. Upon her arrival in the city, Muñ had already walked a great deal. She did not know exactly where to go, nor whom to see, nor whom to speak with. She followed her instincts and surrendered to them. In any case, she had made a choice. She came to this city, and she would not leave until she had found what she was looking for. Muñ was looking for someone. The night when she saw the shadowy mass clumsily heading toward Felix Faure Street, she followed him without thinking. Muñ made the instinctive choice. Upon arriving in front of an doorway, the shadowy mass rushed through. Muñ was unsettled and did not know what to do anymore. What if she kept following the shadowy mass? Where was he going? Regardless, she could not resist the tremendous urge to follow him. She too rushed into that house through a long passageway. It was already late, and people were coming and going in that passageway, always in complete harmony, which was quite simply the result of respect for others and the acceptance of others. Muñ slipped into the narrow passageway, which was like a tunnel. No one was paying any attention to her. The passageway suddenly opened onto a courtyard and from there, several other passageways branched off in every direction. The shadowy mass automatically took a different passageway and Muñ followed him. That was how she saw him settling in atop one of the wooden tables in a space in a courtyard. She retraced her steps and went out into the night. On Felix Faure Street, she blended in with the blissful crowd, ate some kebabs with some bread, drank a lemon-lime soda, and walked around all night long. That was what was remarkable about this street. Everyone had a right to it. It was not a street for the rich or for the poor, or for the prostitutes, or for the muezzins who would masturbate in front of doorways. Felix Faure Street was the street of respect for others. This was how she had gotten to Drianké's place so early the next morning, one November. She came back to where she had followed the shadowy mass. When she arrived that morning, Drianké was already outside, but the shadowy mass was no longer there. There were only big, empty tables and benches. Drianké was sitting in an old leather armchair, whispering the blues, with her eyes closed.

Why had Muñ followed the shadowy mass? Instinct! Had she not, one day, one year later, in the month of November, picked up a typescript in a yellow folder while sweeping the space reserved for the shadowy mass? Ever since that day, she had become increasingly interested in him. At night, when Driankè would retire, she would lose interest in the shadowy mass and shut herself away in the bathroom, located across the way. Every night, there was a lighted lantern in front of the bathroom. There was no electric lighting inside, so that lantern was used. That lantern was one of the lanterns that Driankè took such great care of. In the evening, she would put them out everywhere. In her room, in front of her cottage. Only the space where the shadowy mass was staying did not have a lantern. The light diffused by the lantern, which she would pick up while going into the bathroom, was enough for Muñ to dive back into the typescript in the yellow folder. The lantern's diffused light gave the typescript and its contents a different sensation, a different feeling. The lantern's diffused glow bathed the typescript in light. Reading the typescript went to Muñ's head like the burning wick of the lantern, the odor of which was growing increasingly acrid and choking Muñ. This lantern reminded her of her mother. Her mother was a light. And now she was like a lantern, dying down little by little.

6

THE FELIX FAURE Street Philosopher, who had been designated to go to get the Chief of Police, was taking a while to come back. Tonio, the Cape Verdean hairdresser, had just opened his salon, Chez Tonio, to the sounds of violin music, which was now spreading out onto the Felix Faure Street sidewalk like the red blood of the large, chopped-up leper. He had swept the interior and was now sweeping the sidewalk in front of his hair salon. That sidewalk, witness to a night like so many other nights, to so many other lives wrested away from life. Rolled-up papers, old cigarette filters and hand-rolled cigarette butts, empty bottles, skewers licked clean, paper tissues with traces of lipstick and eyeshadow, matchsticks, were all silent witnesses to these wrested-away lives. The people who had come to experience life on Felix Faure Street had moved on, leaving behind traces of their passage, on the path that led to God, which they were trying to find on Felix Faure Street. Tonio had seen the crowd amassed on the other side of the street but did not approach them. He was in shorts and a short-sleeved shirt. On his feet, he was wearing brown canvas shoes, with no socks. He did not cast a single glance at that crowd, which was increasing in size with all of the people who were passing by and stopping. The Cape Verdeans did not get too involved with the local community.

These were first-generation Cape Verdeans. They had not come to live in the working-class neighborhoods with the locals. When the Cape Verdeans came over, they went to live in the once exclusive Plateau neighborhood, that colonial neighborhood where the colonists lived, with the citizen families of the Communes.* However, the Cape Verdeans were not so well-off. The men were hairdressers for the most part and their wives were seamstresses. Some women might be employed by colonial families as housekeepers or cooks, but not by local families, even well-off ones. Their lighter skin tone gave them an air of superiority over the rather dark-complected members of the local community. Even poor people with lighter skin tones thought they were superior to wealthy, dark-complected Black people! Perhaps this was why some Black people were bleaching their skin with cosmetics and creams made with hydroquinone and mercury!

Tonio, after finishing sweeping, went out with a chair and sat down in front of his hair salon, Chez Tonio. He went out with a small violin and started playing a morna tune, on that Felix Faure Street sidewalk, the street of morna. The sound coming from his violin was piercing, and at that time of morning on Felix Faure Street, it was like a hymn of hope and patience combined. The sound coming from Tonio's violin was like a hymn for the chopped-up body of the large leper whose eyes were now staring at Tonio to tell him the end of the story. The sound coming from Tonio's violin was like an homage to Felix Faure Street. The people in the vicinity of the large leper's chopped-up body, with his tiny genitals stuffed deep into his mouth, were not paying attention to Tonio either. Tonio pressed his violin tightly against himself and played, with his head

* During French colonization, residents of the Four Communes, the first four colonial cities in Senegal—Dakar, Gorée, Rufisque, and Saint Louis—were eventually granted the rights of French citizens and representation in the French National Assembly.

lowered exaggeratedly. Tonio was playing nostalgic tunes from the sea on his violin and Tonio was not paying attention to the people crowding around on the other side of the street, right across from his hair salon, Chez Tonio. With his belly bulging, the large leper's eyes were still telling the end of the story, the end of his story, the end of a story. The large leper's eyes were watching Tonio play his violin, and the large leper's eyes did not understand why Tonio had not come closer to the spectacle. The large leper's eyes did not understand why Tonio was not listening to the story that they were telling. The violin sound was becoming increasingly piercing, and at one point, Tonio started to play a fast-paced tune on his violin and the shiny wood of his violin was reflecting a strange gleam in his downcast eyes. And the Philosopher still had not come back yet.

The Philosopher had nonetheless reached the police station, which was not far from Felix Faure Street. He was immediately seen by the Chief of Police. He knew the Felix Faure Street Philosopher a little from having met him a few times at Drianké's place. The Philosopher reported the facts to him and a discussion had ensued. For the Chief of Police, this type of heinous act was not a crime. In the end, the Chief of Police said this was not a police matter. The Chief of Police said that he had never heard such a story in all of his time in the police force. He had also never heard of any crimes that had been committed on Felix Faure Street, and yet, Felix Faure Street had a reputation for them.

The Philosopher also agreed with what the Chief of Police was saying. For the Philosopher, certain crimes were not crimes. The way in which the large leper's body had been chopped up, with his tiny genitals stuffed deep into his mouth, meant something and that was what they had to find out, that was what they had to analyze. There was a message in that staging. And the four illuminated lanterns, placed at the four cardinal points, were sending other signs. Lastly, the chopped-up body was of no importance. For both the

Chief of Police and the Philosopher, what interested them was the story behind it all. They talked once again about this story that they had to know and made up their minds to go to Felix Faure Street where the others were waiting.

The two fat policemen who had been there since morning were looking defeated. They were still standing, with their legs spread wide. They were hot (even though the sun had not cast a single ray on Felix Faure Street) and they would yawn from time to time. They were kicking themselves for having stayed out on this street so late into the night, only to find themselves in such a mess. All they wanted was for the Chief of Police to arrive, and he was taking his time.

"Did your Philosopher actually go to get our Chief?" said one of the two fat policemen, standing with his legs spread wide. No one answered him.

Drianké was still sitting on the sidewalk, and she was chanting the blues under her breath, a desert blues! This desert blues was like a dirge for the large chopped-up leper. This chanted blues was accompanied by the violin music of Tonio the hairdresser!

The leper's eyes were telling the end of the story when the Chief of Police arrived in the company of the Felix Faure Street Philosopher. The two fat policemen straightened up while making a salute. They did the best they could with their rumpled and dirty uniforms. The fatter of the two fat policemen wanted to begin by making a verbal report, but the Chief of Police stopped him. The Chief of Police, after greeting Drianké, sitting on the curb with her cane beside her, went over to the large leper's chopped-up body, with his tiny genitals stuffed deep into his mouth. Muezzin tried to get the attention of the Chief of Police, who was seemingly fascinated by the large leper's chopped-up body.

"It's extraordinary!

"Come and see," he said to the Philosopher.

"Look at his eyes. One could say that these eyes aren't dead.

"One could say that his eyes are moving.

"Come closer!"

The Philosopher came a little closer and bent down over the large leper's head, severed at the base of the neck.

"No, his eyes aren't dead. It's strange.

"You see!" the Philosopher said, getting up. "I told you that there was a story in this heinous act.

"It is not a crime.

"It is a story.

"A story to know."

Muezzin was still trying to get the attention of the Chief of Police:

"Mister, boss, Chief, I'm the one who discovered the body this morning while going to make the call to prayer. I will tell you . . ."

"No, that's okay," the Chief of Police responded.

"I only wanted to ask you if you noticed anything, a detail or something, when you discovered the chopped-up body, this morning."

Muezzin adjusted his accoutrements and started in:

"It was early in the morning. I couldn't see very well.

"It was still dark.

"At one point, I tripped over something, and it was this chopped-up body that you see here.

"I immediately started thinking about finding a solution.

"I told myself that this was serious.

"So I courageously decided to take matters into my own hands . . ."

"Okay, thanks. That's fine.

"You did the right thing," the Chief of Police interrupted.

Muezzin looked like he had been awarded a French Cross of Merit (if he even knew what that might mean). In any event, he was happy. He had been useful. He had served. He had been heard by the Chief of Police in front of so many people.

And he added:

"When I came back with Drianké and the Philosopher, I noticed the four lanterns placed at the four cardinal points, all around the chopped-up body. I said to myself . . ."

"That's enough, Muezzin. Thanks for the input," the Chief of Police restated.

The Chief of Police asked the two fat policemen to disperse the apprentice philosophers and the people in the vicinity. Which was going to be difficult. The crowd retreated, grumbling. He then asked them to do what was required to reassemble the big pieces of the chopped-up body. Across the street, Tonio, the unflappable Cape Verdean hairdresser, kept on playing his violin. The Chief of Police watched Tonio the hairdresser, with his violin wedged between his chin and his shoulder, as he kept on playing a piercing, overpowering tune. The Chief of Police crossed Felix Faure Street and went over to Tonio:

"Hello, Mister Tonio!"

"Hello, Mister Chief of Police!" Tonio replied, still keeping his violin wedged between his chin and his shoulder.

"Mister Tonio, with your hair salon directly across the street, didn't you notice anything, or hear anything, this morning?"

Tonio pulled his violin out from under his chin and a strange gleam flashed in his eyes.

"No, I didn't notice anything. The salon was still closed. I saw the crowd a short while ago when I opened the salon."

"And you didn't go over to see what was happening?"

"No."

"Why?"

"I'm not curious by nature and I don't want to get involved in matters that don't concern me."

The Chief of Police watched Tonio as he picked up his violin and began playing again. And once again, violin music permeated the sidewalk and the spectacle.

The sun had now risen. It was shining but it was not hot. Instead, the sun was smiling. The sun seemed happy that morning.

"You know, mister Chief of Police," said the Philosopher who had tagged along with the Chief of Police. "Tonio is a man who has been tested. A man who has suffered. He came here with his family. A wife and a daughter. His daughter grew up here on Felix Faure Street, a beautiful girl who the whole street loved. Tonio came to this street from the Cape Verde Islands. He relied on his job as a hairdresser and his wife's sewing work to ensure that their daughter would know something other than the difficult chapters of their life in their home country. Tonio wanted, with his daughter's generation, to break the chains of misery and ignorance that he and his wife had known. His daughter went to school and grew into a good person. His daughter was his pride. She was beautiful, worked hard, and wanted to become a pharmacist. She was in her last year at the university and was hoping, after her doctoral defense, to specialize in natural medicinal plants. And then, one day, a man came to disrupt, to devastate their existence. A large-statured, dark-skinned man with a big belly. He called himself a man of a god. He called himself a muqaddam. He said that he had come to participate in a conference on spiritual and religious paths. He needed to stay a few days before going back home where he worked selling medicines. He also said that he had an interest in plants that could potentially unlock the mysteries of the brain. He said loads of things that fascinated Tonio's daughter. And then, he seduced Tonio's daughter. The blinded girl had even wanted to change her religion in order to marry the large-statured, dark-skinned man. She put all of her father's possessions at the disposal of this man, who said that, although he had come without much money, he had made a bank transfer, which wouldn't take long. His wife, who thought that her daughter had found a good match, withdrew all of her savings earned from her sewing work.

She would prepare the best dishes from islands near and far. She would bustle around like an ant, the minute the large-statured man came into their home. The man eventually moved in with Tonio, who was growing increasingly worried, and his family. That man did not inspire confidence in him. But for his daughter, this was pure bliss, the opportunity of her lifetime. The man who called himself a muqaddam then started casting provocative glances toward the girl's mother, the minute her daughter would leave the house. He would talk to her about his god, about notions of good and evil. He would tell her that his god was speaking to him. And that, according to what his god had revealed to him, she had to be purified. The man asked her to talk to him about her life, especially about her sexual experiences with her husband. Tonio's wife was shocked at first but, reassured by the insistence of the man who called himself a man of God and a muqaddam at that, she went along with it. While she would talk, the muqaddam would grip his penis inside of his pants and stroke it lightly. Tonio's wife would keep talking and the muqaddam would keep masturbating. At one point, he said in a serious tone that she had to undergo a purification session. The muqaddam managed to convince Tonio's wife that she needed to be purified by him. Tonio's wife, swept up in the muqaddam's words, let herself get dragged into the bedroom, and it was like this every day, any time the daughter would go out and her husband would be in his hair salon.

"'My god loves you, you are lucky. You will see that you'll feel increasingly light, light. You will be free of all of your impurities.' And every day, the muqaddam would purify both mother and daughter. The muqaddam had asked Tonio's wife to find him something precious in order to make prayers of thanks to his god who loved her so much. She had given him the family jewelry, those from her own family and those from Tonio's dearly departed mother. For this family of immigrants, the only possessions that they owned and held dear were their pieces of jewelry. That was the bond. Tonio's wife had handed it all over to him. One fine morning, the muqaddam disappeared. Tonio's wife had a nervous breakdown and subsequently went insane. Since then, she has covered herself in veils, stopped going out, and stopped talking altogether. The daughter had a breakdown and died by suicide after her mother told her everything that the muqaddam had done to them both. She was found dead one day in her room, and in her hand, there was a piece of paper on which was written:

"'The scar . . .'

"No one ever knew what Tonio's daughter was trying to say.

"Ever since that day, Tonio has changed. He spends more and more of his time playing the violin, and a strange gleam flashes in his eyes, ever since that time."

Usually, on Felix Faure Street, life resonated louder than death. It was the street of hope and patience combined and not of mourning. *Patiencia y Esperanza*, Tonio's violin had the habit of saying. And the large chopped-up leper's eyes were continuing to tell the end of the story.

7

MUÑ, STILL SHUT away in the bathroom, continued to read the typescript in the yellow folder.

Every day, it was one humiliation after another. Sometimes, I would tell myself that you didn't even realize it. You were exhibiting increasingly strange behavior. In public, you wanted to shine, and you would prevent me from speaking, saying that I didn't let other people speak. In public, you wanted to be noticed. If you weren't, you would do anything to get attention, otherwise, you would get up and leave. One day, you hosted a young couple who had traveled from afar for some unknown reason. Since you didn't tell me about anything, I didn't know the reason for this young couple's journey. I was in such turmoil, which I was calling a divine trial, and this was a lesser evil. Just two days after the young woman arrived, you started taking an interest in her. An interest that far exceeded what one generally offers a married guest, who was with her husband. You liked talking to her, couldn't stand me taking part when you were talking to her. You would praise her for everything, and even for nothing. You would reproach me for not letting her cook. The young married woman immediately realized, a few days later, that you, the famous muqaddam, you were in love with her, well not in love since you were incapable of that, but attracted instead. So then, the game was afoot in the house. Glances were furtively exchanged behind the back of the young husband who was constantly sweating and seemed to be suffering from a strange disease. As soon as I would turn my back, even the slightest bit, you would move closer and closer to her. You would sit down across from her when the young husband wasn't there, spread your legs, and devour her with your eyes. You would masturbate in front of her. Your demeanor was not the demeanor of a man who called himself a man of God and who said that believers had to cultivate virtue. You would masturbate in front of someone else's wife, a young married woman who could be your daughter. I watched your little game, all while going back and forth to serve you tea, coffee, dessert. I was like the little maid who wasn't supposed to say anything, notice anything. As soon as I would try to say something or to ask a question, it was seen as harassment. Never in my entire life had I been in such a situation. I was suffering so much that I was unable to eat. You would laugh out loud, demanding that the food be ready on time because the young wife had an appointment. And I would come running like a little dog to serve a master who didn't want to see me anymore. The young married woman didn't pay me any mind because you yourself didn't pay me any mind. And, in the very house where we lived, you didn't hide that you were infatuated with her. The young married woman's behavior was typical of women whom other people's husbands fell in love with. They tended to ignore the legitimate wife and to despise her. And you wanted me to witness this. Either you didn't hide it from me, or you had trouble curbing your desires. You were only hiding it from the husband, if that. You wanted me to watch the spectacle. Sometimes you would find her in a corner, pinch her, and when she cried out, you would come and sit next to the husband as if nothing had happened, and then, when the wife rejoined you, she would greet you as if she hadn't just seen you. As for me, I pretended to be deaf, mute, she who understood nothing, saw nothing, and was to say nothing—otherwise, it would be harassment.

Was this the test?

What did God want to show me?

All of the house staff had noticed how badly I was being treated, but what could I do or say? I was in it up to my neck. In stories about your god, a god that I did not understand. In all of this, I wanted to remain calm and dignified. I had suggested a boat ride on the lagoon for the couple. I knew the lagoon from having been there several times. You yourself lived nearby, but you had never set foot there. You would play at being the lord, but a lord who knew nothing about the good things in life, the healthy things in nature. You, who said you were seeking God, you knew nothing about His Creation. You only knew about your god and his associates. Everything was planned without my knowledge, and on the day of departure, I was not even aware of it, and at the last minute, someone else, the infamous nephew, asked me to come with you. I didn't want to go anymore, but I wanted to remain dignified, and I accepted. During the trip, you royally ignored me, and when we got into the pirogue, you quickly asked the wife to sit next to you. As if you knew that I had decided to leave you for good that day. Even though the desire and the decision to leave you had been brewing for several months. I had even talked about it with your infamous nephew, who you also envied and badmouthed. I had already left you, long before leaving you forever.

My little girl saw how much I was suffering, how unhappy I was! When we were together again in our house, which I had half abandoned, I threw myself into her arms and cried all of the tears in my body, wounded by the contempt and the hatred that I felt oozing from my pores. This hate, this contempt was coming from you, you who had chased me, hounded me, sought me out, and this is what you had turned me into: a wreck. In my neighborhood, people were worried:

"What's wrong with her?"

"Why has she wasted away like this?"

"Why does she look so pale?"

"What is the deal with that man who took over her life?"

"Ah! What did you hear?"

"That guy is no good!"

"If he was such a good guy, how did she manage to find him in his own country, in the place where he was born, living all alone?"

"He who presented well, he who acted pious, he who would talk about a god on every street corner, to every piece of ass, why did no one else want him?"

"He collects women."

"One comes, one goes."

"Ah, what a shame, this woman who was so good, so respected, look at what she has become!"

"It's terrible!"

"Well, what do you expect, she shouldn't have agreed to be with that man. He has a bad reputation."

And all the while, my little girl continued to suffer in silence.

One day, you made me wash your underwear. A pair that

you had come in while watching women or listening to them talk. If only you could see when a woman was speaking in front of you, you'd be there, with your mouth half-open, ready to drool. You would fixate your attention on her mouth, as if it were a vulva, and you would masturbate. At the beginning of our marriage, I brought you over to my friends' place to introduce you. The husband was away, but the wife was home. As soon as you sat down, right in front of the wife, your jaw dropped, and when I tried to say something, you crushed my hand to make me understand that I had to shut up. I had already noticed this from the beginning, but I didn't understand. I also once hosted a friend who had come to spend the weekend with me to talk about a theater project. You came over to see me and as soon as you saw her, it was over, you didn't see me anymore. You were there drinking in her moving mouth, and if she stopped talking, you would get the conversation going again on topics that didn't even interest her. You wanted to talk to her about your god. You took books that you had given to me and lent them to her to read. I didn't understand, because I, who had things to talk about with this friend, couldn't get a word in edgewise. Whenever I tried, you would stop me dead in my tracks! Embarrassed, I went back and forth, pretending to go and get something when, actually, it was to escape an untenable situation. At one point, you took an interest in me again, perhaps when my friend realized that you had been manipulating her to make her talk. It was only afterward that you'd had sex with me. I sensed that you weren't there with me. You were making love to me while thinking about someone else. I sensed that you were holding yourself back to keep from saying her name. But then, after having masturbated during the day while watching women or listening to them talk, whenever you wanted to call for me, you would say those women's names. You didn't even realize it. My little girl, who would stay at your place from time to time, and I were paying close attention to all of this and putting up with it in silence. Every day, I would cook for guests, young women or young men passing through. Because you also liked to listen to young men talk about their experiences, sexual in particular. You would invite groups of young people over to talk about fornication. You would invite your nephews over to your place of work, close the door, and ask them to tell you about their sexual experiences. One of them told you that, at a very young age, he had been led astray by an older girl. The older girl asked him to make love with her. And so the little man, as soon as school let out, would run to meet up with the older girl and make love to her. At night, whenever you would tell me about your conversations with young people, you would get an erection. And some nights, you would ask me to recount similar incidents, and so I would make something up, and you would start getting an erection. This was the only way you could get an erection. Your penis was in your ears. At night, you couldn't go to bed without watching the latest news on television. You would lie in wait for the female announcers, so you could masturbate. You insisted that I be there too, in front of the television. These were women whose mouths opened up into a certain shape, which turned you on. You would force me to stay there to keep an eye out for the ones with mouths shaped like you wanted. As soon as one of them would make her appearance, you would sit there, all worked up, and say:

"Look at that one, the shape of her mouth shows that she's a slut. What do you think?

"Say that she's a slut.

"Say it loud.

"Say it louder!"

If I didn't say anything, you would look at me with such a gleam in your eyes that it made me shiver. I didn't dare to look at you and see the pervert that you were, but refused to accept.

How could you, a man hiding under the cover of God, be so perverted?

"Look at that one, she's turning me on today, what does she want from me?

"She wants me to fuck her, that's it, yeah, right?"

And you would masturbate. All of this, you did in front of me, and, as someone who wanted to love you, who wanted to admire you, who wanted to show others that, despite your reputation, I would do anything to save our marriage, I was exhausted. I could have put up with anything if it hadn't been for the contempt. Whenever you didn't find masturbation material, you would get mad at me! And you continued to despise me all the more. Sometimes, I wondered how I had managed to meet a man who seemed intelligent but who was ultimately so worthless. This was the lot of people who pretended to be intelligent. Sometimes you would tell me that your sign was that of a hunter. You'd had enough of me, and you wanted to venture out, on the hunt. My grace period was over. You needed a new conquest. You couldn't stand me anymore. I didn't have any money to give you. I didn't have vices galore. You needed money for power and vice to turn you on. Since you didn't know how to make love, I didn't want you anymore either. Making love with you was a painful ordeal. You would put me in uncomfortable positions and think about other women. Sometimes, you would let a name slip.

As your true nature increasingly revealed itself, I was not proud of you, and your company was becoming increasingly onerous for me. I sensed and knew that I was going to leave you. I was treading carefully with what people might say. I was about to be branded irresponsible and reckless in a social circle where I'd tried to fit in and was respected. The family of my in-laws, who I considered my family, had started creating problems for me, especially those who secretly had it in for me for one reason or another. I was starting to be disappointed from all sides.

One day, you were lying on the bed, and you said to me: "Hey, I picked up a letter from a father to his son. And in this letter, the father tells his son, 'This is what your wife should expect from you: you have to house her, dress her, and feed her. But you, you have to marry a wife who is younger, richer, and more beautiful than you.'" I naively replied that you, you were unlucky because I didn't fit this profile. It wasn't until later that I understood that you were speaking for yourself. Incidentally, I pointed this out to you, and you said, "My father isn't the one who wrote that letter."

You would come up with stupid stuff like that several times a day without even realizing it. But this wasn't just stupid stuff, you didn't want me anymore and used every means at your disposal to let me know it. And that was terrible. Another time, you sent your daughter of barely six years old, the one you'd had with the woman of easy virtue, over to tell me that I wasn't pretty, and you, you were off chuckling in a corner, and none of this escaped me. I felt sorry for your child in whom you should have instilled different values. And yet, at the beginning of our relationship, you swore to me that you were concerned about her genetic baggage, because she had been born to a woman of easy virtue.

I was ashamed for you, a man who I wanted to admire but who exhibited such low-life behaviors.

"You know, Arab men don't like widows.

"Ah! They don't marry widows.

"They say that widows bring bad luck.

"They say that widows are responsible for their husbands' deaths."

Whenever your own baseness and contradictions did cross your mind, you would immediately try to pull yourself together by saying that this was why the Book had been sent down, along with a prophet who had married a widow older than himself. And that prophet, throughout his entire life with that widow, never took another wife.

Then, one day while washing a pair of your underwear, which you had soiled with your sperm while masturbating at your job, in your home, in front of the television, in front of women talking (you would even masturbate while watching your sisters talk, your sisters-in-law, perhaps even your mother), I contracted a strange disease without knowing it. It started with little numb areas. I felt like certain parts of my arms weren't feeling heat anymore. This seemed strange to me, but at the same time, with all of the evils I had experienced with you, I thought that this must be yet another manifestation of the suffering that I was enduring. Shortly before that, I noticed that one of my collar bones was sticking out, as if trying to dislocate itself. I spoke to you about it, and you said that I must have had a fracture in my childhood. I was wasting away increasingly. I had become increasingly unrecognizable. My skin, whose softness was legendary to everyone who'd had the privilege of touching it, had become coarse, dull, drab. This skin, which even women would say was so beautiful, so smooth, this skin had become like an old parchment. I no longer dared to look at myself in the mirror. Because every time that I did, I recoiled, as my own face had become so foreign to me. It was unbelievable. That face staring back at me was not my face. People who knew me didn't recognize me anymore. At the post office, one day, an employee who knew me quite well, looked at me wide-eyed, astounded, when I found myself in front of her.

"This can't be, I didn't recognize you.

"It was when I read your name that I recognized you.

"What happened to you? Are you sick?"

And so I was increasingly sure that something was not right, but what? Was it the humiliations that you subjected me to that had transformed me to this extent? No, it wasn't just the humiliations. There were the black fluids that you made me drink while telling me that they were for my protection.

"But protection is in the notion of God, the idea of God, in God, in oneself, in one's own behaviors and attitudes," I said.

"Yes, but that isn't enough!" you replied.

You were someone who would talk about God everywhere, who claimed to leave everything in His hands, but who spent his time believing in other gods. I was devastated. I was all the more so when you started to develop your theory of doubles.

"You know, we were created in doubles. With one twin who is good and another who is evil. It is possible, with the methods that I am researching with friends, to destroy the evil twin."

"How?" I asked.

You laughed, in that self-satisfied laugh. I had been

talking to you about a book that I had read on metempsychosis, thinking that this is what you wanted to talk about, which made you laugh all the more. You came up to me and showed me this middle-aged man whom you had introduced me to the first time that I came over. He was old before his time. He was shriveled, dirty. He was sleeping in a room where I had never set foot before. This room was located in the back of your property, behind your house. You told me that you had met him in front of your medicine shop, where he would often stay, and that you'd brought him back to your place. I thought that you had done a good deed and that this confirmed that you were a man of God. I asked you for news about his family, but you told me that you didn't know where his family was. The man, despite his appearance of advanced decrepitude, seemed to have been a good person in another life. I was horrified when you informed me that it was possible to take someone and to use them to destroy one's own evil twin. He was the one you had brought into your home and were using, so that everything evil inside of you would go over to him. He was one of your sorcerer friends who had recommended using a double, telling you that once you were rid of the evil things that were standing in your way, you would be a powerful and wealthy man. That man was eating rotten food, leftovers that even pigs wouldn't want. He didn't clean himself. He could sit for an entire day, in his filth and in his stench, surrounded by containers of rotten leftover food, wriggling with maggots. He was like garbage. Human garbage. You were keeping him in your home so that he would be your evil twin. You said that if anyone tried to harm you, it would fall upon him. All of the bad vibrations coming into your home would be blocked by

> him. That man was serving as your screen against the evil spirits which were preventing you from being wealthy and powerful like your brothers and sisters. I found this revolting. You told me that there were people created to serve this purpose. That way, you could do whatever you wanted. And you said that the wrath of your god would not descend upon you but would descend upon him. You said that this man could die in your place.

"Muñ! Muñ! Muñ!

"Muñ! Muñ!"

Muñ heard Drianké calling her, but she took the time to put away the typescript, staggering in disgust. That man was heinous, horrible, diabolical. She was making progress in her reading, but wondering if she could keep it up. She put the typescript back on top of the water tank, which she flushed, and then went out.

"Muñ, what are you doing in the bathroom again?

"I think that your mother isn't the one who is sick, it's you!

"You know, it's hard to be with someone who doesn't talk, who doesn't come clean. Ultimately, you're hiding too many things.

"I'm willing to help you, but a person can only help someone who wants to be helped. You're lucky that you do your job well and that you don't worry me. These days, it's hard to meet someone who doesn't worry anyone, with the trend being to constantly worry people, with or without cause.

"Otherwise, I wouldn't have kept you on. You are too weird!

"So, tomorrow morning, on your way to the market, you'll stop by my brother Amoul's place. You'll tell him to come and see me, I need him."

Drianké was in her room, but she was not sleeping. Muñ's situation was weighing on her mind increasingly.

What was wrong with that girl? Ultimately, who was she?

And yet, these were not the type of questions that one asked on Felix Faure Street and even less so at Drianké's place, as she had seen it all. But there was something strange about that girl.

And what was she doing in the bathroom?

Muñ closed the door and laid down on the bed across from Drianké's metal bed. She was not sleeping. In her mind, the story was haunting her.

It cannot be, she thought. How could someone suffer so much and hang on, in the name of God alone?

What was this test? Was it a self-imposed discipline or was it a needless suffering that most people accepted? And so, they would endure this suffering while saying that God was the one who made us laugh and made us cry. Could life be reduced to this simple manipulation? Did mankind have no responsibility then? Everything came from God? The wars in His name, the children dying in His name, the tortures, the atrocities; the women and children crossing jungles and forests, with bloody feet, falling dead from hunger, thirst—that was all God? The women who had seen their husbands killed before their eyes, their children's throats slit before their eyes, that too was God's will? For heaven's sake! Why so much suffering in His name?

Why had this woman been humiliated, ridiculed, scorned, in the name of God alone? While the man who was inflicting this suffering upon her was laughing with others, living well, spending his time chasing little girls in the neighborhood, and masturbating with other people's wives? He, he could live like that in God's name, and this woman had to suffer in God's name? Why?

Was this how women had to accept the notion of God?

The suffering was hers alone, because it was Eve's fault?

And what about Adam, why had he eaten the apple?

Because of Satan?

Who had created Satan?

Muñ tried to fall asleep while telling herself that if this was God, she would rather surrender herself to Him and not make an effort anymore. This would make it easier for her to pursue her objective. But sleep did not want anything to do with Muñ. Muñ could not sleep anymore. What weighed on her mind was finding out the rest of the story, but not the end of the story, which would become her story, and her story did not interest her. What she wanted was to get this hatred, which was burning her heart, out of her blood. What she wanted was to achieve her objective and be done with it.

The next morning, Drianké and Muñ both got up like usual. Drianké sat down in her old leather armchair after taking her cold shower, with a blues song on her lips. Meanwhile, Muñ tidied the bedroom. The lantern in the bedroom kept giving off a weak light and the acrid odor of the oil was making Muñ's throat itch. That smell reminded her of her mother's lantern, far away! Her mother would often clear her throat, and Muñ would tell her to use electric lighting or else a candle. It was no use. She kept her lantern lit night and day, every day, like Drianké.

When Muñ left for the market, after the breakfast they had eaten together in silence, Drianké got her curvy, small-statured self up. Limping, leaning on her cane, she headed over to the bathroom where Muñ had been spending too much time, in her opinion. She opened the door and looked in every corner. The bathroom was clean, which did not surprise her. Muñ was a clean girl. She cleaned everything in her wake. She was practically the only one who used this bathroom regularly. Drianké stayed there for a while, looking all around. She looked up at the water tank, but did not see anything that might concern her. Everything was normal. Drianké was really worried about Muñ.

"What was that girl doing in the bathroom?"

Drianké exited the bathroom, closing the door gently. She limped over to the large tables at the back of the courtyard, those large tables onto which the shadowy mass would creep each night and find a place to sit. She walked among the large tables, picking up a large bench, putting it down somewhere else. Everything was in order. She sat down at a large table, the shadowy mass's favorite, and started to whistle the blues while a strange gleam flashed in her eyes. She stayed there for a long time, pensive, faraway, staring straight ahead—but her gaze had left Felix Faure Street. After a while, she got up, looked over at Muñ's bathroom, and limped back over to the front of her cottage. Drianké settled back in on her old leather armchair and kept on whistling the blues. She was impatiently awaiting Muñ's return from the market. Today, she was not interested in the condiments that she was supposed to bring back. Drianké wanted to know if her brother Amoul had gotten her message. She definitely wanted to see her brother.

Despite her curves, despite her small stature, Drianké was a very beautiful woman. She had to have been the most beautiful girl of her time. This was evident in her aloof air, that of a woman who had seen it all, in her elegant appearance, elegant gestures, demeanor, and in the tone of her voice. Sometimes, a faraway smile would light up her face, and her eyes would crinkle in secret bliss. Sometimes, a sad pout would darken her face, and a strange gleam would flash in her eyes, and she would start to whistle the blues. The courtyard of Drianké's cottage was deserted at that time. It was only in the afternoon that the regulars, clients, acquaintances, and a few family members would come to liven it up. From time to time, a child would run into Drianké's house to deliver a message, and Drianké would always give them something. Some leftover food, a piece of bread, a lemon-lime soda, a coin. Drianké especially loved children. She had a few of her own, but did not live with them anymore. They were grown, and most of them were married, had their own children, and lived somewhere else. Their father had also gone to live somewhere else, when Drianké let him know that, these days, she wanted to be alone. Drianké did not get out often. For one thing, she had her own pace of life, and she hardly ever left her home, except for sometimes in the evening or the very early morning. She would go out for a little walk on the street. The morning was also her favorite time on Felix Faure Street. Drianké could find herself on Felix Faure Street when no one else was out yet, aside from the last few night owls, clinging to illusion. She did not do it as much as she used to, but she still managed from time to time. Apart from these infrequent morning outings, she would sometimes walk in the evening, leaning on her cane, limping up to Maginot Avenue, like the Felix Faure Street nurse had recommended. The Felix Faure Street Philosopher had once said, not so long ago, that he had seen Drianké early one morning, at a furtive hour, walking at a vigorous pace, without her cane. And no one had wanted to believe the Philosopher, not even the apprentice philosophers.

"I am telling you that Drianké has a double life!" the Felix Faure Street Philosopher insisted.

"But everyone has a double life!" an apprentice philosopher said.

"Well, Felix Faure Street will say otherwise one day!" the Felix Faure Street Philosopher concluded.

Muñ still had not come back from the market and Drianké was getting impatient, for the first time. She got up and headed toward the entryway to the house, passing through multiple labyrinths, passageways, courts, and courtyards, ever careful as to where she placed her feet. There were endless comings and goings in these passageways. Dozens of families could be living in this place. Drianké had been living on this street for many years, and without going out very much, she knew all of its nooks and crannies. She knew the entire history of this street. She had spent the longest time in her adult life there. This was the street where she had come seeking refuge after the muqaddam had almost destroyed her. This was the street where she had renounced religions since there were not any temples for God. This was the street where she had tried to heal from all of the humiliations, all of the scorn, all of the exploitation that the muqaddam had made her suffer. For Drianké, Felix Faure Street represented the Savior. Drianké had left her hometown to pursue a singing career in the capital, was all that she said when she first arrived. In her hometown, she had started singing with bands. She had a blues voice. Through her Berber, Black Berber, and Kabylian roots, she had inherited a vocal intonation that came from the deserts of the Atlas Mountains. She had been nicknamed Billie Holliday, Bessie Smith, Sarah Vaughan, Mahalia Jackson, Nina Simone, Ella Fitzgerald—women with whom she was unfamiliar. She had never been to school, and had only her voice. She would sing about her hometown with the languor of that city, with a voice beyond blues. A kind of lament, a loving, weeping lamentation. At that time and even today, women singing with bands in nightclubs were frowned upon. The notion of bad, she had gotten over that a long time ago. The experience with the muqaddam had opened her eyes to the ways in which people manipulated that notion for other purposes, under the cover of God. At that time, she could not resist meeting up with bands that she could sing with until dawn, every night in her hometown, most often for free. She sang and she was happy. She did not see any prospects on the horizon, and yet, people were talking about her, even outside of her hometown. One day, she set off for the capital to try her luck, as she had said when she left her hometown and came to Felix Faure Street. She had heard about Felix Faure Street for its nightclubs, its dance bars, where amateur and professional musicians could always find a band or an improvised group to showcase their talents with, more for enjoyment than the search for prospects. At that time, musicians enjoyed playing together. That was how Drianké, who was in her prime, beautiful, different, with a unique voice, quickly earned a name in the city. She started to find success in the world of artists, filmmakers, actors, singers, et cetera. She got roles in a few films and was eventually hired in the National Ballet. She traveled a lot. But upon her return, she would always look for a band to sing the blues with. What she delighted in and held dear was singing the blues. In the National Ballet, she would sing for national heritage, renouncing her roots to foster national unity, but the blues was always in her heart. Years went by and Drianké was still singing the blues with the same piercing languor that grabbed you by the gut and sent you traveling through inner deserts. Throughout these multiple courts, courtyards, and passageways, she would think about all the time that she had spent in her hometown, up in the North, where life was different. The pleasure, the joy of being together was there, and many talents had blown up through that joy of making music, theater, film, dance, together. There were no managers. All it took was to find two people who wanted to make music, get together, and make music. What a beautiful time! And she was so young and so beautiful! And she was still singing, up until the day when the infamous muqaddam came along and shattered her dreams.

Drianké headed toward the entryway to the house as if going over to greet Muñ. She walked while humming the blues, all along those long passageways branching off in every direction before reaching the street. She noticed that the passageways were never very clean. It was true that these passageways were shared with other cottages, other courts, other courtyards, in this labyrinth of lives that made up the rear lots of Felix Faure Street. The co-proprietors of the passageways had to clean them, and usually they were clean, except for a few inevitable puddles. Drianké wondered what could have happened for the passageways to be so exceptionally dirty today. She limped over to the entryway, and as soon as she got there, she was assailed by noises from this street that she knew so well. But for some time, she had not been going out much anymore. It had been since her encounter with the shadowy mass. People greeted her, calling out to her, and one of them said:

"Drianké, well now, showing your pretty face today?

"You know, we miss you when you don't get out.

"How are you?

"And your business?

"On that note, Drianké, did you hear that there will soon be elections to elect a Felix Faure Street manager?

"In my opinion, I think that you should be the manager, you know Felix Faure Street better than anyone else."

Drianké stopped humming her blues and listened to everything that the other person was saying. She adopted a serious tone and replied:

"The street should not have manager.

"We are all the managers of Felix Faure Street.

"Each of us is a manager of this street.

"Each of us brings something, our talents, our lives, ourselves. Don't let yourself get swept up in these decisions, which all too often lead to tribalism and other things that put Felix Faure Street in jeopardy.

"On Felix Faure Street, we don't need elections to tell us whether or not this or that person is good for the street.

"We are all good for the street.

"So down with elections for our street!"

Drianké was greeting people left and right. Children were coming out from every which way to latch on to her clothing and her cane. She patted their heads and talked to them. Every time she went out on Felix Faure Street, it was always the same thing.

Drianké was Felix Faure Street. This street where people of all different cultures and creeds rubbed shoulders, but with one God! Everyone respected each other and there had never been any real problems. There was a bar almost every hundred meters and a secret bar every fifty. But all of this was happening in perfect harmony. On Felix Faure Street, despite all of its apparent disorder, there was nothing to suggest that this was a street where life was flowing in torrents of alcohol and girls of easy virtue, roaring with laughter. It was a very lively street and a very busy street, where traffic was always dense. Felix Faure Street was an indispensable street in this city. It was an essential street for this city. It was the soul of this city. Drianké was standing there, with her cane in hand, and she suddenly started to sing one of her famous pieces about her hometown. And then, as if by magic, everything in the street stopped and people listened carefully so as not to miss a single note. She sang a little louder as the silence gradually set in, without raising her voice, and in a matter of minutes, she transported Felix Faure Street into the desert. While singing, she had let go of the children and was intending to go back home, when she saw some veiled figures who seemed to have stopped to listen to her. All of Felix Faure Street was hanging on Drianké's voice, and no one seemed to have noticed the veiled figures. The veiled figures suddenly disappeared from her view. She turned her head every which way, but the veiled figures had vanished. She leaned on her cane, limping, and retraced her steps toward her cottage, whistling the blues. It would always take some time for the street to return to its usual frenzy. In Drianké's eyes, outlined with black eyeliner, waves of nostalgia were welling up. The veiled figures that she had just glimpsed on both sides of the street intrigued her. Those veiled figures were four in number, but seemed to be splitting in two, to be multiplying. She had never seen such figures before, neither on Felix Faure Street, nor anywhere else. She tried to figure out if they were men or women, and she instinctively thought that they were women. Those veiled figures took her back a few years. She had found herself in the same get-up, back when the muqaddam had almost destroyed her. She felt a violent pang in her heart, which was racing. She took a deep breath, and began whistling the blues. She had forgotten about Muñ who was coming up behind her. It was only when she reached the front of her cottage, when she wanted to sit down in her old leather armchair, that she saw Muñ.

"Ah! Muñ! You're here?

"Why did you take so long?

"Did you see Amoul?

"What did he tell you?"

Muñ, without looking at Drianké, replied:

"He said that he's going to come by in the afternoon."

Muñ had sweat beading up on her forehead. She was breathing quite heavily, but Drianké did not pay it any mind.

"That's good. I really need him.

"Did you find what you were looking for?"

"Yes, my mother!" replied Muñ who was unpacking all of her purchases into a blue plastic basin. She realized that she just had called Drianké "my mother," momentarily hesitated to say something, ultimately gave up on it, and continued unpacking the purchases. Drianké was also surprised to hear her call her "my mother." This was the first time she had called her that. Drianké regarded it as a slip of the tongue. She watched her unpacking the purchases, asking herself all sorts of questions:

"Who is this girl?

"What does she want?

"What is she looking for?

"She is so strange and so normal at the same time!

"What does she do in the bathroom?

"What illness does her mother have?"

Muñ felt Drianké's eyes on her, but she pretended not to notice and went about her work. She sorted all of the condiments and set each of them aside in the basin, all to make Drianké's work easier. She went to get water, organized the kitchen utensils. She got the stove ready, still under Drianké's watchful eyes. The courtyard of Drianké's cottage was empty at this time. From time to time, a child would come running in and joyfully run back out again, for Drianké had most likely given them a coin. Muñ was bustling around the courtyard like usual. What Drianké liked about her was her diligence and her work ethic. With Muñ, she did not need to repeat the same things over and over again. Muñ was like a machine. She retained everything and even sensed what Drianké wished for or wanted. She was very effective and that was why Drianké did not know how to approach her, how to talk to her about her concerns. Muñ seemed like a normal girl though. A normal girl who did not have any friends, who did not go out. A normal girl who spent a lot of time in the bathroom. Drianké did the cooking as usual, with Muñ's help. When everything was ready, Muñ swept, cleaned, and put everything away. Drianké retired to her room, like usual, to rest and smoke her pipe, after taking a cold shower, while humming the blues. Muñ then immediately ran over to the bathroom and locked herself inside. She grabbed the typescript from the top of the water tank and got back her reading.

> I didn't understand what was happening to me. The decline was so noticeable that I didn't know what to do or say. I was praying morning, noon, and night, asking God to find the best remedies for me. I would speak to Him, telling Him that He knew what I needed, and that I myself didn't know what I needed. I would therefore leave it up to Him, for Him to do what was best for me. I was praying to God, begging Him, getting down on my knees night and day. But day by

day, things were getting worse. The numbness I felt was spreading to more parts of my body. I went in for tests, but according to the results, everything seemed normal. I was just suffering from a little anemia. It was true that I had lost my appetite a long time before that. I couldn't eat anymore. After all of the humiliations that I had suffered with you, I didn't have the heart to eat anymore. You ridiculed me in front of everyone and treated me like garbage. You were never happy and were even less satisfied with everything that I did for you. No matter what I did, you didn't see me anymore, you didn't want me anymore. I pointed this out to you and was always met with hatred spewing from your eyes. You started telling me that you had been attracted to me out of humanism. You started telling me that that there was a plot hatched by your uncle using me to kill you. Your uncle was using one of his connections, a man that I knew, to destroy you through me. This man was supposed to make me take baths in sea water, and upon contact with my body, four big mythical killers would go over to your house to kill you. You would say terrible things. I hung on, telling myself that God only tested the ones that He loved. And I suffered atrociously. In the meantime, my little girl couldn't take it anymore. My little girl looked at me and didn't recognize me anymore. She rummaged through my things to find photos of what I looked like before. She would take these photos with her, and spend hours looking at them. And me, on my end, I couldn't stand my little girl anymore, I was so ashamed of myself, of what I had become. I would yell at her and take all my despair out on her. While talking to her, I would cry, break down. This was when we would run into each other at home, during the daytime. And I would cry like a baby. I would cry my heart out. My eyes would bleed. And you, the muqaddam, you didn't care about any of this. You had started seeing the woman of easy virtue again. You were meeting up with her at your workplace. You would stay there together, in your medicine shop, until late into the night. You would masturbate with her. When you would come home after I had been waiting up for you all night, you'd be almost furious to find me there! I sensed everything, but what could I say? If I spoke up, you would say that I was nagging you and that you didn't like it when people nagged you. Then, you started calling the woman of easy virtue in front of me. You would send her out shopping, make dates with her in front of me. You told me that you were seeing her again because she was having trouble with her children. The woman of easy virtue started coming over to your place as soon as I would leave. You were both communicating by cell phone. When I managed to catch snippets of conversation, you would tell her that you couldn't stand having me at your place anymore, but that you were using me as a screen. There were intermediaries in the house. They would come and go to deliver messages and run errands. And I was there, I knew everything, felt everything, but didn't dare to say a single word. I didn't dare to complain and didn't want to complain. I blamed myself to death. I blamed myself for getting involved in this kind of affair. I blamed myself for trusting you. I blamed myself for believing that you were a man of God. I blamed myself for being so naive. You kept calling the woman of easy virtue with increasing frequency and sending her messages in front of me. She would also call you and you would respond in front of me, without embarrassment. And I was there, powerless, ridiculed. I told myself that this was all God's will. That is what you yourself told me:

"Leave everything in God's hands." But you were thinking about your god.

Increasingly, you no were longer hiding your hate from me, your scorn, but at the same time, you wanted me to stay, to serve as your screen from society, from others. You increasingly ignored me, and did not speak to me anymore. You didn't even want to pray with me anymore. In bed, you would turn your back to me, and I would cry in silence. We had very little sex. The rare times when you did make love to me, you were thinking about someone else. I felt it. And every time I thought that you would let the name of the woman you were fantasizing about while making love to me slip, you would let it slip. I didn't come, but I had to fake it to please you; to make you come. You wanted me to talk, to say that you were good at making love to me, that it was great. When it really sucked. You don't even know how to make love. You only come through masturbation. Whenever a woman was speaking in your presence, that was all it took, you would start to get hard and jack off, even in public. How many times had you not gotten off to other people's wives? You would start thinking about the women you had been with, and sometimes in front of me, you would make dates with them or tell me that you wanted to call them. When you started seeing the woman of easy virtue again—after swearing that things were over between you two—I understood that, this time, it was over between us! That woman was a pervert, and that was what you wanted, but your family didn't want anything to do with it. That woman had stolen money from members of your religious path, for which you claimed to be the representative and the muqaddam, but that was the woman you wanted. That woman cheated on you, lied, stole, but that was what you wanted. She was a woman of easy virtue, you yourself would tell me, but that was what you wanted, because it turned you on to imagine her making love with other men. It turned you on to see her coming back into your bed, with other men's scents, with lies. That was what turned you on. On your own, you couldn't get hard. She was a woman with no morals, but that was what you wanted. And other people did not realize it. For you were playing at being a respectable man in society. You were on your religious path, you were its muqaddam. People would consult you about their problems with your god. You were always in places of prayer. You always had your god on your lips and prayer beads in hand. When you would read the Holy Scriptures, people would get swept up in your voice. But deep down, you were vice incarnate, and vice was your only love. I understood this too late. I thought that you were a man of God, while you were dragging God down. When I realized this, it was too late! You had just given me the strange disease.

I ran away from your place one night, one Friday night. The day before, you had been plotting something against me, which did not escape my attention. You—who weren't speaking to me anymore, or who, as soon as I said a single word, would say that I was nagging you—you served me some tea and I sensed that you had put something in the tea. You wouldn't dare to poison me, you said. But if it was something to make me leave, you didn't have to worry about that. I wanted to leave you from the start. But like the devil, you had lured me into your nets. And I was unable to resist, for the devil was tempting, captivating too. What was I to do then, when I found out that I had contracted the strange disease? I took refuge in my home with my little girl who was so happy that I had left you. She even danced in front of the housekeepers. What was I going to do? I knew that at the stage I was at, no one would realize. There were no marks, nothing to indicate that I had anything. Just a few days after leaving you, everyone who saw me again found that I had changed for the better. I was becoming increasingly recognizable, I was becoming myself again. But people did not realize the inner wound that I had suffered. People did not know that you had given me the strange disease.

A few weeks later, I was feeling better, but I wasn't completely back to my old self. There was something wrong, perhaps it was this strange disease that you had given me. I would look at myself in the mirror every day, keeping an eye out for any mark on my skin, but I still didn't see anything. The tests that I'd had done left no room for doubt anymore. The results obtained confirmed the suspicion. But in the tests, they had also discovered that I had traces of poison in my blood. You had also tried to poison me with all of the strange-tasting liquids that you made me drink, saying that one of your father's friends had seen in a dream that there was a coalition of sorcerers working against you. You said that I had to protect myself too. I had to undergo a treatment in a specialized center to detoxify myself. After that, I had to start another course of treatment for the disease that you had given to me. Since the disease was not yet advanced, I could do the treatment at home, but I had to follow it to the letter. My little girl caught me taking some pills and asked me what was the matter. I replied that it was nothing serious and that I was just taking some vitamins.

My little girl went off to pursue her studies abroad. We didn't see each other often. I didn't want her to come home for holidays, and as an excuse, I would always tell her that she had to travel and see the world. We would talk on the phone nearly every day, and every time she asked how I was doing, I would tell her that I was doing fine. She would ask me to send her my most recent photos. I promised her that I would do it, but as soon as she hung up, I would burst into tears. A few months later, some spots started to appear on my skin. I was covering myself in veils more and more. I was going out less and less. As an excuse, I would say that my job required reflection, silence. I could not go out anymore.

At this stage of her reading, Muñ put down the typescript and said to herself that she now wanted to know this story. This story was about to become her story.

And this was the end of the story that the eyes of the large chopped-up leper were about to tell on a Felix Faure Street sidewalk, the very next morning.

Muñ picked up the typescript again. She felt shaky, but she had to keep reading.

And one day, my little girl decided to come home on vacation, because she missed me. She hadn't seen me in two years, and for her, it had become unbearable. When she came in and saw me, she couldn't help but scream! She had just seen the horror. Her mother had become unrecognizable. She ran out of the house.

What had happened to her mother?

How did she contract this disease?

Who had given it to her? She shouted, spinning all around. Then, she started to remember her mother's history with that large-statured, big-bellied man, who had made her suffer so much and who had made she herself suffer too. But if he was the one who had given her the strange disease, he had to have it too. What had become of him? How would she be able to recognize him if the disease had progressed? Where did he live?

A thousand questions were running through my daughter's mind.

She wanted to ask me some questions, but I didn't want to talk about that painful part of my life anymore. I told my daughter to drop it. The damage was already done. My little girl wanted to know where to find you, you, the large-statured, big-bellied man, with the scar! You, the muqaddam! This was how my daughter decided to go out and find you.

"Muñ, Muñ, where are you?"

Muñ put the typescript back in its place and ran out of the bathroom. Drianké was sitting in her old leather armchair. She watched as she came before her and, looking her in the eyes, said:

"Muñ, can you explain to me what you're doing in the bathroom?"

Before Muñ could find something to say, Drianké's brother Amoul arrived, and she exclaimed:

"Amoul, I've been impatiently waiting for you!"

Amoul, sweating, started to explain away his delay without formally greeting Drianké, who hadn't done so either.

"I've been on your street though, but you know how it is. There's always something happening on Felix Faure Street. People have told me that, lately, they've been seeing four veiled figures on both sides of the street, and that they seem to be multiplying.

"It seems like people have been seeing them here for the past two days. No one has seen their faces. These must be people from sects, which are popping up everywhere. Now that women are getting involved in them, we are in for it! Well, we don't know if they are women, but apparently, they look like women."

A strange gleam flashed in Drianké's eyes.

"Yes, people are talking about it. But you know, these days, there's a little bit of everything. Personally, I don't like sects, associations, groups, groupings, categories. People are afraid of themselves. So they can only function within the group and in line with the group. And the individual is dead. The individual doesn't exist anymore. Instead, it's the clan, the group, the single mindset—let's go toward God together.

"We will never go to God's place together. Each one of us has a pathway to God. I don't know much, but at least I do know that it's every man for himself. Being in a group is all about repetition, normalization. Personally, I don't like all of these groupings. Life, we have to face it alone. Life is a battle, a battle with oneself to become One with God.

"Come here, sit down."

Drianké pointed a bench out to her brother.

Amoul was not Drianké's real brother. He was her first cousin, but she preferred to call him her brother.

"You know, I called you because of Muñ. Do sit down.

"She is on my mind so much that I don't know where my head is at anymore."

The bench that Drianké's brother Amoul was sitting on was not level, and Drianké was trying to fix it.

"There. Sit down.

"How are you?"

"Everything is fine," Amoul responded before following up: "When Muñ came and told me that you wanted to see me today, I was a little worried! What's up?"

"Ah! I don't even know where to begin!" Drianké said, resting her chin on her left hand.

"Actually, I am worried, but not about anything in particular.

"It's about Muñ. Muñ, come here."

Muñ came over.

"Sit down," Drianké told her.

Muñ took another bench, one that the afternoon regulars would use, and sat down.

"Well then! You know Muñ, she has been working here for almost a year. She's a good girl. I don't have any problems with her for her work. She told me that her mother has been suffering from a serious illness. I suggested that she bring her here, or give me her address so that you could go and get her, but it's been no use. She is stubborn in her silence, saying: yes, soon, no, it's not serious, et cetera. And she shuts herself away in the bathroom too much.

"What is she doing in the bathroom?

"I went to look in the bathroom, and I didn't find anything. But she stays in there for too long and I can say that she spends nearly all of her free time in the bathroom. This girl is a mystery to me. That is why I called you."

Muñ shuddered when Drianké said that she had gone into the bathroom to see what she might be doing in there. The typescript was tucked away on top of the water tank. Perhaps it was because of her small stature that Drianké had been unable to see an edge of the yellow folder that contained it.

"Muñ, well, what do you think about everything that Drianké has just said?" Amoul said, looking at Muñ, whose eyes were lowered.

"Nothing!" Muñ replied.

"By the way, where are you from?" Amoul abruptly asked.

"From Hogbo."

It seemed as if Muñ had let this response slip.

"Hogbo, that rings a bell!" said Drianké's brother, thinking.

"Wait, wait, Hogbo, Hogbo!

"Ah, yes, it's coming back to me.

"Isn't that in the valley region?"

Muñ gave herself away but took on her most natural expression.

"Yes."

"I've never been there.

"It's far from here, from what I hear.

"But how did you manage to get here?"

"I took the bus."

Muñ was relieved. Drianké's brother Amoul had never been to Hogbo.

"Wait, someone told me about that area once," Amoul corrected. "It will come back to me."

Amoul sat there, thinking, trying to rack his brain.

Drianké had a glimmer of hope on her face. "So we will be able to go and get Muñ's mother to get her treated!" Drianké thought.

"But it was here that I heard about Hogbo," said Drianké's brother Amoul.

Muñ shuddered.

Drianké shuddered.

This did not escape Amoul.

"What's wrong with you two, are you cold?"

Drianké and Muñ did not respond.

Ever since Muñ and Drianké had heard "Hogbo" connected to someone here, they stopped looking at each other, stopped speaking to each other. Drianké and Muñ were hanging on Amoul's every word. Amoul picked back up after a moment:

"This is where I heard about it."

Drianké and Muñ stifled a strange cry in unison.

"One night, I stopped by here to see you, and while heading out, I caught sight of the shadowy mass sitting over there in his space. I went over to him. Incidentally, I'm not sure why. I felt drawn to him that day. He was talking with your friend, the great young man, the one who makes movies, Djib, I believe. The shadowy mass said that he wanted to tell a story to that great young man, a story that had been troubling him for several years, but that he didn't know where to begin. The shadowy mass said that he had lived in Hogbo or, even, that he was from Hogbo."

Muñ tried to suppress her shivers.

Drianké tried to suppress her shivers.

They seemed to be in sync.

"The shadowy mass, Muñ, do you know him?"

Drianké's brother Amoul did not give Muñ the time to answer because he kept talking.

"You know, with Drianké, you have to be ready for anything. She is so generous, she feels so sorry for people! She's the one who asked the shadowy mass to come here to sleep at night and to leave early in the morning. At first, I was not okay with it."

Drianké did not say anything. She was looking off into the distance and pursing her lips tighter and tighter. And Amoul kept on:

"People are even starting to say that this shadowy mass looks like a leper who, by night, lures in young people, whom he asks to recount their sexual experiences. He is a scumbag, a pervert, and, apparently, this leper says that he is seeking God.

"Drianké, you know, you and I, we are more than a brother and sister from the same mother. You are my cousin, but I consider you more than that. Nonetheless, we don't always have the same opinions on things. You, you've spent your life with artists. Me, I have my little life. I'm a manager in my neighborhood and there are some things I cannot accept."

Drianké still did not say anything. And Amoul kept talking.

"You know, I don't like your business here. But since it's discreet, I close my eyes to it, since you are alone, it gives you company, and you earn a little money to live on. I know that you aren't making a living on your royalties, or if you're even getting them at all! Long story short. I also know that you suffered greatly with that infamous muqaddam who cheated on you. I know that this guy has ruined your life."

Drianké still did not say anything.

"But in this life, we have to move on.

"We have to know how to forgive and forget.

"God did not demand forgiveness, I know.

"It's a matter of choice.

"If you want to, you forgive; if you don't want to, you don't forgive."

A strange gleam flashed in Drianké's eyes.

All of the sudden, Drianké started whistling the blues.

Her brother Amoul smiled and kept talking:

"You're only happy when you're in your songs.

"So the shadowy mass told me that he had an incredible affair with a woman in Hogbo. He said that he'd married a widow several years before, and he admitted that he'd made her suffer tremendously. Now, seeing what he himself has become, he wondered if this woman had been infected and also what had become of her. The shadowy mass wanted to tell his story to the great young man who wanted to make it into a film! Only he didn't know how to tell the story.

"That is how I heard about Hogbo.

"That is what I know about Hogbo.

"Perhaps I could ask the shadowy mass for some clarifications tonight, no, not tonight. I have plans with my friend Joseph. His son wants to marry the daughter of a man who is leading a so-called religious path. He wants to talk about religious matters. With all of these false gurus, false muqaddams, and new prophets, he doesn't want to sacrifice his child to these new gods. With all of the downward spirals, mass suicides, stripping of fortunes, sex games for purification, romantic difficulties, and other issues, he is distrustful. And he is right. But tomorrow night, I will be here, and I will ask the shadowy mass for more information about Hogbo and how to get there. Drianké, you see that we're on the right track."

Drianké, who had stopped whistling her blues and had once again shut down into her silence, quietly said:

“There’s no need anymore.

“We just found the answer.”

“What answer have you found?” Amoul asked, surprised.

Drianké only said to her brother:

“See you tomorrow. Let’s spend the night in peace!”

Drianké’s brother Amoul was heading out when suddenly he retraced his steps, pensive. When Amoul got back to her, he looked Drianké in the eyes and said:

“Actually, Drianké, wasn’t your infamous muqaddam from Hògbo?”

“Yes!” Drianké replied.

“It’s a small world, indeed,” Amoul said, and then he headed off.

On the night of that same day in November, the great young man, the filmmaker Djib, came to Felix Faure Street. He went straight to Drianké’s place. Only a few clients and friends were there. They had a drink or two and left. There was not a crowd that night at Drianké’s place.

“What’s going on today?

“Is it not my day or what?

“There aren’t many people, and everyone seems to have something important to do or to say! Something extraordinary is definitely brewing today. Even the sky seems to be in a different mood. Even the clouds have changed their face.

“Even the stars don’t feel like shining!

“Even the Kiravi Valpierre wine seems to have turned!”

Drianké was humming everything that she was saying, like a prayer. Once again, she turned toward the great young man, the filmmaker Djib, who was making the rounds in her courtyard.

“How are you, Djib?

“Do you want to drink something?”

Every time that Drianké saw Djib, it was like this.

She was happy, excited.

But that evening, her excitement had a different vibe about it. Drianké had a strange gleam in her eyes, and she was beaming. She herself got up to serve a glass of rosé to Djib who had started to smile.

"You seem happy. I'm glad!

"I love seeing you happy, because you're a good man.

"You've helped us all, those of us they call everyday people.

"You could have been like the others, those who look down on everyday people, those who don't pay us any mind, those who don't even see us. May God grant you a long life! As long as you live, we will be dignified people. May God help you in all things!"

"That's enough, Drianké, stop!" the great young man, the filmmaker Djib, gently said. He was still standing, with his glass of rosé in hand. With his great height, he towered over Drianké, the petite, light-skinned woman, who would walk with a limp every now and again.

"What's the matter, Djib?"

The great young man, the filmmaker Djib, took Drianké by the shoulders and, looking her straight in the eyes, said:

"I don't like hearing about this fictitious god, this god that people are dragging out left and right, this vilified god, this god who is in the thick of every sauce. I don't want to hear about this puppet god found in most places of prayer. I don't want to hear about this god who tortures some, sends others to hell. I don't want to hear about this threatening god, this god who is with some and not with others. I don't want to hear about this god that the false muqaddams are using in their unhealthy desire for prestige, for their own vanity, their own interest. I don't want to hear about this god who is being dragged out among charlatans and sorcerers. I don't want to hear about this god whose name is pronounced, recited, chanted, whispered countless times to get rich, become famous, have opportunities, power, potency, to dominate anyone and everyone. I don't want to hear about this god that the false muqaddams and other false gurus and prophets are using to subjugate men and women, exploit them, take their money and their dignity. I don't want to hear about this god used for personal purposes by false muqaddams and new prophets with personality disorders. I don't want to hear about this god used to scorn anyone and everyone. I don't want to hear about this god used for fornication, masturbation, vice, hate, scorn, moral and physical violence."

"I completely agree with you," Drianké said. "I'm not talking about that god, not anymore. I'm talking about the God who is with us, in us. The God who is in our veins. You know, Djib, soon you will understand. There is a part of my life that I have never talked to you about. If I am grouped in with the everyday people, the marginalized who you love and respect, it is because this is what I have become. I wasn't born like this. A muqaddam was the one who put me in this state. A muqaddam who used his god to scorn, humiliate, exploit, and break me. A man without virtue, a man who almost killed me. He is the one who taught me not to believe in religions anymore. I will tell you about it later."

The great young man, the filmmaker Djib, who had taken Drianké in his arms, hugged her very tightly. And once again, the strange gleam furtively flashed in Drianké's eyes. This did not escape Djib when he pulled away from her.

"You know, for me, your blues songs are the most beautiful prayers I have ever heard, and these are the prayers that God hears, and you know, with my glass of rosé, I am praying too. We have to reread Hafiz and the other poets. You don't need to say anything more. I know everything. The screenplay is ready, and we start filming very early tomorrow morning.

"Tomorrow, yes, tomorrow, November 29th."

Drianké burst out laughing and the strange gleam flashed all the more brightly in her eyes.

Djib was happy because he was sure that he was close to finding the end of the story that the shadowy mass wanted to tell him but did not know how to tell. Djib was happy because he felt that the end was near. An end worthy of this story. The only puzzle that he could not solve was the appearance of the four veiled figures in the Kermel market, and that he had never seen those veiled figures ever again.

"Those four veiled figures are the crux of the end of the story.

"I have to find those four veiled figures," he said, as if talking to himself.

"Here, on Felix Faure Street, people are starting to talk about those four veiled figures spotted on the street on several occasions.

"They come by, come back," Drianké told him.

Drianké asked about the short-haired, light-skinned young woman, who had not been back since the rumors started. Djib smiled and said:

"She left. I haven't seen her since the day of the incident.

"That was the day I lost my story. But she will come back. I don't know how, but she will come back.

"I am sure that she will be here tomorrow for the film.

"She said that she was looking for a man she met a few years ago, and who she tracked down, by a scar that he had on his belly. This was the story that I used to develop the story I thought I had lost. It's unbelievable! She told me that she tracked down this man who had exploited, humiliated her. She tracked down this man who she'd been looking for, by his big belly and his scar, his small penis and his stench.

"In the end, I don't need the story that I've lost anymore. The film shoot is happening tomorrow, and I don't need to look for the four veiled figures anymore either. They will be in the film. They have come for the film. The main character of the film is missing, but I know that this character will be there too.

"The character is even already there.

"I feel it."

Drianké shuddered and shivered.

In that moment, Djib noticed Muñ, sitting on a bench, in silence.

"What! Your girl is still with you?"

"Djib, you aren't paying any attention to Muñ, one might think. She'll have been here for a year to the day, tomorrow, November 29th, on the dot. Muñ has told me that she knows you well.

"She's very interested in you, and she says that she is getting to know you better and better. In the evening, I often catch her over there, when you come to visit the shadowy mass. She glances at you and, sometimes, she looks at you for a long time. I've even wondered why she is so interested in you and the shadowy mass. She doesn't give the impression of being interested in anything but at least I noticed that. You know, Muñ is a strange girl."

Djib called to Muñ with his very gentle voice:

"I too know Muñ, and I am very interested in her. Muñ, come a little bit closer."

Muñ approached Djib, hesitantly.

She was trembling, shivering, almost sweating.

It was getting increasingly late, but Drianké's clients and friends were not streaming in. And the shadowy mass had not yet arrived.

What did Djib—that great young man who often came over with that short-haired, light-skinned young woman with a sexy kind of beauty—want from her? Muñ was afraid that Djib would make the connection between her, the typescript in the yellow folder, and his lost story. She was afraid that Djib would unlock her secret, her secrets, her hate, her desire for vengeance, her search for a muqaddam who had made her mother suffer, a muqaddam who had a scar running across his big belly. When Muñ found herself in front of Djib, he laid his big eyes on her and looked at her intensely.

Drianké wondered what could attract Djib to Muñ.

"Djib, do you want to cast her in your film or what?" Drianké asked, laughing.

"She is one of the film's heroines, like you," Djib replied.

"This girl just gave me the end of the story.

"She is not only going to be in the film.

"She is the film's connecting thread.

"Muñ, come a little closer."

Muñ came a little closer to Djib, who grabbed her by the shoulders. Muñ raised her eyes toward Djib and suddenly burst into tears. And Drianké got up, stumbling before grabbing her cane:

"Muñ, what's wrong?

"Djib, what's going on?"

"It's nothing, Drianké, sit down. Muñ is the character I was missing. She is the main character of the film," Djib said.

While sobbing, Muñ remembered the part of the story that related to her in the typescript, which she didn't need to read anymore.

One day, she found herself alone with the muqaddam in her home. He started to reproach her for all of the stupid things that she had done with the friend from somewhere else. Then, he asked her to tell him about the sexual experiences that she had already had. She replied that she barely had any, but he insisted on the details of those sexual experiences, however negligible they might be.

He was strange when he spoke to me. He kept getting closer and closer to me and breathing heavier and heavier. He insisted that I keep talking and he was staring at my mouth in a strange way. At one point, he got up, went into his bathroom, and came back with a bottle containing a black fluid. He slathered my entire body in it, after taking off all of my clothes while telling me not to worry about it. He ran his hands over my breasts, my vulva, and at one point, he started taking off his clothes and talking, as if talking to himself:

"I must do my duty.

"I must take care of you.

"You are the daughter of the woman I married.

"You are the daughter of my deceased cousin.

"I must help you and protect you.

"You must undergo a purification, for you are dirty and you are possessed by the devil. I see, through the gifts that my god has given me, a devil who often comes to make love with you. I see the devil mounting you and I hear you gasping, panting. You come, and after the devil has finished having sex with you, you curl up into a ball, sighing, with your pagne untied next to you. I told myself that if I had a camera, I would film this scene. My god shows me so many things! You were also a victim of witchcraft by one of your aunts. This aunt doesn't like you. Actually, it's not you that she has it in for, but your mother. She doesn't like your mother. She is jealous of her. She doesn't understand how she can get by with the only job that he has. She spends her time badmouthing your mother, denigrating her in front of others. She would like your mother to leave your house. Since she can't get to her directly, she goes through you, her daughter, to undermine her. I have to do something. I must do something. It's a duty. It's my duty."

I could never talk about what he made me do. He purified me, he said. I never wanted to tell this to my mother. It would have killed her, and me too.

That evening, the great young man, the filmmaker Djib, did not wait for the shadowy mass. He headed out, wishing Drianké and Muñ good luck on the film shoot early the next morning on Felix Faure Street.

That night, Drianké's clients and friends had cleared out from the front of Drianké's cottage very early.

That night, Muñ did not shut herself away in the bathroom, and went to bed very early.

That night, Drianké, after the hasty departure of a few friends and clients, did not take a cold shower.

She went to bed and closed the door herself.

She did not do her bookwork.

She did not smoke her iron pipe.

That night, Drianké just whistled the blues.

Early the next morning, very early, four multiplying veiled figures slipped into the labyrinth of courts and courtyards through the long passageways leading to Drianké's place. It was cool that morning. The four multiplying veiled figures stopped in a corner. They were all silent.

Another small-statured human shadow suddenly emerged in that semi-darkness, holding four unlit lanterns and a cane. The four veiled figures, which seemed to be multiplying, moved back a bit toward the large doorway, as if to avoid detection by that shadow, who was walking with a vigorous step. The human shadow who had just arrived positioned herself at the first passageway of this interior courtyard, with the unlit lanterns next to her. Once the shadowy mass, who left early each morning, moved past her, the human shadow pounced and struck him violently on the head with the cane.

The shadowy mass collapsed without making a sound.

Meanwhile, on the sidewalk, across from the Chez Tonio hair salon, with the Chief of Police and the Philosopher still standing in front of the large chopped-up body, the eyes of the large leper, with his tiny genitals stuffed deep into his mouth, continued to tell the end of the story. Drianké had asked the Chief of Police and the Felix Faure Street Philosopher to come to her place to cool off or do some more thinking if they wanted to.

"Ah yes, I need something cool to drink, but I don't need to do any more thinking.

"That leper killed himself.

"That leper chopped himself up.

"That leper stuffed his own genitals deep into his mouth," the Chief of Police solemnly declared.

The Philosopher was watching Drianké, who had gotten up from the curb where she had been sitting, still chanting the blues. The Philosopher gently took Drianké by the hand that was not holding on to the cane, and when Drianké raised her eyes to him, he said: "Drianké, you are an extraordinary woman. I knew, ever since you arrived here, on Felix Faure Street, that you did not walk with a limp. I sensed that you had a weight upon you that was making you limp. You know, Drianké, you are truly a part of Felix Faure Street!"

Drianké did not say anything, but kept looking at the Philosopher, and at one point, she freed the hand that he had been holding on to and headed over to her cottage, with her cane on her shoulder.

The Chief of Police commanded the two fat policemen to take care of the large chopped-up leper.

"Hẹy, you two fatties, go and get a van to haul out these chunks of flesh.

"Take this leper to the hospital morgue.

"I'll do the report. He'll be thrown into the common grave, if no one claims him. Which would be surprising for a chopped-up leper on Felix Faure Street."

Just as the no-longer-limping Drianké, chanting the blues all the while, was bringing the Chief of Police back to her place, followed by the Felix Faure Street Philosopher (who was smiling while bobbing his head), four veiled figures suddenly appeared at the four cardinal points, each one holding a lantern with a dancing flame. The four veiled figures seemed to be multiplying. They moved along the sidewalk where the body of the large chopped-up leper still lay, with a scar running across his belly from top to bottom. His tiny genitals, stuffed deep into his mouth, had gone limp. Once in the vicinity of the chopped-up body, the four veiled figures set down the four lamps that they had been holding. The wicks of the lanterns, placed at the four cardinal points, seemed more ablaze. It felt like the sun had descended upon that Felix Faure Street sidewalk. The four veiled figures surreptitiously lifted their veils in unison and burst out laughing, with their heads turned up to the sky. That sky on that morning was so luminous! That sky was blue, a radiant blue. The sun was laughing in the sky, in fits of uncontrolled laughter. The sun could not hold back any longer and started to dance. The four veiled figures blended their laughter with that of the sun, which kept on moving and grooving.

"Go on, get out of here, you lunatics," said one of the two fat policemen, who was wondering which big chunk to start with, in order to transport the large leper's chopped-up body in a red van located at the nearby police headquarters.

The unveiled women were beautiful, with a supernatural beauty, with a radiantly brewing-rage kind of beauty. Their faces were ethereally luminous. They kept on laughing with the sun and, putting their veils back on, went out as they had come in, at the four cardinal points, after picking up their four lanterns. The wicks of the four lanterns, still placed at the four cardinal points, were burning increasingly intensely. The light that they were giving off was competing with the Felix Faure Street sun, which was out of control.

The eyes of the large leper, with his tiny genitals stuffed deep into his mouth, continued to tell the end of the story, as he was being transported in pieces in a little red van, toward the hospital, located not far from Felix Faure Street. The large leper's eyes were laughing out loud as they finished telling the end of the story by going back over the events from the beginning, starting with the cane strike.

The cane strike in the passageway, which had knocked out the shadowy mass, rang out like the sound of a broken violin.

“Take that! From God, who you’ll be seeing!” said the shadowy human who struck him with the cane. Upon seeing this, the four veiled figures approached. One of them drove a long knife into his guts.

“For exploiting and scorning others!”

The second veiled figure seemed quite young and was strong.

A strength suppressed for so many years! A strength sustained for so many years! The shadowy mass was writhing in pain, but no cry escaped his lips. The shadowy mass was now stripped of the clothes that had been covering him, by the veiled figures. A scar ran across his stomach, from top to bottom, a deep scar which, on that big belly, seemed to want to burst open. The shadowy mass was a leper, a leper whose entire body was ravaged by a strange form of leprosy. He had scabs all over with pussy fluids oozing out of them. The leper was large in size, and his big, protruding belly took center stage on his midsection, like a mound. The third veiled figure broke his arms with a small axe and chopped them up into pieces. She severed his legs at the knees and chopped them up into pieces. She broke his legs and chopped them up into pieces. His entire body was chopped up this way, in big pieces, from head to toe. At the same time, two twins appeared like angels and were dancing around the large leper’s chopped-up body, to the sound of violin music, which was oozing through the shuttered windows of the closed Chez Tonio hair salon.

“We are not dead. You are the muqaddam who sleeps with other people’s wives and makes them get abortions. But with the twins, you will pay!”

The eyes of the shadowy mass, who was nothing but a large leper, with a big belly with long scar, were witnessing the scene of his large body getting chopped up into big pieces.

"Take that! From the woman whose son you are keeping from her!"

His small penis and tiny genitals, which he had used to harm all of these women, seemed to be begging the veiled figures. That small penis, which he had used to masturbate on women who he would ask to talk, say crazy things that turned him on. That small penis, which he used to make women (who most of the time did not come) suffer. He would exhaust them by asking them to massage him all over his big body. During that time, he would think about a woman he had spent time with, listening to her or watching her, and masturbate. He would do everything to hold himself back while the woman he was with was suffering in uncomfortable positions. That small penis, the other veiled figure tore it off without batting an eye. His tiny testicles were also torn off, and the entire package was stuffed deep into his mouth, which he had been using like a passport to seduce women and lead them to their downfalls.

"You claimed to be a handsome guy, a seducer, a hotshot, an athlete, a lord, a tiger, a hunter! You took yourself for a god, a muqaddam of a religious path, when you were really just a vile man hungry for power and potency!"

At that moment, Muñ appeared, with the typescript in the yellow folder in hand, with the emboldened flames of the four lit lanterns trying to rise up into the sky. The veiled figures were panting, sweating. The first call to prayer was about to ring out. The veiled figures began carrying the large leper's chopped-up body parts out onto the Felix Faure Street sidewalk, one by one. Muñ set the four lanterns and the typescript down on the ground, and helped the veiled figures by taking the leper's head with his genitals stuffed deep into his mouth. She spit on it and started chanting the blues. The twins took the four lit lanterns that Muñ had put on the ground and placed them around the leper's chopped-up body at the four cardinal points while saying:

"To the four cardinal points scorned by the muqaddam!"

Muñ had seen Drianké, breathless, sweating, return to the front of her cottage, cane in hand, without limping. Drianké had taken the four lanterns out there beforehand, where she had left them and lit them. She had placed them all around the space that the shadowy mass was occupying. She went to sit down in her old leather armchair, wrapped in her big blanket, with her cane and a lantern with a bold flame beside her. She was looking out straight ahead. In the back of the wooden cottage, through the half-open door, a lantern was burning exceptionally brightly, with an invigorating glow.

Drianké was not whistling the blues anymore.

Drianké was not humming the blues anymore.

Drianké was not singing the blues anymore.

Drianké was not whispering the blues anymore.

Drianké was chanting the blues.

Muñ dropped the leper's severed head, with his tiny genitals stuffed deep into his mouth, on the Felix Faure Street sidewalk and, as she got up, directed her gaze toward the closed shutters of the Chez Tonio hair salon, from which a piercing violin sound was oozing.

Muñ went back to Drianké's place while chanting the blues. She had picked up the typescript in the yellow folder as she walked by and dropped it in the space where the four veiled figures had gone to sit down on the large tables and benches, with four lanterns illuminated in the vicinity. It was in this space that Muñ had picked up the typescript entitled "Vengeance" on November 29th, one year ago to the day. The yellow folder opened up, and the pages of the typescript flew away with that morning breeze, which was coming from the nearby ocean. Muñ went back into Drianké's room, gently closed the door, and kept on chanting the blues. The four veiled seemingly multiplying figures watched the pages of the typescript fly away in front of them, one by one. They got up and left just as Muezzin was getting to Drianké's place.

In one of the veiled figures, Muñ recognized her mother.

In one of the veiled figures, the Felix Faure Street Philosopher recognized Drianké.

In one of the veiled figures, Tonio, from behind the shuttered windows of his hair salon, recognized his daughter.

In one of the veiled figures, the twins recognized their mother.

In one of the veiled figures, one might recognize the mother of a son being kept from her.

In one of the veiled figures, one might recognize a woman with a food stand.

In one of the veiled figures, one might recognize a woman betrayed.

In one of the veiled figures, one might recognize a woman scorned.

In one of the veiled figures, one might recognize a humiliated woman.

In one of the veiled figures, one might recognize an exploited woman.

In one of the veiled figures, one might recognize an abused woman.

In one of the veiled figures, one might recognize the short-haired, light-skinned woman.

In one of the veiled figures, one might recognize the hairdresser Tonio's wife.

In one of the veiled figures, one might recognize the woman with the suitcase.

In one of the veiled figures, one might recognize the woman encountered in the Holy Land.

In one of the veiled figures, one might recognize Muezzin's oldest daughter.

In one of the veiled figures, one might recognize every woman, except for the woman of easy virtue who had given the muqaddam leprosy.

The four veiled figures went off, seeming to multiply on Felix Faure Street. They were like an illusion, like a mirage. They were light and moved away slowly, each one holding an illuminated lantern in hand, whose increasingly emboldened flame was bathing Felix Faure Street in a supernatural glow at that time of morning. From the still-shuttered Chez Tonio hair salon oozed a violin music, a rousing morna, a morna that invited love and pleasure. It was five-thirty in the morning.

At the hospital morgue, the large chopped-up leper's eyes had stopped moving once and for all, but were still wide open. The morgue employee, while putting the pieces in a red crate, did not notice that the unmoving eyes were staring at an image. He tried to close the leper's eyes, but realized that they would never close again. He drew a little closer and there, he saw the image, the last image burned into his eyes forever, one might say, just before death. He pushed the red wooden crate into a corner and delivered a eulogy for the infamous muqaddam: "They got you good!"

That was one November 29th.

APPENDIX

Author's Preface in the Original French

Ken Bugul

JE SUIS VENUE à la littérature par nécessité. Mes trois ouvrages, *Le Baobab fou*, *Cendres et braises* et *Riwan ou le chemin de sable*, qui constituent une trilogie autobiographique romancée, ont été écrits dans une démarche thérapeutique, dans l'urgence, par nécessité. J'étais dans une telle précarité existentielle que je n'avais plus le choix. C'était une question de survie à la folie et à la mort. Cette folie et cette mort qui donnèrent le titre de mon premier ouvrage de fiction socio-politique, *La Folie et la mort*. Et c'est avec cet ouvrage-là, que ma passion pour l'écriture est née. J'alternais ensuite autobiographies romancées ou auto-fictions et livres socio-politiques. J'étais emballée et excitée par l'écriture qui non seulement me réparait, mais me faisait voyager dans des imaginaires qui aiguillaient tous mes sens. Je ne pouvais plus me passer de l'écriture, mais ce qui me motivait le plus c'était la création et la créativité dans l'écriture. Un éditeur d'une collection de romans policiers avait sollicité la participation d'auteurs africains pour une collection dans une prestigieuse maison d'édition française. Le projet me tentait mais il n'y eut plus de suite. Et c'est longtemps après, une aventure douloureuse avec un moqadem qui m'avait entraînée dans une relation destructrice dont je devais me guérir, m'a fait revenir au projet. Je cherchais une approche, une manière d'écrire un livre sur cette histoire traumatique. Et c'est ainsi que j'ai écrit *Rue Félix-Faure* comme un roman policier, alors qu'en réalité c'est du vécu que je ne pouvais pas relater dans un genre autobiographique. C'était trop douloureux pour que je puisse utiliser le "je." Ce serait insupportable. Je ne pouvais pas accepter, digérer, ce qui m'était arrivé. Je devais me venger du moqadem. Je ne pouvais pas imaginer avec tout ce que j'avais vécu, l'apaisement que j'avais trouvé dans ma vie tourmentée jusque lors, le niveau de stabilité que j'avais atteint à cette époque-là, que je pouvais me faire avoir, me faire manipuler, sous le couvert de Dieu. C'était tellement énorme que pour raconter cette histoire j'avais besoin de faire preuve de créativité pour exprimer tous les ressentis et j'ai utilisé la forme d'un texte policier scénarisé, en profitant pour rendre hommage au cinéaste Djibril Diop Mambetty qui m'avait fait mieux connaître rue Félix-Faure, une rue atypique et célèbre de Dakar, la capitale sénégalaise. J'ai choisi cette rue pour y situer le roman. Cette rue aux nuits interlopes, me permettait de me noyer dans son décor et ses personnages et y perpétrer ma vengeance. Et c'est cette approche que j'ai utilisée, qui m'a permis de raconter cette expérience douloureuse où j'ai été exploitée et humiliée, dans des mises en scène de personnages féminins hors normes qui par leur détermination m'ont épaulée tout le long de l'écriture du livre. Je me suis cachée derrière la puissance des personnages de Drianké, de Muñ, des quatre femmes voilées, qui ont été toutes des victimes de manipulations et d'exploitation sous le couvert de Dieu, par le même moqadem. Ce sont ces personnages qui m'ont inspirée et soutenue pour en finir avec le lépreux, dont le corps a été retrouvé découpé en morceaux, un matin, rue Félix-Faure, rue des philosophes, des Capverdiennes aux teints caramel, rue des bars et des salons de coiffure d'où s'échappe de la musique de morna. J'avais créé une atmosphère cinématographique d'ombres, de lumières, de sons et de silences pour y plonger tout ce que j'avais subi et que je n'osais avouer à personne même pas à moi-même. Et cela m'a permis d'assouvir ma vengeance et de me remettre, de me guérir en grande partie de cette douloureuse expérience. *Rue Félix-Faure* fait partie de certains de mes ouvrages où la magie de l'écriture et de la créativité s'est le plus opérée pour moi. Écrire *Rue Félix-Faure* a contribué à me faire comprendre qu'il n'était pas nécessaire de passer par qui que ce soit pour atteindre le ciel. Et depuis, je trace mes propres chemins.

Translator's Acknowledgments

Thank you, Mariètou Mbaye, for giving me the opportunity and for trusting me to translate *Felix Faure Street* into English. Thank you for your receptivity to my questions and your generosity of spirit. I offer this translation as a thank you for your kindness and encouragement toward the younger me, when we found ourselves stranded together in a snowstorm en route for the African Literature Association Conference in 2008. Your words gave me the confidence to simply be myself, at a time when I was struggling because I did not fit neatly into anyone else's idea of what or how a young woman was supposed to be. Thank you for encouraging me to be true to myself, to not be afraid to take up space, and to step into the light of the sun, the moon, and the stars.

Thank you to the editorial team at Vanderbilt University Press for providing a platform for Global Black Writers in Translation and for supporting this project. Thank you for the time, attention, and care that you have given to this edition. Special thanks to Gianna Mosser and Joell Smith-Borne for your attentive feedback on the manuscript.

Thank you to the organizers and presenters at the 2022 Dakar Translation Symposium and the 2024 Dakar Translation Symposium-Accra Edition. You have all inspired me to hone my craft and to do my part to translate works by authors from Africa and her Diaspora. Special thanks to Alba Rodriguez-Garcia for helping me to reconnect with Mariètou Mbaye after all of these years.

Thank you to the organizers and presenters at the Sel et Piment (Salt and Pepper) conference in Schoelcher, Martinique in 2023. To Patrick Chamoiseau, thank you for using your voice to speak to the importance of recognizing and elevating the matrimoine culturel vis-à-vis the patrimoine culturel. Thank you to Manuel Norvat for reminding me that translation is poetry and that translators are poets.

Thank you to my colleagues and students at Marymount Manhattan College. Your presence, collegiality, and support have meant so much throughout the process of translating this book. Special thanks to Michael Colvin and Jerry Williams, my first office mates and longtime friends, for being my sounding boards. Thank you to Jennifer Brown and to the students in my Reading Contemporary Africa class for providing feedback on early drafts of the first few chapters.

Thank you to Khadim Sylla for helping me with my Wolof and always being there to answer my questions.

Most importantly, thank you to my partner, Nick, and to my canine assistants, Milo and Werner. Thank you for taking the time to listen to all of my wild thoughts and lyrical puzzle-work. Thank you for your unconditional love and support throughout this process, and also for letting me know that dancing the mayonnaise deserved some sort of mention in the translator's introduction.

Lastly, thank you to the friends and family who leaned in to support me in translating this wild, sublime, horrific, and resonant tale. Special thanks to Dani Blum, Caryn Cast, Ann Huntington, Lisa Huntington, Mary Judd, Jason Meketa, Erin Nau, Carrie O'Dell, and Wenona Williams. Thank you to Dad, in memoriam. Forever in my heart. Stars forever.